A LONG WAY DOWN

A Selection of Recent Titles from Ken McCoy

The DI Sep Black Series

DEAD OR ALIVE *
A LONG WAY DOWN *

The Sam Carew Series

MAD CAREW
TRIPPER
HAMMERHEAD
LOSER

* *available from Severn House*

A LONG WAY DOWN

Ken McCoy

This first world edition published 2017
in Great Britain and the USA by
SEVERN HOUSE PUBLISHERS LTD of
19 Cedar Road, Sutton, Surrey, England, SM2 5DA.
Trade paperback edition first published
in Great Britain and the USA 2017 by
SEVERN HOUSE PUBLISHERS LTD

British Library Cataloguing in Publication Data
A CIP catalogue record for this title is available from the British Library.

ISBN-13: 978-0-7278-8730-6 (cased)
ISBN-13: 978-1-84751-844-6 (trade paper)
ISBN-13: 978-1-78010-904-6 (e-book)

All Severn House titles are printed on acid-free paper.

Severn House Publishers support the Forest Stewardship Council™ [FSC™],
the leading international forest certification organisation.
All our titles that are printed on FSC certified paper carry the FSC logo.

MIX
Paper from
responsible sources
FSC® C013056

Typeset by Palimpsest Book Production Ltd.,
Falkirk, Stirlingshire, Scotland.
Printed and bound in Great Britain by
TJ International, Padstow, Cornwall.

PROLOGUE

C harlie Santiago departed both his office and his life through an open window with the gusto of an Olympic diver, leaving splashes of his viscera all over the stone-cobbled yard fifty feet below. The overnight rain had washed most of the blood into a nearby gulley grate and thence into the city drains. It was an ignominious end for such a man. In life, Charlie had been a successful businessman: handsome, respected by some, feared by others and wealthy. In death, his destroyed and bloody remains had lain there all night in a misshapen heap in the cold rain; saturated, alone and unobserved. His fall from health, wealth and happiness was as terminal as his fall from the window. A lone face at the window looked down at Charlie's body. It was a face without emotion or concern.

With Santiago being an important member of the community Detective Chief Inspector Wood of the West Yorkshire Police decided to lead the investigation himself. It had been initially reported as either an improbable suicide, or a probable murder. The man had fallen a distance of over fifty feet, from an office window to the cobbled yard and had landed on his head.

Forensic evidence would prove the death to have been suspicious, possibly a murder. There were signs of a struggle. The disarray in the office including one of Santiago's shoes left behind and the grazing on his knuckles was sufficient evidence of that. He'd fought a losing fight and had been dispatched out of the window which had been conveniently wide open.

It would have been an exhausting, terrifying and probably noisy death. Murder was the initial finding but a murder with no suspects, no clues, no evidence and no apparent motive, just a dead body down there in the yard. It was a seemingly senseless murder, of which DCI Wood and his team had failed to pick up any leads. The inept DCI had therefore labelled it a possible suicide and had handed it over to the Cold Case Unit while it was still very much lukewarm. DCI Wood, an unpopular officer and the beneficiary of at least two sideways promotions to get him out of someone's hair, was a major contributor to the West Yorkshire Police cold case files. Detective Superintendent Jane Hawkins, the officer in charge of the Cold Case Unit, was becoming heartily fed up of picking up the pieces after Wood had dropped a case before it had been properly investigated.

ONE

March 2015

Detective Inspector Sep Black found himself confronted by three known felons. Known to him, because at some time in their past he'd arrested all three of them, albeit separately and now they were all out of prison and together and bearing deep grudges against him.

They were outside a pub he'd just left, trying to track down a man he'd been looking for in connection with a cold case he was working on. He'd had a call from a reliable snout to say the man was in there, but the information was wrong, which had puzzled him as his snout was usually most reliable. But it was a puzzle no longer. It would appear that the snout had been 'got at' and he was worrying that his snout, Gerry Beddows, was still in one piece. Gerry was by no means a young man, nor was he much of a fighter or fast on his feet, but Sep's major worry was that Gerry would come out of this all right. He was both of the things that his snout wasn't, but Sep was also just one man.

He was in a pub car park, which was deserted because it wasn't exactly a popular pub. Deserted to the extent that whatever happened here wouldn't be seen by any witnesses. All three of these men could be classified as thugs. All three were wearing knuckledusters, a weapon Sep wouldn't have minded having right now. His ideal plan of action would be to run. *He who fights and runs away may live to fight another day* and all that. But turning and running was out of the question because he was surrounded. One in front, one behind and one over to his right. All he could do was his best, which was usually considerable. He did a 360 turn to assess them all and, knowing them all of old, he decided that the one on the right would be the easiest to take, but he would need to take him before the other two joined in. Speed was essential here. Without actually looking to his right he shifted in that direction with his eyes on the man in front of him until he was no more than three yards away from his target. Then he spun around, took two strides, brushed aside a wild punch aimed at his head and in one twisting movement, took the man in an armlock, broke his arm, and pulled the duster from the man's fist. Then he backed away from the other two who had advanced, warily, having been reminded of just what he could do and knowing that he also was armed with a knuckleduster. Sep was the biggest man there and the toughest and the one filled with the most rage. It was a rage fuelled by the certainty that these men had come to kill him and they had probably already killed old Gerry Beddows.

The injured man was staggering around, out of action and howling with the pain of a badly broken arm. Sep scowled impatiently and shouted at him over his shoulder, 'Stay down there and don't get up, you whining bastard!'

The other two had experienced the rough end of his ire before and neither of them wanted to be the target of his next attack. His violent rage, plus the casual way he had disabled their crony, had them on their guard.

Once again Sep assessed the situation. If they had any sense they'd both move in on him at once, launching a two-pronged attack from opposite sides, but it would appear these men had other ideas. One was tall and not as stocky as the other. Sep thought he'd leave him until the last, but the tall one came for him first. Sep closed the gap between them with one long stride and, ducking under the thug's first blow, landed a heavy blow himself with his right fist, on which he now wore the knuckleduster. It took the man on his left cheek and knocked him onto his back with a broken cheekbone. The third man was now right behind him and he jumped on Sep's broad back trying to take him in a headlock. Sep dislodged one of the man's fingers and bent it back far enough to snap it. This caused the man to lose his grip to attend to the acute pain in his broken finger, as the second man tried to get to his feet only to be met by Sep's boot in his face, slamming him back to the ground, unconscious. Sep now surveyed the damage he'd done. The two conscious men with broken bones were hurrying to a car, so he ran after them and thumped them both in the backs of their heads with his knuckle-dustered fist. Both went down. Sep dragged the unconscious one over to join his two companions

'Stay down, boys,' he told them. 'Anyone tries to get up, they'll get the toe of my boot in the teeth and these boots have got steel toecaps.'

Sep allowed his fury to simmer. It had been part genuine, part theatrical, but it had served its purpose into making them believe they'd been dealing with a dangerous madman. He took out his mobile and rang the station. 'This is DI Black. I need a van to the Ostler's Arms car park to pick up three customers and I want it right now!'

Sep followed the van to the station, went inside and asked the desk sergeant, 'Has there been a report of a man being attacked in the last few hours? Small man, about seventy.'

'We've had a report of a man's body being found, sir.'

'Description?'

'Erm, hang on . . . five feet six, old feller. They have a name for him. He had a driver's license.'

'Gerald Beddows,' guessed Sep, hoping he was wrong. His hopes were dashed.

'That's him. Did you know him, sir?'

'Yes, I did. In that case, the three who've just come in are the main suspects in his murder. They might need a bit of medical attention. If they have to go to hospital they need to be under twenty-four-hour guard.'

Sep went through to Detective Superintendent Ibbotson's office – the CID boss.

'Afternoon, Sep. What's Cold Case doing in here?'

'I've just brought in three men who attacked me in the course of an investigation and I've good reason to believe they killed my informant, Gerry Beddows, who was found dead earlier. I'm very upset about that, sir.'

'Yes, I know about the Beddows killing. Didn't know he was your informant. We'll try and make a DNA connection with the people you brought in. Thanks for what you did, but I think you need to get over to your own people in Cold Case before Jane Hawkins accuses me of poaching you.'

'Just keeping you informed, sir.'

'Before you go, Sep, these men you brought in. They attacked you, did they?'

'They tried to, sir. Old customers of mine when I worked with your lot. I think they had it planned and I think they made Gerry Beddows set me up with a false lead; after which I'm guessing they killed him, sir, which is what I think they intended for me.'

'Will they need any medical attention?'

'They will, sir. They were quite violent.'

'I'd best get an ambulance over here.'

'Any luck at the Ostler's?' enquired Detective Superintendent Jane Hawkins.

'Only bad luck. My snout had been got at by three of my old customers, It was a set-up, ma'am. I managed to bring all three of them in to the station. They're in custody now. My snout was found dead.'

'What? Old Gerry Beddows . . . oh no!'

'I'm afraid so, ma'am.'

'Well, I think I'd better tell CID that I want a word with those three scrotes myself before they get at them. You'd better sit in with me. If they went to such trouble to set you up, they must know something about the case you're working on.'

'Maybe, maybe not, ma'am. Personally, I think I just walked on their patch, they saw me and decided to take advantage of the situation.'

'Your reputation has you treading a very dangerous path, DI Black. Are they all in one piece?'

'More or less.'

'Well they'll be stuck with less till I've had a word with them. I expect forensics and DNA will put them bang to rights for Gerry's murder so they won't have much to lose by coming clean.'

'They're all in a bit of pain, ma'am, and villains tend to be not so stubborn when they're in pain.'

'Sounds like you roughed them up a bit.'

'I broke one or two bones that's all.'

'And you're OK? No injuries?'

'None at all, no.'

'Good. I'll tell them how lucky they all are to have found you in a good mood. Did you get any further with your case?'

'I didn't, ma'am.'

TWO

March 2015

James Boswell double-checked the name of the Grimshawe Hotel. Yes, this was the right place – more of a downmarket workman's lodging house, unworthy of the label 'hotel', he reckoned. Maybe it had been a hotel a hundred years ago when the district had been a habitat for professional people who had brass plates outside their doors advertising that they were doctors, lawyers, dentists and architects, but the last of the professionals had moved on sixty or more years ago when the district began its descent into decrepitude. Leeds was a big and booming city with huge, modern developments ongoing in the city centre but none in the district where the Grimshawe Hotel was located. This was a building that had been well-named. James wasn't surprised that the classy woman whom he was to meet in there had chosen such a dump. He knew her reason, but it was even more of a dump than he'd anticipated.

The reception at the Grimshawe was a serving hatch in a wall that might have once led to a kitchen in days gone by. There was a brass bell which he banged with his palm a couple of times to summon the attention of whoever was going to book him in. He looked about him and gave a sigh. Was this really the right place? No way would this woman set foot in a dump like this. She said she had information that would be invaluable to him. He must have got it wrong, but how? It was her choice, not his. Or did this dump have some connection with her information? Yeah, what else could it be? An old woman appeared in the hatch. The cigarette she was smoking was down to its last half-inch with a good inch of ash still attached. She looked to be in her late nineties and not ageing well. Her manner was belligerent, albeit tempered by her voice being little more than a croak.

'What?'

'I booked a room. The name's Boswell.'

She looked down at a ledger that was open in front of her and squinted at it. The ash dropped off her cigarette as she wiped her nose with an elaborate sweep of a forefinger and put on her glasses to take a closer look.

'That'll be twenny quid.'

'I've already paid by card over the phone.'

'Card, eh? We don't get much o' that bollocks. It weren't me yer paid. I wouldn't know how ter do it.'

'Yes, I did it yesterday evening. It was a man I spoke to.'

'That's why it weren't me. I'm only on till six. Anyroad, yer woman's already up there, waitin' for yer. Just one night, is it?'

'Just an hour or so, maybe less.'

'Quick shag, on yer way 'ome ter the wife, eh? Yer dirty bastard!'

The hotel was matched in class by its receptionist.

'No, it's not—'

He gave up on his protest. Why should he worry what she thought?

'Well, it's still twenny quid. It's upstairs, room 7 and don't make too much bleedin' noise. It's right above here. I'll be able to hear every squeak o' the soddin' mattress.'

He went up the stairs which had been carpeted sometime in the dim and distant past, probably around the time it had last been cleaned. Cobwebs, dust and dirt abounded. He passed a man coming down, followed by a woman who was cursing him for not paying for some extra service she'd rendered. She paused and called back to James.

'Are yer lookin' fer business, darlin'?'

'Er, no, thank you.'

James got to the top of the stairs which led to a dimly lit corridor with a single strip of jaded carpet running down the middle. He came to room 7, knocked and pushed the door open. The woman was standing at the window, smoking and looking out, with her back to him. It was her all right. From the back she looked well-groomed and elegant, with glossy black hair down to the shoulders of her expensive-looking coat. It wasn't her normal colour hair, probably a wig. He knew that and he knew she'd be totally out of her comfort zone in this place. But it had been her choice, not his. For the purpose of this subterfuge she was calling herself Winona. Shabby meeting place, wig and a false name? James thought she was overdoing the secrecy bit.

'Hi,' was the last word he'd ever say.

The woman didn't turn or respond. She just continued looking out of the window at the dingy street beyond and smoked her cigarette. She winced at the sound of a blow to the back of his head striking James to the floor, unconscious. Two more blows killed him. Winona and James's assailant left immediately, with Winona sparing James a brief but troubled glance. The old woman in the reception area was aware of them leaving but she hadn't got her glasses on so she wasn't entirely sure who it was. She put them on only to look out of the window and was fairly certain it was the woman who'd only arrived a few minutes ago. She shook her head. Strange goings on in this bloody place, still, it wasn't her job to worry too much. People leaving were of no interest to her, they will have already paid their dues on arriving. Her grandson paid her well enough to go to the bingo three nights a week and the pub four nights. He also gave her a roof over her head free of charge.

Unfortunately, this was the roof.

THREE

Black Horse Hotel, Leeds, July 2015

'**M**r Black?'

Sandra Boswell had been directed there by Winnie O'Toole, Sep's lady friend. He was sitting outside, enjoying a pint and reading his paper. He was a big man, ex-special forces with both a Military Medal and an MA in English Language and Literature. A rare combination in any man.

'Who's asking?'

He said it with a polite smile as she was pretty enough to distract his attention away from his newspaper. Her long dark hair was blowing in the breeze and the wind did the casual style of it no harm at all. It was a style seemingly designed for such weather. She held it away from her face as she looked at him.

'I'm thinking you're Mr Septimus Black.'

'That's good thinking.'

'Winnie O'Toole told me I'd find you here. Not many men would fit the description she gave me of you.'

'Did she now?'

'Yes. I'm hoping you can help me.'

'In what way?'

'I'm told you do private detective work.'

'I'm actually Detective Inspector Black. I've been back on the police force quite some time now.'

'Ah.'

'Is this something a proper copper couldn't handle?'

'It's something a proper copper failed to handle.'

'What sort of case is it?'

'It's a murder case. I'm told you do murder cases.'

'Murder? Well, yes. It's usually us police who deal with murders.'

'The police gave up on it almost before they started.'

'Are we talking about the local police? By local I mean around here.'

'It happened about a mile from here. The Grimshawe Hotel.'

'That wouldn't be a Detective Chief Inspector Wood by any chance?'

'It would, yes.'

'In that case, sit down,' he said, then he got to his feet. 'What can I get you?'

'Just a glass of orange juice, please.'

Sep returned with the orange juice and sat down opposite his visitor. 'OK, tell me what you've heard about me.'

'Well, I know you're ex-army and you're as tough as you look.'

'Winnie told you all that, did she?'

'Not all of it, you were in the papers a lot last year with that child abduction case which you solved while under suspension from the police.'

'I wasn't suspended. I was sacked.'

'But you proved to the police that you were better than the lot of them, which is what I'm looking for.'

'Tell me who you are and all about this murder.'

'My name is Sandra Boswell and it's not just the murder, it's the circumstances I need to clear up.'

'Who was murdered?'

'My husband, James Boswell.'

'Right . . . Oh, sorry to hear that. Hang on, James Boswell? I read about that. A few months ago wasn't it?'

'Four months ago. March the twelfth to be exact. And if you heard about it, I imagine you heard he'd been meeting a prostitute in a sleazy hotel – a knocking shop to put it crudely.'

'The name rings a bell – James Boswell.'

'The famous James Boswell was a writer.'

'Of course. He wrote a book about Samuel Johnson.'

'Hmm, Winnie mentioned you were a man of letters.'

'That's not how I'd describe myself. I had to read Boswell's book about Johnson for my degree.'

'Anyway,' said Sandra, 'what I was saying about the prostitute is what bothers me. That just wasn't my James. He'd never go with a prostitute, especially in a horrible dive like where he was found. He was a good man.'

'I'm sure he was,' said Sep, who now felt he knew enough about this woman to know she would never settle for anything less than a good man.

'He was a freelance journalist,' said Sandra 'although he did a lot of work for just one or two newspapers. He was working on a story when he was killed.'

'And you think the story was why he was killed?'

'I can't think of any other reason why he'd be in such a place as where he was murdered. Apparently a woman was in the room with him, but she was never found.' She looked at Sep to determine whether he believed James to be such an innocent man. 'I need you to believe James was not meeting a prostitute.'

'As it happens, Mrs Boswell I happen to be working in the cold case unit right now. What we take on isn't entirely up to me, but the DCI Wood connection might swing it with my boss. Anyway, I need to believe everything you tell me. So, go on.'

'There's not much to tell. He didn't come home that evening, but he told me he was working on a story so I didn't panic, but when he stayed out all night without phoning me I rang the police to report him missing. Even then I was worried that he'd go mad with me for doing that when I knew he was working on a story, but there are limits to how much worry I can take. I gave the police his name and description and half an hour later they were knocking on my door. They told me that a man fitting James's description had been found killed in a hotel.'

There were tears in her eyes now.

'It was James,' suggested Sep, knowing her speech had dried up. She nodded and took a deep breath.

'He'd been battered about the head. I had to identify him – it was awful to see him like that.'

'I imagine it was,' said Sep, mustering up genuine sympathy. 'And the police got nowhere?'

She shook her head. 'No.'

'I can check all that myself. How's the orange juice?'

It was small talk designed to give him time to think of what to say next. Sandra sipped her drink and smiled.

'It's actually very nice thank you. I've read about you in the papers, Mr Black, which is what brought me to you. I gather you've had problems with the police.'

'That's all in the past I hope.'

'I understand you got a colleague of yours locked up for trying to frame you for something you didn't do.'

'My word, you have been talking to Winnie.'

'I call into her shop now and again. She sells some interesting clothes. Second-hand of course but really good stuff all the same.'

'Well, she does get new stuff in now and again. She opened the shop about a year ago. Winnie has a lot of good contacts.' He omitted to mention that Winnie's contacts were somewhat shady to say the least, but she herself was an excellent informant at times. A service she provided in exchange for immunity from police prosecution for her shady dealings.

'It would help if you didn't make it known that Winnie had any ties to me,' he said.

'Oh yes, she's already sworn me to secrecy about that.'

'She shouldn't have told you about me in the first place. I never go into her shop in case anyone recognizes me.'

'Normally, she wouldn't have told me about you, only she's aware of my problem and mentioned you as the only person who might be able to help me . . . and like I said, I'm sworn to secrecy.'

'It's important that you mean it.'

She leaned over the wooden table and spoke confidentially as if to prove her trustworthiness. 'I'm told you're a good man, Mr Black, and in case you're wondering if I can pay you for this, James had his life insured for a quarter of a million pounds. I'm willing to pay fifty thousand to get to the bottom of what happened and clear his name. It will also do no harm for me to finish his story for him, which might recoup some of the money.'

'If I took money from you I'd be drummed back out of the force. They've been looking for an excuse ever since I proved them wrong the last time they sacked me.'

'In that case I'll give it to Winnie and she can give it to you . . . if she wants.'

'You know about the story James was working on, do you?'

'Only some notes on his computer. It should be enough to give you a start. By the way, I'm also a journalist, or I was before I became a mum. We have—' she paused for thought – '*I* have a three-year-old daughter.'

'I see. Did you show this information to the police?'

'Yes. I printed it all out and gave it to Detective Chief Inspector Wood. You obviously know him.'

'I do.'

'What do you think of him?'

'Not a lot. He got where he is through a lot of sideways promotions from people trying to get rid of him.'

'Yeah, that pretty much describes him.'

'He's a rank above me and he's got no flair for detective work. He should have stayed in uniform, helping old ladies across the road.'

'And you've got this flair, have you?'

'I have my moments.'

'So I've heard.'

'What else have you heard?'

'Mr Black, I read the papers. Your reputation precedes you.'

'The papers have always made up stories about me. I'm a real handy target. None of it's true of course.'

'I'm here simply because of your reputation as a crime solver. So, are you taking the job?'

'I need to check with my superintendent. I think that case is already on file, but with it being one of Wood's many failures it's not being treated with any urgency. We have a whole filing cabinet of Wood's failures.'

'That explains a lot.'

'Don't mention that to the papers, or my opinion of Wood. They'll know where you got it from.'

'OK.'

'My boss'll probably let me look into it for a week or so and if I come up with anything at all concrete I imagine we'll make it an official case.'

'Is it something you might go undercover for?'

'Bloody hell! What has Winnie been telling you?'

'Like I said. I read about you in the papers last year. Down-and-out Glaswegian, weren't you?'

'Well, if I do go undercover it won't be as Scottish ne'er-do-well Jimmy Lennon again.'

'Do I call you Sep or Mr Black?'

'Sep.'

'If you call round to my house, Sep, I can show you everything James had.'

FOUR

S ep paused at the gate and looked up at the house. It was a good, solid, pre-war house on a small development just north of Leeds.

'Hello, Sep, bang on time. Come in.'

He followed Sandra through to a living room that needed a good tidy, a bit like his own living room, apart from the absence of dust.

'Excuse the mess . . . I . . . actually I haven't got an excuse except that I'm so messy nowadays.'

'If you think this is messy you should see my place.'

'Sit down.'

'Thank you.'

She had no make-up on and she hadn't brushed her hair. 'I'm having a really bad morning, I'm afraid. I still get them from time to time.'

'Yeah, I know what it's like to lose a loved one.'

'You mean you lost your wife?'

'My wife left me for another man. In fact, she didn't have the decency to leave me, she just moved him in and me out.'

'That must have been awful, Sep – and have you got over it?'

'Completely. Should never have married her in the first place. It's actually my daughter I miss. Anyway, I've got Winnie now.'

'Right. The computer's through here.'

In James's office, Sandra had turned the computer on. 'Let me open the file. It hasn't got a proper title. The file's just labelled NEW JOB.' She stood to one side as he sat down in front of the monitor.

'OK,' he said, checking the page count, 'is it just this page?'

'That's it she said. 'It's all on this page. Like I said, there's nothing much, but there are a few names you can conjure with.'

'And a date,' said Sep. 'Date of death 12 March 2014. Here we go . . . *Circumstances of death . . . fall from high building . . . cause of death . . . unknown, probable murder.*' He looked at Sandra. 'Does he tell us who's dead?'

'Further down.'

Sep scrolled down further and read out loud, '*Charles Francis Santiago, more commonly known as Charlie. Born 15 November 1962, died 12 March 2014. Managing Director and majority share-holder in Santiago TechSys Ltd. Turnover 2012–2013, £6.8 million net profit . . . £1.7 million* – that's a lot of net profit. I'm guessing he didn't top himself because he was broke.'

'The police don't think he topped himself at all. As coincidence would have it, DCI Wood was working on that case as well.'

'Santiago TechSys? Sounds like it's something to do with computers. Could that be what we're looking at? Was he bumped off by some rival computer company who stole his rights to some system or other?'

'Do you know anything about computers, Sep?'

'Well, about enough to fill out paperwork, but I know someone who does and if this case is why James died we might just unravel what happened to James and who did it – two birds with one stone as it were. Do you know if Wood was working along those lines?'

'I've no idea what lines he was working on,' said Sandra. 'The last I heard he said something about it being a cold case, just like my James. What exactly does that mean?'

'It means they've run out of ideas and it's been put on ice until something new turns up. It's the very unit I work for right now.'

'But you've never heard of it.'

'I haven't. It could be that we haven't made a start on it yet, but if the James Boswell case is one we're working on, it's high time we made a start on Mr Santiago.'

'I wonder what their line of enquiry was.'

'Well,' said Sep, 'that's something I can possibly find out.

Knowing Wood I'm guessing it was just one line of enquiry. There
may be several other lines of enquiry I need to follow. What about
Santiago's family, will they be cooperative?'

'Once again I don't know.'

'Right, let's see what else James uncovered . . . Olivia Hardacre,'
said Sep. 'She's been given very special attention, but I wouldn't
have thought throwing a man out of a window was a woman's
style of thing, unless she's huge and he was tiny.'

'Once again, I wouldn't know. All I know is what's in this file.
I know I'm a journalist but I wouldn't know how to start investigating it all – that's a detective's job.'

'Did James say anything at all to you about this story he was
following up . . . I mean, anything or anyone?'

'To tell you the truth, Sep, when he died I was so grief-stricken
my brain seemed to switch itself off and I'm not quite right even
now. I loved James very much.'

'Yes, I can see that and now you want to do his memory justice.'

'Something like that. I don't want this thing to be left hanging
in the air with no proper resolution. James would have hated that,
especially this horrible prostitute connection.'

'Yes, you need to tell me all about that as well, I'm afraid.'

'I think it might be more helpful if I showed you where he
died.'

'Can you manage that?'

'I can show you the grotty hotel, but I don't want to go inside.'

'That's fine. Going inside is my job.'

'Are you allowed to go in without a warrant or something?'

'I'm allowed into the public area. For me to enter the crime
scene I would need a warrant or its equivalent.'

'What's the equivalent of a warrant?'

'A twenty pound note usually does it – or a fifty if they're
reluctant. This is where I start to run up my expenses bill.'

'I'll give you five hundred in advance if it helps.'

'Hmm, it probably would, providing my work never finds out
about it. Tell you what, give it to Winnie. She's the one I'll have
to account to with all my expense claims and she's very strict – on
the client's behalf.'

'I'm impressed.' said Sandra. 'So, do I take it there's a reasonable chance of success?'

'I can't guarantee that at this stage. In fact, I might not be able to guarantee anything at any stage but it seems there's quite a lot to go on that the police have missed. I'll follow it up as much as I can.'

The ancient receptionist stared up at Sep with rheumy eyes and Sep accurately guessed that she wasn't able to see him too well.

'What name did yer say?'

'Boswell, James Boswell.'

'Is that your name?'

'No, my name's Sep Black.'

'What? Are you that foreign bugger what got kicked out of his football job fer bein' a crook?'

'No, Sep Black, as in . . . black and white.'

'Why didn't yer say so first time? And who's this James Boswell?'

'He's the man who was murdered here recently.'

'Murdered? In here? Oh aye, I remember now.'

'I was actually wondering about a woman he had in his room. Did you see her?'

'Nay, I can't see bugger all wivout me specs.' She put her glasses on. 'I can see you all right now but I couldn't see her. She wasn't booking, see. She only wanted ter go to a room what had been booked and paid for. Prozzie most like. Not a bad looker for a prozzie – as far as I could tell.'

'Paid for by who?'

'Him – he paid usin' one o' them cards.'

'Boswell paid by card for a prostitute?'

'Just for the room. We don't supply tarts. As far as the law knows we're a respectable hotel.'

Sep could have told her the law knew exactly what sort of a place it was, but that would give him away as a copper.

'So you've no idea what she looked like?'

'Sep Black, yer say. I've told all this ter them coppers what came. No, I've no bloody idea what she looked like. We get all sorts o' bleedin' trollops come ter this place. It's not my idea ter run it as a knockin' shop, it's me grandson's place. I just sit here all day and watch telly when I'm not bookin' folk in and out. I'm what yer might call a fucker booker.'

She turned her back to him and laughed at her own joke. Sep didn't. He could see a TV over her shoulder. She was watching the *Jeremy Kyle Show*. He leaned through the hatch and tapped her on the back. 'Could I see the room Mr Boswell was in – is it vacant?'

She turned round. 'What?'

'Mr Boswell's room, is it vacant? I'd like to take a look at it.'

'It's twenny pound a night – twenny-five if yer want bed and breakfast, but I wouldn't recommend it – it's shite.'

Sep took out a twenty and gave it to her, saying, 'I just want to look in it for a few minutes, not to stay overnight. There's another one of those for you if you can give me any proper information about who was in the room with Mr Boswell.'

'Yer norra a copper, are yer?'

'No,' lied Sep.

'I thought not. Coppers don't go round handin' out twenny quid notes.'

The old woman took the money and looked up at him over the top of her glasses, which meant she probably couldn't make him out at all.

'Another twenny, yer say?'

'Yes, but only for proper information. I don't want you making stuff up just to get the twenty. I'll know if you're making stuff up.'

'Will yer now? Some sort of fuckin' mind reader are yer?'

'Try me,' he challenged.

She closed her eyes as if in deep thought. 'Well, she weren't a tarty sort like we usually get here. In fact, she weren't from round here at all. She talked a bit posh but I reckon she had a bit of Scouse in her.'

'Posh Scouse, eh? That should narrow it down a lot.'

'Eh, don't be so fuckin' cheeky. I'm from Liverpool meself.'

Sep was trying to detect the Liverpool accent from her voice but it was too hoarse.

'My apologies.'

'No need to apologize, lad,' she said. 'But there's some nice spots around Liverpool what she might have come from. North Liverpool I'd say. Maybe even Formby. It's nice up in Formby.'

'How old would you say?'

'Well, I thought she'd be fairly young with her bein' on the game, but maybe I were wrong. I don't think she were all that old. I know she had dark hair, I could see that – and I can tell yer what scent she had on. It were that Chanel stuff. I know that cos one o' the tarts ended up wi' some on what a punter had bought her. I think he must have wanted ter shag someone what smelled nice.'

'This Mr Boswell and the woman, had either of them been here before?'

'Well, I'd never seen 'em an' I'm the only one bookin' people in and out. I work from ten till six. Anyone wants to book in before or after can go bollocks. All our reg'lars know the rules.' She pointed to a notice on the wall that said, *I only take bookings between the hours of 10 a.m. and 6 p.m.*

'Anything else you noticed?'

'Well,' she said, 'and I never mentioned this to them coppers cos I thought it had nowt ter do with owt. A feller came in just after her and followed her up. Straight in, straight up without stoppin' here.'

'And you thought this had nothing to do with the murder?'

'Why should it? There's blokes comin' in and out all the bleedin' time in here. Half the time I don't know who's who. I'm ninety-three, yer know.'

'Do you know if he went to the same room as her?'

'I don't know, but I do know he wasn't a reg'lar. Big bloke, heavy-footed when he went up the stairs, like a bleedin' elephant . . . and yeah, he did go to her room cos I could hear him go in, real noisy bugger, now I come ter think of it. That room's right above here.'

She jabbed an arthritic finger at the ceiling. Sep leaned through the hatch and looked up, as though there might be something to see apart from a cracked ceiling that needed a good dusting and a coat of paint.

'So, when Mr Boswell went upstairs there were two other people in the room. The Chanel woman and the bloke with heavy feet.'

'That's right.'

'Here's the other twenty. If you think of anything else while I'm up there I'll give you another twenty, but don't make stuff up, mind.'

'I know – yer, a bleedin' mind reader,' she cackled. 'Here's the key. It's number seven.'

Upstairs, Sep turned the key and pushed the door open. He was guessing this was probably the last thing James Boswell had done. He was also guessing that the heavy-footed man was in some way attached to the Scouse woman. Husband, boyfriend, hired heavy, hired hitman, who knows? Not Sep Black, not yet anyway.

The room was cleaner than it had been for some time. The fingerprint dusting had been polished off and the rug on the floor on which James Boswell died had been replaced with a slightly newer one. He was just three steps into the room and he was standing on it.

It was a wretched room and not just because it was a murder scene. Sep switched on the lone bulb that dangled by a dirty flex from the ceiling and was rewarded with forty watts of miserable light. The curtains were worn and dirty and thin; the woodchip wallpaper, long ago painted in magnolia was now grubby and decorated with illiterate obscenities; the double bed looked worn and stained enough to repel all but the most desperate of fornicators; and there was a dank and unpleasant odour about the place; an odour of unwashed bodies and vomit. Now it was a murder scene and Sep felt sorry for James Boswell whose life had come to an end in this abominable room. No man should have to end his life in such a place. It struck Sep that twenty pounds a night was at least a hundred pounds too much.

He looked around at the door he'd just come through and guessed the assailant had been behind it with his blunt instrument at the ready. Thud! One blow to the head, down goes James. The police report, which had mentioned three blows – *thud . . . thud . . . thud*! James would have been most likely on the floor to take the second two blows, the ones that killed him. Blows delivered by a heavy-footed man, probably a strong man, certainly a ruthless man. Was he a paid hitman or an angry lover? Or was James's death as much of a shock to the woman as it was to James? Might she be the main witness he was looking for? A woman who hadn't been expecting her lover to be killed. A woman who might be of great help, who could point Sep in the right direction. If she *were* James's lover, it wouldn't please Sandra, who wanted him to prove otherwise, but all he could do was find out the truth, whether or not it was what she wanted to know.

He went to the window and slid it open to let in some fresh air. Then he stood in the middle of the room and did a 360-degree turn to see if anything out of the ordinary struck him. If everything was still as it was when James Boswell was murdered, then there was nothing that stood out. He didn't expect anything but it was always useful to visit the scene of a murder in case a visual memory was required at some time during his investigation. He took out his mobile phone, turned on its video recorder and repeated the circle three times, different views each time – high, medium and low level, videoing everything in the room. He played it back to check he'd missed nothing, stuck the phone back in his pocket and asked himself what he knew that DCI Wood didn't know.

He knew that James had *not* been killed and robbed by a common prostitute. His wallet was still in his pocket so robbery – the obvious line of enquiry for DCI Wood to have taken – had been immediately discounted. No wonder they'd come to a dead end so quickly. James had been killed because someone wanted him dead and that someone was either a jealous husband or lover, or for some other reason. The most likely other reason being the story James was following up on. This was the motive Sep was hoping for.

He smiled to himself. This was an enquiry that should keep him clear of St James's Hospital A&E ward, for a change; an enquiry that just required brain and not brawn. Proper detective work. It might not turn out like that, but Sep was an eternal optimist. He had one last thought. On his way out he stopped at the reception hatch and spoke to the old woman.

'I can't think of nowt else ter tell yer,' she said. 'Bit of a shit'ole, isn't it?'

'That's an insult to shit'oles,' said Sep. 'But there is something you might help me with. When this woman left, did she leave with the heavy-footed man?'

'D'yer know, she bloody did! I forgot about that. Mind you, no bugger asked me.'

'After Mr Boswell went up how long before they came down?'

'Bloody hell, yer asking me some right stuff now. It's bloody ages ago all this. After he went up, eh? Let me think . . . they came in first, then him as was done in came in a few minutes later and went up . . . then they came down and *he* didn't – well, of course he didn't. Then I went up and knocked on t'door.'

'So how long after Mr Boswell went up did the other two come down?'

'If yer'd gimme a bloody chance that's what I'm tryin' ter remember! It weren't long at all as it happens. In fact, it were only a couple o' minutes before her and that first feller came down.

I did wonder meself what she were up to, which is why I went up and knocked on t'door.'

'So, Mr Boswell is now in the room on his own and the other two are leaving together. Did they seem all right with each other? I mean, did she seem scared or anything?'

She scratched her head as she thought back. 'No, not that I remember. No, they left together in a bit of a rush. Hey, and I make no bloody wonder after what they'd done! I put me glasses on and looked through t'winder. I can be a proper nosey bugger at times. They were in a car and she were drivin'. She got in and, er . . . that's right she got in and he lit a ciggy and had a smoke before he got in. I remember because he only took a couple o' drags then threw it away. Waste of a bloody ciggy, if you ask me.'

'So she could have driven straight off and left him there if she'd been scared of him?'

'I suppose she could, yeah. I don't suppose he'd have been so suited.'

'So they more or less came together and left together?' mused Sep. This could eliminate the jealous lover theory. He took another twenty from his wallet and gave it to her, along with a card containing his personal mobile phone number and nothing else. A card that would be frowned upon by the police, but a card he often found handy.

'And when you knocked on his door, what then?'

'Nothin'. I mean I didn't know he were dead. Why would I think he were dead?'

'Did you look in the room?'

'No, I didn't. He might have been undressed for all I know. Yer don't just go bargin' in people's room – 'specially not in a place like this.'

'No, I don't suppose you do. So who found the body?'

'That were me grandson, our Paul. He came the next mornin'. I told him the room was let for a night and he went up ter check it's been left in a decent state.'

'You just said it was a shit'ole.'

'I know, but what can you expect for twenny a night? We might be a knockin' shop but we do have standards. We're very popular, yer know. We do very good business.'

'Yeah, I can imagine. So Paul found Mr Boswell's body?'

'He did.'

'Did you go up to look at it?'

'I did as a matter of fact – only a quick look. It were a right mess, blood all over t'rug.'

'And you rang the police?'

'No, that were our Paul.'

'If you think of anything else would you ring me on the number on that card?'

'Such as?'

'I don't know. What sort of car was it?'

'I don't know cars.'

'What colour?'

'Sort of grey . . . silver, mebbe. Yeah, shiny grey. Is that worth another twenty?'

'It'll be worth forty if you ring me with more good stuff.'

'Right, I'll give it a right good think, shall I?'

'You do that. What's your name, by the way?'

'Agnes, although most people call me Aggie.'

'You look more like an Agnes to me. Thank you, Agnes.'

FIVE

'He was set up,' Sep told her, 'it was a planned murder.'

They were in his car, driving away.

'How do you know?'

'The woman had a male accomplice. They came together and left together in a grey car. That's a lot of planning and trouble just to rob a man of what he might have in his wallet. For all they knew he might have been skint.'

'They didn't take his wallet. He only had twenty-five quid in it.'

'So, your husband was lured there to be killed and for no other reason. It's a knocking shop all right, no question, but James wasn't a knocking shop customer and she wasn't a prostitute. For a start, he hadn't been there before, nor had the woman. It was just a rendezvous, probably chosen by her to make the police think he was killed by a prostitute.'

He looked at her and detected a faint smile and he knew it was a smile of relief. He'd pretty much confirmed that her James hadn't been killed by a prostitute he was visiting.

'I imagine that's something you wanted to hear,' he said.

'It helps.'

'I can only assume it was a story he was working on and this mystery woman was involved in it. She found out about him chasing the story and decided to have someone shut him up.'

'How come you've found all this out in no time at all and the police found nothing.'

'The senior officer on the case isn't the sharpest tool in the box. He and I had many differences. Especially before I moved over to the Cold Case mob.'

'Is he the one who got you suspended?'

'No, that feller's doing serious time in prison.'

'You're not a man to cross swords with, are you, Mr Black?'

'That doesn't mean I can be careless. If Wood finds out I'm working on it for you, he won't be too pleased. He'll no doubt find out eventually, but rather later than sooner. He can't obstruct me in my enquiries without getting himself into trouble. My job is to bring the killer in with enough evidence to nail him. Woody will hate it, but I do get a certain kick out of that.'

'I imagine you do.'

Sep sniffed the air and detected Chanel No 5. He recognized it because it was Winnie's favourite perfume. Pricey, but very popular, it would seem.

'She wore Chanel Number Five, like you,' he said.

'Really? It was James's favourite, mine too when I could afford it. I hope that doesn't put me in your frame.'

'Not at all.'

'So, what's next?' she said.

'What's next is we find out what we've got on file.'

'Who's we?'

'There'll be a police file on the case that I wouldn't mind taking a look at.'

'What about James's computer?'

'If this was a story worth killing for I suspect James might well have information hidden away on his computer behind a password or something.'

'Well, you're welcome to take a look at his computer. Are you an expert?'

'Me? No way. But it's not *what* you know it's *who* you know. We might need you to help with the password. It's usually a word or name familiar to the user. We live in an IT age where most things can be hacked, even if you don't know the passwords. I also know someone who's an expert hacker.'

'I bet he's young.'

'It's not a he it's a she and you've met her.'

'What? Winnie?'

He grinned and nodded.

'No! You've got to be kidding!'

'Hey, I didn't believe it when she told me, but she's grown up with computers since she was a girl. They had one in a children's home she lived in. In fact, she stole it when she ran away with another girl. To a girl like her, who'd had a real rough time growing up, it was the best thing ever and when the Internet came out it opened up a whole world to her. Winnie O'Toole's a genuine genius on a computer.'

'So why doesn't she work in IT instead of running a second-hand dress shop?'

'No formal qualifications. She's doing an Open University degree in computer science, although she thinks she's years ahead of what she's being taught. So do her tutors for that matter.'

'A prodigy, eh?'

'Apparently so. She's helped me out on one or two cases, although I claim all the kudos myself.'

'Of course. Why waste a bit of kudos on someone who doesn't need it?'

'It's all part of the mystery I surround myself with when I solve impossible cases. Mostly I just use ingenious lies when questioning suspects. It's how I got to be a DI, apparently.'

'Well, we'd better get Winnie over to the computer straight away.'

'I think first I need to take a look in the police system to see what the officers originally investigating the case came up with. Did James have any particular publication in mind who might buy his story?'

'Not really. He had contacts in the *Mail* and the *Telegraph*, although he did most of his work for press agencies. They took fifteen per cent off him but they hawked it around and got much better deals than he ever did . . . and better money.'

'Any particular agency?'

'There's one called Tyke News he worked with a lot. I think he'd have taken it there with it being a local story. They'd have sold it to the *Yorkshire Post* and then to the nationals, maybe even television and radio if it's a big enough story.'

'Well, it's certainly a big story now – if James was killed to suppress it.'

'Yes,' said Sandra. 'I'm more than aware of that and I'm going to tell it, if only to get some sort of justice for James. The only story the papers have run about it so far is that he was murdered in a downmarket hotel, probably by a prostitute.' She glanced at Sep and added, 'There is one thing that bothers me now.'

'What's that?'

'If James was murdered to suppress his story it means you're up against some very dangerous people and I'm worried about what I've got you into.'

'Sandra, I'm not sure if I've got enough to persuade my boss to take the case on right now. I need to plod away on my own for a while. Either that or I hand what I have over to my colleagues and see what they can do for you.'

'The trouble is,' she said, 'the police haven't impressed me so far and you have. But what if you end up like James?'

'Let me do the worrying, Sandra. I've been in tricky situations before. So, who's it to be, me or the West Yorkshire Police?'

'Is it all right if I go along with you until things become impossible for you?'

'Fine by me. If I think I'm getting nowhere, you'll be the first to know.'

'OK, I'll stick with you.'

'Good, is there anyone in particular at this press agency?'

'James dealt with a man called Lovell, Patrick Lovell.'

'Right, I'll have a word with Patrick Lovell before I do anything else.'

Patrick Lovell was an ex-feature writer with the *Daily Express* who now spent his time covering crown courts, inquests, tribunals and breaking news of murders and similar mayhem, but he couldn't be everywhere and do everything which is why he had relied on the likes of James Boswell who had been a press association-trained journalist, to bring him stories. Sep was in Lovell's office.

'So, you don't know what story James was working on?'

'No idea. I usually ask people to bring me a finished article, or at least the bones of one. From what I hear James had only just begun his investigation into this, whatever it was.'

'Did you know James well?'

'Fairly well.'

'His wife thinks that no way he'd go with a prostitute.'

'I think she's right. He was a good-looking, personable bloke was James. He wouldn't need to pay for it.'

'What about not paying for it?'

Patrick looked at Sep with humour in his eyes. 'You mean, was he having a bit on the side?'

'Yes.'

Patrick twiddled a pencil around in his fingers as he gave this matter some thought.

'I'm thinking an angry husband,' added Sep.

'He'd have to be really angry to commit murder.'

'Jealousy can drive a man to insane lengths . . . well?'

Patrick sighed 'Yes, he did. But I'm a bit reluctant to tell you because I promised him faithfully I'd keep my mouth shut about it.'

'He's dead.'

'I know, but Sandra isn't.'

'What did the police ask you?'

'The police didn't ask me anything. They never came here.'

'Really? I'm amazed . . . or I should be, but knowing who was in charge of the investigation I'm not so amazed. Is this woman married?'

'Yes.'

'Have you met her husband?'

'I have.'

'Well?'

'You're asking me if he's capable of murder and I don't know.'

'Who is this woman?'

Patrick nodded at the glass partition behind which two women were working. 'Actually she works here, but she'll be mortified if she finds out I've told you.'

Without looking round, Sep said, 'I'm guessing the young blonde.'

'Good guess. Her name's Julie Rogerson. You're not going to talk to her, are you?'

Sep shrugged. 'I need to eliminate her and her husband from my enquiries. If I can't do that, then I'll need to tell my colleagues in the police . . . who will.'

Patrick pressed a key on his intercom. 'Julie, can you come through, please.'

'Yep.'

A few seconds later a pretty woman in her twenties, entered the office and stood beside where Sep was sitting. Her hair was shiny blonde and cut in a short bob. The rest of her matched the beauty of her face.

'This is DI Sep Black,' Patrick told her.

'I know. I recognized him. We have his photo in our files.'

Sep tried to catch a hint of Scouse in her accent. She had no regional accent at all.

'Really?' he said.

Julie smiled at him and sat down in another chair. 'Yes, one of our photographers will have taken it, which means it belongs to us to do with what we want.'

'You'd be best not annoy him, Julie,' said Patrick.

'She's not annoying me,' said Sep. 'I was just surprised that anyone would want to keep a photo of me.'

'You're a very newsworthy person at times, Mr Black,' said Julie.

Sep turned his chair to face her. 'Julie, I'm investigating the murder of James Boswell, I gather you knew him well.'

Julie's friendly expression switched itself off. 'I gather this is a private investigation,' she said, looking daggers at her boss.

'No, it's a police matter,' said Sep.

'Julie,' said Patrick. 'If I hadn't told him, more police would have come round asking questions of both you and Martyn. You can talk in complete confidence with DI Black.'

'Mrs Boswell's not happy how his murder was reported,' said Sep.

'You mean, by a prostitute?'

'Exactly.'

'Well, I don't believe that. James didn't need to go to prostitutes.'

'Julie, I absolutely believe you.'

The implication had her blushing and looking down at her hands.

Sep went on. 'The police don't appear to know that you were having an affair with James and there's no need for them to know, so long as you're open with me.'

'I wasn't having an affair with him and you're the police so you can put them straight, should it ever arise!' Her forceful manner had Sep almost believing her.

'I'm not the regular police,' he said, 'I work for an arm's-length unit and I don't exchange information with them unless it's absolutely necessary. And they're not working on this case anymore but, with it being a cold case, I am.'

Julie looked up at Patrick, who took the hint and got to his feet. 'Look,' he said, 'this conversation needs to be private. I'll make myself scarce for half an hour.'

Julie watched him go then said to Sep, 'He'll have gone downstairs for a cig, then across the road for a coffee.'

'Good for him. I didn't want to embarrass you.'

'No? You've done a poor job of that so far.'

Sep grinned. He was beginning to like Julie and was sincerely hoping she wasn't involved in the murder. His gut instinct said she wasn't and it was usually reliable. 'Look, I'll get straight to the point. I'm trying to eliminate anyone who might have had a motive for killing James and I'm afraid one of the candidates appears to be your husband and he's a candidate the police don't know about – as yet.'

'Martyn?'

The name almost exploded from her mouth. 'He doesn't know about it and he wouldn't harm a fly. Oh God! You mustn't tell him you think I was having an affair with James.'

'Julie, if I don't check him out, the police will mention it, no matter how innocent you are.'

Tears appeared which she wiped away with the heel of a hand. 'Mr Black . . . Sep . . . if Martyn thought I was having an affair he wouldn't be able to hide his feelings. I feel really sad about James dying. He was a dear friend I used to exchange information with.'

'Who else knew about your friendship? Obviously your boss did.'

'No one at all. Patrick only knew because he saw us together and put two and two together and made five. He told me not to be so careless or to pack it in. I told him there was nothing to pack

in. He liked both Martyn and James. In fact, Martyn liked James
– considered him to be a friend.'

'Do you know Sandra?'

'I don't actually, no. Never been in her company. It wouldn't
do her any good to think that James had been having an affair.'

'I know that. Describe your husband to me . . . physically I
mean.'

'Physically? He's an ex-rugby player, a big man, but that doesn't
mean he's violent. He's a real pussycat to me.'

'Rugby player? A lot of rugby players are surprisingly light on
their feet. Is Martyn?'

'Not that I've noticed. I think Martyn must be the exception.
He was a prop forward, whatever that is.'

'It's a position requiring a lot of strength.'

'Enough to kill a man, you mean? Mr Black, to kill a man you
need a killer's capability. Martyn wouldn't harm a fly. I may look
young, but I'm a twenty-eight-year-old ex-crime reporter. I've been
around a few killers and you can somehow sense the, er . . . the
capability in them. Martyn hasn't got that. I can't explain it any
better I'm afraid.'

Sep has also been around many killers but he hadn't been
able to sense any such thing. In his opinion, given enough
provocation, any person can turn killer in the blink of an eye.
Maybe he just didn't have her intuition. He held her gaze. He
knew that pursuing this line of investigation would damage three
lives, those of Julie, Martyn and Sandra. Hell, for all he knew,
his gut instinct might be miles off track. Julie might be up to
her neck in it.

'OK,' he said. 'What I'll do is this. I have other lines of
investigation that I can follow. If I come to an eventual dead end
I'll give everything I have over to the CID in the hope that with
their powers they can dig deeper than I can, but I'll let you know
before I do because they'll need to interview both you and Martyn.
It'll give you a chance to warn him and convince him that you
and James weren't having an affair. In the meantime, if you know
anything of the story he was following, I'd be grateful if you
told me.'

'You think it's that story what got him killed?'

'I think that's the hot favourite.'

'It was something to do with a murder in Leeds last year.

The police didn't get anyone for it. James was working on a lead.'

'What sort of lead?'

'I'm not sure,' she said, 'but I'd heard from another source that a local heavy had been somehow involved and I wanted to warn James to stay clear of him.'

'Who's the heavy?'

'A man named Redman, Carl Redman. That's all I know, just a name. James could be quite secretive about his stories, especially to people in the same business, even me. We only saw each other about once a month and that was only for an hour or so in some pub or other. It wasn't a fling or anything, just an exchange of information. We liked each other and enjoyed each other's company, which is why we made it a regular thing. I'd never leave Martyn and James would never have left Sandra. You're a copper who gathers information, you know how it is.'

'Julie, if anything comes to mind please let me know. It'll be in both our interests if I get to the truth.'

'The truth would be good for me.'

SIX

It was the following week when the woman calling herself Winona rang old Agnes at the Grimshawe and asked if the police had been enquiring about her. Since James's murder she'd had weeks of anxiety, knowing she was a party to a man's murder.

'I don't know who y'are, so how am I supposed ter know?' croaked Agnes. 'I'm norra fuckin' mind reader. Coppers are allus round here askin' their stupid questions. Mind you. I'm not surprised wiv the types what we get in 'ere. We've gorra shit reputation.'

'I was there on the day of the murder.'

'Oh, I remember that. We don't have murders every day. Are you that tart what was up there when that feller were done in?'

'I'm not a tart, but yes, I was there at that time, only when I left he was alive,' said Winona. 'I want to know if the police were asking questions about me.'

'Well, it were a few weeks ago, but they did come round askin' stupid questions.'

'So, what did you tell them?'

'Nowt really. I told 'em a woman had gone up before 'im and I reckoned she were a prozzie. I didn't get a right good look at yer, mind.'

'Did you tell them anything else?'

'No. As a matter o' fact I forgot all about that feller what came out wiv yer.'

'Good, because he had nothing to do with it either. It was all just very bad timing on our part. It would suit me if you didn't tell the police any more than you have.'

'I don't know no more.'

'Well, I'll know if you do because I know people in the police.'

'Oh heck!' said Agnes, worried.

'There's no need to worry if you haven't said anything more to the police. You haven't, have you?'

'Not to the police, no.'

'What does that mean? Who have you been talking to?'

'A bloke called Black came round a few days ago askin' questions. He's a private detective, I think.'

'Black? What did you tell him?'

'Same as I told the police. It's all I know. I told him I'd seen a woman, which was yerself but I couldn't give a description, with me not having me glasses on.'

'That's all you told him?'

'I told him that bloke what she was wiv yer were clumpin' round like a soddin' elephant.'

'He wasn't with me.'

'Mebbe not, but he were very 'eavy on 'is feet.'

'Agnes, I'm going to send you fifty pounds in cash and if I don't hear anything from my people in the police I'll send you the same every month.'

'That'll be very acceptable. At my time o' life money gets a bit scarce.'

'You can expect a registered envelope tomorrow with fifty pounds in it. Who should I send it to?'

'Agnes McGinty. D'yer know me address?'

'I do. And do not tell anyone I'm sending you this money. I will know that as well.'

'Why would I tell anyone? They'll only take it off me pension
. . . the bastards!'

Agnes was watching *Jeremy Kyle* on the television when the
heavy-footed man walked in the following day, only this time he
wasn't heavy-footed. The woman known as Winona had warned
him about this, so he trod lightly. Jeremy Kyle was opening an
envelope and about to give the result of a DNA test when the
heavy-footed man crept up behind Agnes and placed a small pillow
over her mouth. He was a powerful man and forced her head over
the back of her chair, cutting off her breathing which wasn't good
at the best of times. The shock and terror of what was happening
to her paralysed her limbs to the point that her arms hung limply
down by her sides as the man choked her to death. She died in
complete silence apart from Jeremy Kyle announcing to a young
man, whose emaciated face was decorated with tattoos and assorted
bits of metal, that he was the father of a child whose mother was
now weeping with joy at the news. The heavy-footed man checked
that Agnes's pulse had beaten its last and left the room as silently
as he'd arrived with Agnes slumped in the chair as the young
father stormed off the Jeremy Kyle set using many deleted F words.
Despite the care the killer had taken, a post mortem—usually
required when someone dies suddenly outside a hospital, would
reveal petechiae—broken blood vessels around the eyes and fibres
in her oesophagus, indicating that she had most probably been
murdered. A natural death is a difficult thing to fake.

'Fiona, I've rung you six times and all I get is a woman telling
me that you're unavailable.'
    'With respect, sir, I *am* unavailable when I'm on police
business.'
    'This is a murder – which I believe is police business.'
    'What murder's that, sir?'
    'The Santiago murder last year.'
    'That's a cold case, sir. Nothing to do with us anymore.'
    'I know, but I've had a look at the police file, having found
Robin Wood's password.'
    'Oh, well done, sir. What is it?'
    '*Cock* as in *Who Killed Cock Robin.*'
    'Oh God! I might have known.'

'I wish *I'd* known. Winnie and I went through the whole of Sherwood Forest searching for it. It took her smutty mind to find it.'

'Well done, Winnie. No wonder the DCI in Wood was reluctant to give us it. He obviously has an inflated opinion of his sexual magnetism. Was there anything in the file of any use to you?'

'Not really. It isn't a very comprehensive file, Fiona. I suspect even you lot gave up on it. I trust you'll keep me up to date on any useful information that comes your way.'

'Sir, if we gave up on it, there'll be a good reason.'

'Oh, there's a good reason all right and that reason now has a name . . . Cock Robin.'

There was a pause and Sep knew he'd hooked his pal, DS Fiona Burnside. She had even less time for DCI Robin Wood than had Sep. He decided to add to the temptation.

'In fact, there are two murders . . . both connected. Charles Santiago last year and James Boswell four months ago. I'm guessing Woody didn't spot the obvious connection and I'm wondering if you did . . . or if anyone down there did?'

'What was the obvious connection?'

'James Boswell was a freelance reporter working on the Santiago killing.'

'Was he? Oh shit! James Boswell was the last murder case I worked on. I did a lot of legwork on it for the DFCI but no one made the connection with Santiago.'

'Well, I did and it took me just one visit to Boswell's wife to make that connection.'

The DCI thought that Boswell had been killed by a prostitute,' said Fiona, 'but we had no luck in tracking her down.'

'That's because he wasn't killed by a prostitute – didn't you do *any* work on the Santiago job?'

'I did a bit of legwork, that's all. I believe DCI Wood put that case down to suicide, but handed it over to you all the same.'

'Suicide was a bit too convenient. What did you put it down to?'

'Sir, I'm a lowly sergeant. I wasn't party to all the available information. I was on another job.'

'Anyway,' said Sep, 'the Boswell killing was four months ago. The Santiago killing was over a year ago. Exactly how much work did you do on that one?'

'Not much.'

'I'd like us to meet up, Fiona.'

'Oh dear.'

They met later that day in Sep's local pub. Fiona was amazed at how much Sep knew about both cases.

'James had a possible mistress called Julie Rogerson who was employed by a news agency he did some work for. Her husband might well be a suspect and I'm also not happy with the man who owns the hotel. His ninety-odd-year-old grandmother works there and she practically runs the place.'

'What's a *possible* mistress?'

'She might be, or she might be just a business colleague passing on information.'

'What's your take on that?'

'I don't have one,' he said.

'So you think the hotel might have some connection with the Santiago killing?'

'Actually, no. It's the Santiago connection that lets the hotel off the hook.'

'I'll tell you something that might put them back on the hook.'

'What's that?'

'A ninety-odd-year-old woman was found dead in there this morning.'

'That must be Agnes? How did she die?'

'It seems she just stopped breathing. There'll be a post mortem which will tell us exactly why she died.'

'She was murdered,' said Sep, 'no question.'

'It's possible but she might simply have run out of life – it happens.'

'No, it doesn't. Everyone dies for a reason, no matter how old they are.'

'The odd thing about it was that a registered envelope containing fifty quid cash and addressed to her arrived this morning as well.'

'Can the sender be traced?'

'I doubt it, sir. Whoever sent it will have been very careful. Gloved hands and no DNA, I'm guessing.'

'Trouble is, that could be two people who wanted to keep her quiet – one by bribery, one by murder.'

'Most likely one and the same person, sir.'

'Yeah, poor old Agnes. I reckon she'd have seen the century

out had she been allowed to live. That's three murders. Fiona, are you up to helping me?'

She shrugged, dismally, then said, 'I'm a detective sergeant who does what she's told by her bosses and that that doesn't include you right now . . . sir.'

'Excellent, what do you have for me?'

'Why would I have anything?'

'Because I know you, Fiona. Once you found we'd taken the case on you wouldn't be able to resist doing a bit of checking on the police computer.'

'I did some background work on Santiago. It wasn't very successful but I found a few notes that pointed to something that might be of interest to you.'

'What's that?'

'Well, it was to do with one of these dot-com companies and something to do with share dealing.'

'What have you got?'

'Just a name, really.'

'What name?'

'Snowball dot com. I checked with Companies House. The company was registered but it was declared dormant not long after it started trading, which was just after Santiago's murder.'

'What were its aims and objectives?'

'Pretty standard for that sort of company, but they often are with new companies. They like to keep their options open until they're up and running. All I can say is that it seems to be some sort of share-dealing company.'

Sep took a long drink of his beer as he gave the matter some thought. 'You know,' he said, at some length, 'it could be that I'm going way off track here.'

'Why's that?'

'Well, it's not actually Santiago's murder I'm investigating. Trouble is, I'm struggling to believe that the murders of Charlie Santiago and James Boswell are unconnected. Who's in charge of his firm now that he's gone?'

'Well, his wife's the sole shareholder.'

'And is she a grieving widow?'

'I don't know.'

'You mean you've never met her?'

'I was never asked to interview her.'

'I wouldn't mind a word with her. Do you have an address?'
'I do, but not one you can ever say you got from me.'
'You know you can trust me, Fiona.'
Fiona gave him a look that placed a big question mark over that statement.

SEVEN

'**M**rs Santiago?'
'Yes.'
'My name is DI Black. I'm investigating a murder that might well be connected to your husband's death.'
'You mean you're Sep Black the detective?'
'I am, yes.'
'I think I have enough problems without the likes of you adding to them, Mr Sep Black.' She clicked her phone off. Sep gave a mild curse. What he needed was a tempter, something she wouldn't be able to resist. He dialled her number again and spoke without introducing himself.
'Did the police ask you about Snowball?'
'What? Is that you again, Black?'
'It is. Sorry to be so troublesome, but I may have a lead that the police didn't follow.'
'Mr Black. I haven't heard from the police for well over a year and they didn't follow any damned leads *then*! Right now I'm just getting my life back on track.'
'I'm sorry about that, but I assume you'd like to see his killer brought to justice.'
'His killer? The police seem to think he threw himself out of that window, when I know he didn't.'
'I believe that also, Mrs Santiago.'
'Do you really?'
'Yes, I do and it'll cost you nothing to tell me what you know – and what you know might be of great assistance to me.'
'You'd better come round in the morning. Do you know where I live?'

* * *

Mrs Santiago lived in a fine house in a small, select village ten
miles north of Leeds. Sep pulled up his Jaguar – an XKR sports
job that he'd bought from the proceeds of a lucrative private
investigation he'd done while on suspension from the force.

She was in her late forties and well-preserved. Not Sep's type
at all. Back in her shop Winnie would be wearing torn jeans and
a faded Celtic top – the football team of her choice – probably
the O'Toole Irish in her. She might well have an ink mark on her
nose where she'd been scratching an itch with a biro. Here was a
woman as fragile as a Ming vase. Squeeze her and you might
break her. Squeeze Winnie and she squeezed you back.

'Mrs Santiago?'

'Mr Black, I assume.'

'Yes.'

'Please come in.'

He followed her into a room as flawless as its owner. Sep was
glad he'd got changed into his one and only suit before he came
and was not in the casual gear he usually wore. It was a dark suit
with a faint pinstripe, Marks & Spencer's finest. His shoes were
well-polished, black Oxfords that he'd had for ten years and worn
no more than a dozen times. His shirt was crisp and white and
had been in a drawer for three months, wrapped in cellophane
until he'd taken it out that morning. She sat down in a blue velvet
easy chair and, with a wave of her hand, invited him to do the
same in the chair's partner.

'Do you have a list of questions you wish to ask me about
Charles's business?'

He noticed she called Charlie by his unabbreviated name, the
only person he'd heard do this.

'Did you always call him Charles?'

'I did, on account of my name being Lilian. Had I called him
Charlie he'd have called me Lil. Do I look like a Lil?'

'No, you look like a Mrs Santiago.'

'Then that's the name I'll accept from you.'

'You can call me Sep and yes, I do have a few questions . . .
question one: what do you know about Snowball?'

'Not much. I declared it a dormant company after Charles died.
I've tried to pick up the reins of Santiago TechSys since he died,
which is over a year ago. I do have some professional qualifications
in that area and I seem to be getting the hang of it.'

'Snowball is actually a company in its own right as far as I can tell,' said Sep. 'I wouldn't mind taking a look at its memorandum and articles of association. Would they be here or in his office? I'd like to know who the directors are . . . or were.'

'Well, there were just two directors, me and Charles. I'm now the only director and with it being a dormant company I don't need another director or a company secretary until it starts to trade again – if it ever does, which is unlikely. I've got enough on my hands with Santiago TechSys.'

'So Snowball's not trading?'

'Not since Charles died and even then it didn't do much trading. If you want to see the memo and articles you're free to have a look at them, but they're pretty standard. Do you want to see them?'

'Maybe not, if it hasn't traded for sixteen months.'

'Do you think Snowball had something to do with Charles's death? The police never mentioned it to me.'

'I think it's possible, but right now it's just one avenue of investigation. In fact, the crime I'm investigating is the murder of a young journalist who was murdered four months ago and who, I believe, was investigating your husband's death.'

'And you believe one might lead you to the other?'

'Yes. There again, my man might have been killed by mistake, or by a jealous husband or for some reason I haven't thought of yet. What I'm doing right now is investigating what's staring me in the face.'

'What's staring you in the face, Mr Black, is me. I suppose you've got to start somewhere and I'm that somewhere, am I?'

'You are. I often find that following one lead can bring to light all sorts of other information that can eventually send me down the right road. Or it may well be that my first lead is the right one. In a way, I'm hoping it isn't – I know very little about computers, or the stock market for that matter.'

'Is Snowball legal?'

'Would your husband dabble in anything that wasn't?'

'Only if there was no chance of him being found out.'

Sep looked at her with raised eyebrows.

'Why so surprised?' she asked him. 'He was a successful businessman. Many successful businessmen find it necessary to step over the line from time to time. Charles was a sharp operator, but I don't think he did anything too illegal.'

Sep's look of surprise turned to one of disbelief. Mrs Santiago smiled. 'Look, he has an office in this house with a filing cabinet. A safe as well.'

'Mind if I have a browse?'

'Not at all.'

'Did the police have a browse?'

'I found their man a bit objectionable and told him if he wanted to search the house to get a warrant. He said a search wouldn't be necessary.'

'This would be Detective Chief Inspector Wood, would it?'

'I think that was his name, yes.'

'And did you tell him about the filing cabinet and the safe?'

'No, I didn't. I know I should have been more helpful, with him searching for my husband's killer but he got on my nerves, whereas you have an amiable manner. I like amiable men. I just wanted Wood out of my house,' she said. Then added, 'Are you married, DI Black?'

'Engaged,' said Sep.

EIGHT

S ep sat back in his chair and put his feet on his coffee table. He and Winnie were in his house – a modest semi-detached in a good area of North Leeds. He'd lived there on his own since his divorce. Marriage had done him no favours, which made him disinclined to try it again. Winnie, the widow of an iniquitous man, who had died a drunken death beneath the wheels of a bus, didn't share his distrust of marriage.

'I gave what I had to my super,' he told her, 'and she's given me the go-ahead to work the Boswell case on my own. The unit's pretty tied up right now. If I need troops to help me, they'll be made available.'

'Are you OK with that?'

'I think so. It gives me a free rein to come and go as I please, with no one to worry about but myself, only reporting in every other day or whenever necessary.'

'Did you get anything useful from Mrs Santiago?'

'She's the only living director of Snowball and that the police didn't impress her too much with their investigation, especially DCI Wood. I had a browse through a lot of company documents which Woody never asked to see.'

'Did you get any names?'

'Not in the documents – just found some in note form in a folder. Two people who I assume are employees of Santiago TechSys Ltd and have something to do with Snowball. I asked Mrs Santiago about the employees. One is a brilliant IT expert and the other is his brother who has mental health issues and is employed in some low-level capacity.'

'Mental health issues?'

'It's the term Mrs Santiago used, although I think she was trying to be kind. He's good at what he does, but what he does isn't all that important. The IT expert is called Adam Piper and his brother's called Simeon. Both of them completely harmless, according to the CID boys.'

'I've already spoken to them both. Adam got on his high horse and told me I had no right asking him questions. Simeon was scared to death of me.'

'Do you think they know anything that might give you a lead?'

Sep left her question unanswered for a while, then said, 'To be honest, I'm seriously thinking of knocking the whole thing on the head. Telling the super I'm up against a brick wall.'

'That's not very professional, Sep. You've taken the job and there's a woman out there relying on you to restore her husband's reputation from being a man killed by a prostitute he was said to be having it off with.'

'That's the problem. I'm working for two bosses, one of which would sack me on the spot of they knew I was also working privately.'

'How would they ever find out?'

'Dunno. How do I find stuff out?'

'Yeah, I suppose you have a point.'

'Winnie, did I by any chance tell you that Mrs Boswell offered me fifty grand from her insurance money if I solved the case to her satisfaction. I told her I couldn't take the money with me being a copper so she said she'd give it to you. Did I tell you that?'

'No, you didn't tell me that! Are you saying that's why I want you to stay with the case?'

'Just wondering if she'd mentioned it to you, that's all.'

'Well, she hasn't and I'm bloody insulted!'

'OK, OK, I'll stay with it. As far as the job's concerned she's just a useful witness and there's no money coming my way.'

'Good and you can tell Mrs Boswell that I'm not too proud to take her money.'

'I'll tell her no such thing. By the way, her James was probably having it off with another man's wife. Do I tell her that?'

'Not if it has nothing to do with the case.'

'Good point. There are three deaths connected to these cases and I haven't got a clue who's done what to whom. I could be the next when they find out I'm on the case and I hate it when people try to kill me.'

'Do you think Wood was threatened?' Winnie asked. 'He seems to have dropped the two cases like hot bricks.'

'You could be right. He's definitely a man who can be scared off and I've been surprised at how little he's done on both cases. I think I'll run that one past Fiona . . . what?'

She was giving him a funny look.

'I hope that's the only thing you run past Fiona.'

'Winnie, Fiona would be more interested in you than me.'

The professional killer who called himself Mr Wolf gave a grunt of satisfaction and started the engine when his mark appeared. This was to be a dangerous hit on a man who'd be aware of such danger; a hit on a busy road with any number of unknowns hampering a clean getaway. He'd asked for four grand and finally agreed on three, plus expenses which included the cost of the van he was driving. He felt he was selling his services too cheaply. The sun was behind him and low in the sky, which was to his advantage. If the cop turned and saw him coming he'd be blinded momentarily by the sun and blinded for one second was enough for Wolf. At forty miles an hour the van would travel twenty yards in one second. Wolf didn't know much but he knew that.

He knew the copper would have to cross the road to get to where his red Jaguar was parked. Stupid bastard, driving around in a flash car like that, advertising his whereabouts to anyone wanting to do him a mischief – anyone such as Wolf.

It was a busy road and these jobs don't work too well on busy roads, unless you could slip off down a side road that took you well away from the scene. He had that very side road in mind as he watched his mark dart out into the middle of the road and wait until the traffic on Wolf's side had cleared. Wolf was the last in that line of traffic. He gave himself a decent gap between him and a car in front, then picked up speed as he approached the copper standing in the middle of the road, awaiting a gap in the traffic on the other side; it was a gap which had closed by the time Wolf arrived. With two turns of the steering wheel the job was done. The copper flew clean over the van roof and landed in a heap on the road behind it. The killer caught a glance in his wing mirror of the man landing in the road and what he saw pleased him. He swung left down a side road and was a quarter of a mile away before anyone reached Sep Black, who wasn't looking good. Winnie had heard the commotion and dashed outside, knowing immediately who it was lying there with blood pooling around his head. She slid to her knees beside him.

'Sep!' she screamed, cradling his bloodied head.

'Looks ter me like he's had it,' said one spectator, dolefully. Winnie looked up and glared at him, knowing that there's always someone hoping for the worst on these occasions.

'I've rung for an ambulance,' said a more helpful one. 'I told them they need to be quick. They reckon ten minutes ETA.'

'He'll never last ten minutes,' said the doleful spectator.

'You won't last ten bloody seconds if you don't shut up!' screamed Winnie.

A queue of traffic was forming with many impatient horns sounding but Winnie had no awareness of this. She was only aware that Sep was showing no sign of life. She tried to find a pulse but she had never been any good at that. Still cradling his bleeding head in her arms she spoke to him.

'Sep Black, don't you die on me now, don't you dare die on me, Sep Black. I love you, Sep. If you can, you need to speak to me. Show me you're alive. Any sign at all. Please, Sep.'

But Sep said nothing, did nothing. He just laid there, lifeless. A passing police car stopped. Officers got out. One of them knelt beside Winnie.

'Do you know who he is?'

'It's S . . . Sep Black . . .' was all she could say.

'DI Sep Black?'

'Yes.'

'Hit-and-run,' someone called out. 'There's an ambulance on its way.'

The other officer was asking for witnesses. He rang it into the station: 'We've got an RTA on Warbuoys Road. The victim is DI Black . . . yes, *our* DI Black. An ambulance has been summoned, but double-check that please. It looks very urgent. It's a hit-and-run. Could be attempted murder. Small, dark blue unmarked van is all I've got. Headed off down Rathbone Terrace, possibly heading for Wakefield Road. It happened five minutes ago so it's still in the area. We need to alert all available units.'

'Is DI Black still alive?'

'My partner can't find a pulse. It's touch and go. He's in a bad way. The hospital needs to be alerted.'

Three hours later the man in the van was no longer in the van, because the van was now a compressed metal cube in a Rotherham scrapyard. He was a large, heavy-featured and heavy-lidded man with gnarled teeth and a pock-marked complexion. He called himself Mr Wolf after a character in the film *Pulp Fiction*. He considered it was more intimidating than his real name – Stanley Butterbowl.

Wolf had returned from Rotherham by train and was watching the evening news on the TV in a hotel room. It said the man in the road accident was seriously injured but still alive. This meant Wolf's payday would be delayed until the man was dead. Either that or he'd need to finish the job. If it was the latter he'd demand an extra grand – no, two grand. The man was a cop. A second attempt would be so much more dangerous than the first. In fact, it occurred to him to go in heavy with Redman and demand to be paid his three grand now for work in progress. The idea had been to scare Sep Black into not investigating Santiago's death. Wolf figured he'd already done that. Even if Black hadn't been scared off he wouldn't be in a fit state to investigate anything. Wolf had hit him good and hard and had seen him bounce on the road through his mirror. If Black lived, he'd most likely be in wheelchair for the rest of his life. That should be good enough for Carl bloody Redman.

NINE

Fiona and Winnie sat side-by-side outside the Intensive Care Unit in St James's Hospital. Fiona looked at her watch. 'His daughter and her mother should be here soon. I hope we get some encouraging news before they get here. You know, it's not fair on them, putting them to all this worry.'

'This isn't really Sep's fault,' Winnie said. 'He was talking about giving up on this case before he got knocked down. Trouble is, knowing Sep, if he recovers, he's bound to go after whoever did this to him.'

'Well, I don't wish him ill,' said Fiona, 'but it'll be a miracle if he makes a full recovery.'

'Fiona, this is Lazarus Black we're talking about.'

Fiona gave a wan smile, appreciating Winnie's optimism. 'Yes, he has truly magical powers of reincarnation.'

'I'm guessing you've said a prayer for him.'

'I have indeed. I've asked the Lord to forgive him his trespasses and to balance them against all the good work he's done down here.'

'Do you think one balances out the other?' Winnie asked.

'Only if you don't include all the aggravation he's caused me over the years.'

'And me,' said Winnie. 'I forgive him, though.'

'That's the problem with Black. He's such an easy bugger to forgive. If he gets well, you must insist on him marrying you and taking a desk job.'

'I *must insist* on Sep marrying me? Yeah, that's gonna work. We're supposed to be engaged but he keeps forgetting. I think his first marriage put him off the idea.'

'Winnie, he should never have married her. Marrying you is his only chance of survival into old age. What he needs is a desk job. All this running around after villains is taking its toll of him.'

'Maybe, but you must admit he's had some good results in the past.'

'Not for a while.'

A registrar appeared, still wearing a green surgical gown. Fiona and Winnie examined her face for optimism. Was he alive or was he dead?

She chopped off their doubts with one sentence.

'Miraculously, he's still with us.'

'Is he going to make it?' Fiona asked.

'Too early to say I'm afraid. We brought an orthopaedic surgeon over from Leeds Infirmary to do the bone work – best man in his field. I knew he'd worked on Mr Black before so I rang him on the off-chance. He's certainly given your friend the best chance he'll ever have of getting his bones back in working order. Anyway, he'll be out in a minute to speak to you. His name's Callaghan.'

Two minutes later the surgeon appeared, having removed his scrubs. 'Hi, my name's Peter Callaghan, I've been working on your friend, I believe. Does he have any relatives here?'

'He has an ex-wife and a daughter. I can't imagine what's keeping them,' said Winnie. 'I'm his fiancée.'

'Ah, you'll do then. Erm, as far as we can tell he was knocked clean over the vehicle and landed on his left side, with his left shoulder taking the brunt of the fall which was as well, as it cushioned the effect such a fall would have had on his skull, which is fractured but not disastrously. He may well develop a subdural haematoma but we have an excellent neurosurgeon who'll keep an eye on that.'

'Will he be paralysed in any way?' Winnie asked.

'Well, our first job is to keep him alive but, having mended him before, I know Mr Black has an extraordinary determination to stay alive. I keep coming across pieces of my old work. I've completely rebuilt his left shoulder which should work OK once it's all healed, although it may well give him arthritis in his old age.'

'We're hoping he has an old age to have arthritis in,' said Winnie.

'Quite. Tomorrow I'm going to work on his leg and his ribs where the vehicle impact was, but before that another surgeon will need to fix his internal damage. As far as paralysis is concerned none of his vertebrae were damaged.'

'So he should walk again?' Winnie asked.

Rachel, Sep's ex-wife appeared, very flustered, along with Phoebe, his daughter.

'Is he all right? I've had a devil of a job getting here. Only found out half an hour ago.'

'Is Daddy awake?' Phoebe asked the surgeon.

'No, he's still under anaesthetic and we'll keep him asleep until all the work is done, which will be tomorrow afternoon.'

'Is he going to be all right?' Rachel persisted. 'I'm his ex-wife. This is Phoebe, our daughter.'

'All I can say is that the odds are in his favour.'

'That means he'll be OK, Mum,' said Phoebe. 'Daddy always beats the odds.'

Rachel remembered Winnie's last question, still unanswered and asked it herself. 'Will he be able to walk again?'

Winnie looked at Rachel and suspected she still had feelings for her ex. She couldn't fault her for that. He was the father of her daughter, which surely counted for something, but Rachel had been a poor wife; betraying him with a cruel lie and taking a lover when he needed her support the most. Winnie would never be a poor wife. Her love for him was real . . . unquenchable.

'All I can say,' said Callaghan, 'is that I see no reason why not . . . at the moment. Just as long as he doesn't take a turn for the worse.'

'Daddy never takes a turn for the worse.'

The surgeon smiled at the young girl's optimism. 'Even if all goes well it'll be several weeks before he's up and about again. He has severe bruising all down his right leg where the vehicle hit him. That alone will keep him off his feet for a few weeks.'

He took Rachel and Phoebe into a small room to repeat every-thing he'd just told Winnie and Fiona, both of whom sat there in a daze, still not sure if Sep would live or die.

'He's been in some bad situations,' said Winnie, 'but never as broken up as this. God, he must be in a thousand pieces!'

'Winnie, under all this anaesthetic there'll be an awareness inside DI Black. He'll have no intention of dying and if Sep Black doesn't want to die, he won't die.'

'How do you know?'

'He told me about it once. He plays it like a game of life, but it's a game he reckons he knows how to win.'

'Did you believe him?'

'Not sure. I've been under anaesthetic a few times and I don't remember dreaming, so I've got no idea how it works, but there again, who knows how Sep Black's mind works. I know he's not ready to die just yet.'

The registrar appeared again. 'Has Mr Callaghan been to see you?'

'Yes, he's in that room talking to Sep's ex-wife and daughter. Is everything OK?'

'Well, yes – other than Mr Black woke up out of his anaesthetic which shouldn't have happened. He woke up, grinned, winked and me, then he went off again. He shouldn't even know where he is or what happened to him, so why is he grinning and winking?'

'It's what he does to good-looking women,' said Fiona.

'What? Me dressed like this?'

'According to Sep the prettiest thing a woman can wear is a smile. I'm guessing you smiled at him.'

The registrar reddened slightly. 'Oh . . . I, er . . . I need to tell Mr Callaghan.'

'Yes, I think you should,' put in Winnie. 'It'll cheer his daughter up, if nothing else.'

As the registrar left, Fiona turned to Winnie with a grin on her face, 'Looks like he's decided not to die today.'

Winnie shook her head, not believing this hocus-pocus. She'd believe it tomorrow when Sep was better mended; alive, conscious, talking sense and not winking at pretty registrars.

Fiona knocked on Mrs Santiago's door quite tentatively. Not a policeman's knock at all. In fact, when she came to the door Mrs Santiago took a very close look at Fiona's warrant card to confirm she was who she said he was.

'You don't look like a police detective.'

'Thank you, that's very much to my advantage.'

'Yes, I suppose it must be. I heard about Sep Black. How's he doing?'

'He has his own unique life force, has DI Black. What would kill a normal human being is little more than an inconvenience to him.'

'So he's going to be all right, is he?'

'He'll live, yes, but this was more than an inconvenience. He'll be laid up for quite a few weeks.'

'Well, I'm glad to hear he's going to be OK. He seemed a

decent sort to me. I assume it's his accident you're here to talk about, is it?'

'It was no accident, Mrs Santiago.'

'I know that, I meant—'

Fiona cut her off. 'We haven't got many leads as to who might do this to him and I'm hoping you might point me in the right direction.'

'I'll help if I can, but I'm not sure how.'

Fiona followed her through into the sumptuous room in which she'd spoken to Sep. In fact, she sat in the same velvet chair.

'My theory is,' she said, 'that someone doesn't want your husband's murder investigated and I'm obviously wondering who that might be.'

'In other words, you want me to tell you who Charles's enemies were.'

'Something like that, yes. Perhaps business rivals or something more personal.'

'You mean a jealous husband?'

'Is there such a person in the picture?'

'Possibly, possibly not. My husband had several affairs, the latest being a woman called Magda Feinstein. I know her husband knew about it, because I told him.'

Fiona looked at her notes. 'Ah yes, Jacob Feinstein. We had him investigated and he had a solid alibi. I'm wondering about any previous affairs he might have had.'

'Well, he was with her for over a year. I imagine any other husband's anger might have cooled by then.'

'Possibly.' Fiona studied her. 'It seems to me that you tolerated these affairs of your husband.'

'We had what you might call an open marriage.'

'An open marriage might well enrage a lover's spouse into murder.'

'Possibly, but not in our case.' She examined Fiona for a few seconds then added, 'There is one name you might want to investigate. His name is Graham Feather. He was the company accountant for many years until he was locked up for embezzling the firm. He was released about a month before Charles died. He served three years.'

'Really?' said Fiona, looking at her notes. 'I'm wondering why we didn't follow that up.'

'Because I didn't realize he was out until quite recently and nor did the police, apparently.'

'If that's the case, it was very remiss of us.'

'Yes, it was. Your Inspector Wood doesn't inspire confidence. I hear Graham still bears a grudge – his story is that Charles took the money and set him up for it.'

'And what's your take on that?'

'How do you mean?'

'I mean do you think your husband might have done such a thing? It'd certainly have provided a motive for revenge.'

'True. I struggled to believe Graham would embezzle us for a few thousand pounds. He came from a wealthy family and he wasn't short of a money. He only worked for us to occupy his time.'

'Why would your husband do such a thing?'

'Because the missing money had found its way into Charles's account and he found a devious way to place the blame on Graham than admit to it himself. There are few minor shareholders in Santiago TechSys who wouldn't have looked too kindly on Charles embezzling company money.'

'Where can I find this Graham Feather?'

'I believe he's living in Leeds. His wife divorced him and ended up with a big house and their two children – she got married again, so I hear. She used his prison record against him in the family court so he's got very restricted access to his children.'

'Is he working?'

'Doubt it. As I say he wasn't short of money. I think he's bought a decent place for himself. He'll be in his late forties now. I suspect he'll be looking forward to a very lonely old age.'

'Hmm,' said Fiona. 'A man like that would hold a lot of bitterness if he'd been set up for a crime he didn't commit. Is he a man capable of murder, would you say?'

'I don't know what a man like that would be capable of. I know he'd have money to pay someone else to do his dirty work for him.'

'How would he know such people?'

'He's been in prison, hasn't he?'

TEN

St James Hospital Leeds

'Good grief, sir!' said Fiona, 'You're bandaged up like the invisible man!'

The reply came through a hole in the head bandage. 'So how do you know it's me?'

'It's written above your bed and whoever wrote it knows you of old.'

'Why, what's it say?'

'Septimus Black. Treat with caution.'

'Ah, they like their little jokes, these nurses.'

'How many times have you been brought into Casualty over the years?'

'Seventeen, according to their records, mind you, five of them were when I was a boy. So, what news from the world of crime detection?'

'Ah, I've got myself seconded to the Cold Case Unit, pending your return,' Fiona told him. 'The super's given me your job to do.'

'Well, you know everything that I know, except for one thing.'

'What's that?'

'You need to know how to keep your head down.'

'Well, I'll take no advice from you on that. The super's let it be known around the station that the Santiago case is being put on hold because of your injuries. I've been told not to mention to anyone that I'm working on it. As far as the station's concerned I've joined the Cold Case team to help out in your absence.'

'Was it Hawkins who told you not to touch the Santiago case?'

'Yes and no, sir. She wants me to stay on it, but not tell anyone.'

'I wonder who she's worried about down there?'

'Sir?'

'The super obviously thinks that the way to get the word out to the bad guys is to tell the station that the case has been put on hold, so the bad guys drop their guard. She thinks there's a leak.'

'She never mentioned anything like that to me.'

'No, but she'll have done it to protect you. I think Cock Robin might be the hot favourite.'

Fiona smiled at Sep's use of Wood's new nickname, as Sep added, 'I think he's already been got at, which is why he had the case dropped before it ever got started.'

'I think we have a hot favourite for the killings, sir, his name is Graham Feather. He used to be Charlie Santiago's accountant until he got sent down for embezzling three grand from the firm. He claims Charlie framed him and took the money himself. He was released a month before Santiago was murdered.'

The bandaged head nodded as thoughtfully as a bandaged head can nod.

'That's all very neat and tidy.'

'Oh heck!' said Fiona. 'You mean *too* neat and tidy.' She knew Sep only too well.

'You know I never trust neat and tidy. What makes you think he was framed?'

'Because Graham Feather was a man of means and he'd no need to steal three grand. He had ten times that in the bank in cash, plus a good house.'

'Ah,' said the hole in the bandage. 'Was he a vengeful man by nature?'

'I don't know.'

'I assume you got this information from Mrs Santiago.'

'How did you know?'

'Educated guess. Did she not know him well enough to answer that question or did you forget to ask her?'

'Of course I asked her. She wasn't sure how vengeful he might be after three years in prison.'

'How long had he been working there?'

'About seven years prior to him being locked up.'

'She must have met him quite a few times in that seven years and yet she couldn't tell you if he seemed a vengeful man.'

'During the seven years she'd known him he'd never been an innocent man locked up for three years.'

'Good point, but he'll have had three years of vengeful thoughts boiling up inside him as he sat in his cell. The question is, could it turn a good man into a killer?'

'Who knows?'

'Not me, that's for sure. Maybe it's a double bluff to point the blame at him.'

'And who's pointing the blame?' asked Fiona.

'I don't know . . . Mrs Santiago?'

'Sir, I have no idea how that brain of yours works. Maybe you being wrapped up like that has confused it.'

'Or maybe all this darkness and solitude has enabled me to see through the smoke screens these people put up.'

'Why would Mrs Santiago try to frame an innocent man for her husband's murder?'

'Well, she wouldn't, would she? Look, Fiona, I think there's a lot more to this than we know about, a whole lot more. You know, Winnie's a genius with computers, maybe she also knows a thing or two about share trading. I'd have her working with me on this, so should you. Forget the cuckolded husbands for the time being and try to open up a lead down the share trading route. Have a talk with the two brothers who work for the firm, but don't rule out this Graham Feather chap.'

Graham Feather's ex-wife watched as the two children ran up the drive of their father's house for their monthly visit. Their ambition was always to get to the door before their father opened it. Jenny felt the usual pang of guilt, wondering if she'd been too hasty in divorcing him while he was in prison. Her new husband didn't match up to Graham in many ways, certainly not in the children's eyes and there was always the problem of whether or not he was actually guilty of the crime. He still maintained that he'd been set up by Santiago and if that was true she'd only added to the injustice the world had heaped upon him. Her new husband was handsome and ten years younger than Graham. He was also jobless and bone idle. She was lucky that Graham hadn't contested ownership of the house, but she wasn't surprised. He'd done it for the sake of the kids. It was their home. The children reached the door before it opened and banged on it, shouting, 'Daddy, we're here.' But the door didn't open. They knocked again but the door remained closed. This was most unlike Graham.

The children, a ten-year-old boy and an eight-year-old girl turned to look at their mother. She got out of her car, walked up the drive and tried the door. It was locked. She banged on it herself but to no avail.

'I don't believe this. It seems your daddy isn't in.'

'Maybe he's gone to the shop.'

Jenny bent down and opened the letter box, looking through into the hall. She let it slam shut and sat down on the step with her head in her hands. With shaking hands she took out her mobile and stabbed 999 into the keypad.

'Emergency, which service, please?'

'Police and ambulance, please.'

ELEVEN

Fiona was standing beside Sep's bed once again. The *Treat With Caution* had been removed from his name board and replaced with his name and the name of his consultant.

'Are you inside there, Mr Black?'

'Who's that?'

'Me.'

'Mr Black's not available at the moment, would you like to leave a message?'

'Yes, tell him to ring me when he's able. I have news of his attack.'

Fiona turned to go, with a grin of triumph on her face. The hole in the bandages called after her.

'Come back, you lunatic!'

'Me, a lunatic? With respect, sir, it's you who's been in here seventeen times.'

'What news?'

'Graham Feather has committed suicide. All the evidence points to him being behind the murders, plus the attack on you.'

'How did he do it?'

'Hanged himself in his house.'

There was a silence from under the bandages as Sep considered this news. 'Was there any sign of forced entry to the house?'

'None. All the windows and doors were locked.'

'Locked? I wonder why? Did he live in a dodgy area? I only lock my door if I'm out or going to bed.'

'What's suspicious about the doors being locked?'

'Because it tells the police that he hanged himself and that no one else was involved. If any of the doors or windows were left open, there would be a possibility of murder. How old was he?'

'Same as you – forty-eight.'

'A lot of ex-cons don't like to lock themselves in, did you know that?'

'No, I didn't. Maybe he locked himself in because he didn't want to be disturbed. I imagine he didn't want to be jumping off the landing with a rope around his neck just as someone was coming through the front door.'

'What was the estimated time of death?'

'OK, forget that one. I think it was early hours.'

'Did he have life insurance, because if he did, suicide would invalidate it? An accountant would know that. Have you checked on his life insurance?'

'No.'

'I'm guessing the beneficiaries,' Sep said, 'would be his children, certainly not his ex-wife. Who was the pathologist?'

'Bloody hell, Sep! What is all this?'

'This is me being an old cynic. One simple suicide solving three murders and one attempted. I think I'd be digging a bit deeper. Did Cock Robin accept it as suicide?'

'Yes, it's his case. How can I argue with him?'

'Probably you can't, but I know someone who can. Have you met Feather's ex-wife?'

'Yes, she seems a decent sort. Her name is Pilkington now. Very shocked at her ex-husband's death. Not an easy thing to tell the children.'

'Fiona, could you find out about his life insurance and the name of the pathologist.'

'His name's Dr Missingham.'

'Ah, the copper's regular man and well-named too. I'm guessing Cock Robin had a word in his ear about it being suicide before he did his post-mortem.'

'Sir, I think you should get out of the habit of calling the DCI Cock Robin and you can't go round accusing pathologists like that.'

'Fiona, Missingham's a regular police expert who rarely suffers the inconvenience of being up against a second opinion. Do you think you could get Feather's ex-wife to come and see me?'

'I wish *I'd* never bloody well come now.'

'By the way, Cock Robin is a name the DCI gave himself.'

'I'm aware of that, sir.'

'Fiona, just the insurance details and Feather's ex-wife is all I'm asking you to bring me. If we solve the case, you'll get all the kudos.'

'Kudos? Is that another word for blame?'

Jenny Pilkington was fuming as she drove towards St James's. Her pillock of a husband had tried to lay the law down with her and had forbidden her to visit Sep Black.

'Why?'

'Because it'll be to do with Graham's death and I don't want that thieving bastard haunting us after he's dead.'

'If you must know, I don't think he did it. I think Charlie Santiago set him up. Why would he embezzle three grand when he had a fortune of his own?'

'I notice he never gave you any of his fortune.'

'He gave me this house, which is more than I ever got off you.'

The only good thing about the argument was that the kids weren't there to hear it. They were at school. She had no idea why Sep Black wanted to see her, other than that lesbian cop had told her that Black had his doubts about whether Graham had committed suicide. That was enough to get her there. She was now regretting taking Danny Pilkington's name and had taken care to leave the kids with their father's name. This has annoyed Danny.

Jenny identified Sep from the name at the back of his bed. The fact that he was encased in bandages offered her a further clue, but this was a hospital and plenty of people wore bandages.

'Sep Black?'

Sep was dozing and the voice only just punctured his subconscious.

'Huh?'

She placed a hand on his shoulder, just enough to alert him to her presence but not enough to hurt this badly damaged man.

'My name is Jenny Pilkington. You wanted to see me.'

'Jenny . . . erm . . . ah, Jenny Feather, as was?' said Sep, through his mental haze.

'Jenny Feather, as I wish I still was,' said Jenny, still cross from her confrontation with Danny.

'Ah . . . er, yes. I asked Fiona to get you to come and see me. Give me a moment, I'm trying to remember why. Being mummified like this tends to affect the brain.'

'I assume it's to do with my ex-husband's suicide.'

Sep's voice came through the hole, which was surmounted by two eyeholes through which she could just see his eyes. 'Can you see me all right?' she asked.

'Just about. You're very pretty. Am I right?'

'That's not for me to say.'

'You have brown hair and . . . brown eyes. Very beautiful brown eyes, if I may say so.'

'Mr Black, if you're trying to chat me up for some reason, I must tell you that I'm forty years old and I know every chat-up line that was ever invented.'

'Yes, a pretty lady like you would experience many chat-up lines. Have you heard that one before? Damn! I thought I'd just made it up. Sorry, forgive me. It's very boring inside all this lot and along you come to brighten up my dark world.'

'Why did you want to see me?'

'Erm . . . that's a good question. "Why" is always a good question. Ah, I remember now. Do you know if Graham had any life insurance? No, that's information I wanted Fiona to bring me. Would you know, by any chance?'

'He did but it was invalidated by his suicide.'

'Who was the beneficiary?'

'Our two children. They'd have got a quarter of a million between them. He kept up the payments during his time in prison and even after our divorce.'

'Ah, a man doesn't divorce his children.'

'That's right. I understand you were once married.'

'Yes, it was a poor marriage. Tell me, Jenny, how are you fixed financially?'

'Not fixed at all. My present husband is out of work, although Graham left me five thousand in his will, which amazed me.'

'Would you be willing to risk a couple of thousand in an attempt to prove he was murdered?'

'What?'

'You see, in this living tomb of mine I have time to think things through with amazing clarity and it strikes me that Graham would have made some attempt to disguise his suicide as an accident, if only for his children's sake. A car crash perhaps, or a drunken fall under a bus. Both of those would have triggered an insurance payment and would have been far less awkward than hanging himself.'

'I never thought of that. How would spending two thousand help me prove it was murder?'

'By investing in a second opinion. You need to see a solicitor and tell him you're not happy with the pathologist's report and you want your own pathologist to take a look at him. But you need to do it quickly before they dispose of the body.'

'Two thousand? Is that how much they charge?'

'That's what it'll cost. Possibly on the top side but you don't want to get caught out.'

'And am I allowed to do that?'

'A quarter-million-pound insurance policy says you are. It might not work but I'd say the second pathologist, if he's told what to look for, might find evidence that Graham was murdered and his murder made to look like a suicide. It's the only thing that makes sense to me.'

'Are you saying the first pathologist was bent?'

'Not at all, but he might well have been influenced by a conclusion that the police had already arrived at. Some of them are very busy people and overlook tiny but important details. A second pathological report often turns up things missed by the first pathologist.'

'Do you think there's a good chance? It'd be great for the kids. He left them all he had but that five grand he left me was all he had in readies. He left them his house which has only about twenty grand equity in it and that's if we get a decent market price. It could be we owe money on it.'

'It could be I'm wrong,' said Sep, 'but I think it's worth a two-grand gamble.'

'Well, the two grand will come from Graham, so maybe I owe it to him to get the truth. But who would want to murder him?'

'Jenny, let's take this thing one step at a time. See your solicitor and instruct him to set the wheels in motion. If nothing else that'll keep his body available. I'll give you the name of a pathologist who won't miss a thing.'

'I'm guessing it's a woman.'

'That's a very good guess, Jenny . . . and very true. Her name's

Alicia Tempest, she's very good and very thorough. I know her well, so I'll prime her with my own suspicions.'

'What if you're wrong?'

'If I'm wrong she'll soon let me know.'

'So will I, if it costs me two grand.'

Jenny walked away, smiling to herself that she'd been charmed by a heap of bandages and even more determined to dump that useless husband of hers; especially if the kids had a quarter of a million coming their way. Knowing him, he'd get his hands on it somehow and that would be the end of it. Thank God she'd resisted his many entreaties to put her house in joint names. Oh, how she wished she'd stood by Graham, who was ten times the man Danny was. If he'd been murdered, it was her duty to help as much as she could to find the killer. It fleetingly crossed her mind that it might be Danny. He'd done six years as a soldier in Iraq and Afghanistan, so killing wasn't beyond his capability. But why? What would he gain from it? He knew she'd still carried a torch for her ex-husband, a torch that had shone brighter by the day. He must have noticed that. If it turned out that Graham had been murdered she'd mention Danny to Sep Black. It'd be one way of dumping him.

She was smiling to herself as she left the hospital and headed for her car – her first smile since she'd seen the suspended body of her ex-husband through his letter box. She was also wondering what Sep Black looked like under his bandages. She already knew he was divorced.

TWELVE

September 2015. St James's Hospital. Leeds

It was seven weeks since the attempt on Sep's life and Fiona had made scarce progress with her investigation. She and Winnie had gone together to bring Sep home. The bandages were no longer on his head and his body, apart from his left shoulder, was no longer trussed, but he still had a pain in his right leg. It was why he needed the wheelchair they'd brought him. He wasn't entirely happy with it.

'Couldn't you have got me one of those motorized ones?'

'The doctor recommended this, as the exercise will do you good,' said Winnie.

'I'm doing physio four times a week. That's exercise enough for me.'

'I've arranged for a physio nurse to come round to the house so you don't have to be trailing here all the time.'

'How much is that costing?'

Winnie pulled an exasperated face and said, 'Oh, shut up, Sep, you curmudgeonly old sod! You can limp here four times a week, if you prefer.'

'That'd be good exercise,' suggested Fiona.

'Did you check on Danny Pilkington?' Sep asked her.

'I did. He claims to have been at home in bed when Jenny found Graham Feather's body. She confirmed he was there when she and the kids left the house and he'd been there all night and at home the previous evening.'

'And the time of death was what?'

'Between four and six in the morning.'

'I suppose that rules him out. Jenny will be disappointed.'

'She's his alibi,' said Fiona. 'She's managed to kick him out though. Apparently she gave him a couple of thousand and told him to clear off.'

Winnie gave Sep a suspicious look. 'I gather she's been to see you a few times.'

'Yes, she has, purely business. Alicia Tempest, our new pathologist, found signs of manual strangulation. His death wasn't caused by the rope he was found hanging by. She ascertained that death occurred prior to the hanging.'

'How would she know that?' said Winnie.

'No idea, but it was fairly apparent according to Alicia Tempest. The first pathologist should have spotted it. Tempest, who has an impeccable reputation, presented the new findings to the coroner, hence the new verdict of unlawful killing. With it no longer being a suicide verdict, the insurers have agreed to pay out in full.'

'Ah, I wondered why she went for a second opinion. I imagine Dr Missingham no longer has an impeccable reputation.'

'You imagine correctly. A pathologist should deliver an opinion that's not influenced by the police. Trouble is, the police like a tame pathologist to make their lives easier and pathologists like to get regular police work. We needed a name to be reckoned with and Tempest was that name. It was my idea – suicide invalidated Graham Feather's life insurance, which would have been another travesty of justice.'

'Another?' said Fiona.

'Yes. I strongly suspect he was set up for the fraud by Santiago. I'm not sure why.'

'It was because three grand went missing from the company accounts and ended up in Santiago's personal account. Santiago wanted to keep it from his shareholders, so he somehow moved it into Feather's account,' Fiona told him.

'Why would he do that?'

'Who knows? Maybe he just had a grudge against Feather for some reason. So he set him up for a fall.'

'Sep,' said Winnie. 'I thought this investigation was just for Mrs Boswell's benefit. To prove her husband wasn't killed by a prostitute he was visiting.'

'Well, that's how it started out, but it seems to have snowballed since then, in more ways than one. Why do you ask?'

'I just got the impression that her interest in you was more than just business.'

'She was very grateful for all my help, if that's what you mean.'

'I'm wondering just how grateful she is.'

'She's a good-looking woman,' said Fiona, teasing Winnie, 'and a woman without a man.'

'Yes, she is,' said Sep, going along with this, 'and I seduced her with my sexy bandages and naked feet. How could she resist me?'

He caught Winnie's gaze and added, 'Winnie, I have no interest in her, other than I believe her husband's murder to be part of this whole affair that started with Charlie Santiago taking a flier through a window.'

'And have you come to any conclusions while you were mummified?' Fiona asked.

'I'll tell you what conclusion I've come to: Charlie Santiago was murdered by being chucked out of a window; James Boswell was murdered because he was investigating Santiago's murder; the old woman in the Grimshawe hotel was murdered because I was using her to investigate Boswell's murder; I was run down for the same reason; and Graham Feather was murdered because he knew something that might have incriminated the person behind all this. So Graham Feather is the key to everything and the murderer assumes that his death stops us finding out what he knew. And talking of keys, can we get access to his house?'

He was looking at Fiona, who said, 'Now that I'm off the Cold Case team you're assuming that I'm now working on the Feather murder.'

'Fiona, you're the best detective Cock Robin's got on his team. He needs to make up for his mistake somehow.'

'Sir, one of these days you're going to get into trouble calling him Cock Robin. They're all calling him that down at the station and they know it came from you.'

Sep looked at her accusingly. 'DS Burnside, they can't possibly have got it from me. I haven't been near the place for weeks.'

'OK. I might have let the name slip, but you know what they're like down there.'

'Not big fans of Cock Robin?'

'DCI Wood does need to make up for his mistake but it's only been a murder since the coroner's latest verdict. The man's been dead well over a month.'

'After which no doubt Cock Robin sprang into action like a coiled sponge,' said Sep. 'That house should have been locked up and guarded until the coroner made his verdict. Any decent forensic evidence will have been trampled into the floorboards by now.'

'Sep, for the first two weeks we had a pathologist's verdict of suicide and no reason to think otherwise. DCI Wood was spitting chips when he found out you were behind ordering the second pathologist. It makes him look a prat, with him saying it was suicide.'

'Cock Robin is a prat,' said Sep.

'I know, but he blames it on me, with me being your stand-in.'

'You should have told him Jenny ordered the second pathologist on your advice. That way you'd have got the credit for finding out it was a murder not a suicide.'

'You mean I'd have got the credit for making DCI Wood look a prat.'

'That as well, yeah.'

'The *Yorkshire Evening Post* did him no favours.'

'No, I didn't think they would.'

Fiona glared at him. 'It was you who gave them the story, wasn't it?'

Sep gave a slight wince that might have been pain or it might have been guilt – bit of both in fact.

'It was too good an opportunity to miss. Hey, they don't know his nickname yet,' he said.

'Oh, you can't tell them that, sir!'

'I won't, but I bet one of our constables might let such a thing slip to a persistent reporter.'

'Sir, you have a highly developed sense of irresponsibility,' said Fiona.

'Talking of responsibility,' said Winnie, 'you've still got a job to do proving that James Boswell wasn't murdered while visiting a prostitute.'

'I've convinced his wife that he wasn't and that's half the battle,' said Sep. 'She needed to know that for sure. Fiona, you need to look through all Graham Feather's stuff in his house. Any note-books, computers, any paperwork at all; anything concerning Santiago's firm; in fact, anything at all that might give us a clue as to why the murderer was worried about what he knew. He spent most of his time in that Cat D prison near Wetherby. Go there and have a word with his prison mates. He might well have confided in them. He might well have been planning revenge on Santiago.'

'You think he might have killed Santiago?'

'Well, I'm sincerely hoping he didn't, otherwise it only adds to the mystery of who carried on with the killings after Santiago died. For all I know, the whole thing could be Graham Feather taking revenge on the world and not just Santiago. But if so, who killed Graham Feather? It could well be that we've already spoken to that person. We've got a lot of work to do.'

'We've also got to get you home,' said Fiona.

'Good job I'm in the peak of physical condition,' Sep said. 'Ouch, go steady with me!'

His transfer from hospital bed to wheelchair was more awkward and painful than he anticipated, thanks to his good friend DS Fiona Burnside.

Back in his house Winnie looked down at Sep after he'd settled into the chair she'd bought him; a high armchair suitable for a person with his physical limitations. He was within reach of his wheelchair and had practised the transfer from one chair to the other until he could do it without falling to the floor.

'I reckon with my elbow crutches I can get about without the wheelchair. The physio reckons I should try crutch-walking as much as I can. I'll give that a try tomorrow. It's not as though my leg's broken, it's just the wrong colour that's all. Mind you, most of that's gone now.'

'I'll be staying with you until you're able to walk with a stick,' Winnie told him.

'Are you not worried about the man who tried to kill me?'

'Yes. Do you think he'll try it again?'

'Possibly.'

'You know what I'm wondering, don't you?' said Winnie.

'You're wondering if I still have a gun in the house.'

'Have you?'

'None of your business.'

'Is it fully loaded?'

'An empty gun's not much protection.'

'Sep, it's an unlicensed gun. If you use it, you'll be in so much trouble.'

'I'd say it was his gun.'

Sep mimed the scenario, holding out his right arm.

'Picture this. He comes towards me with the gun held out at arm's length. When he gets near me I kick it out of his hand with my good leg. As luck would have it I catch it and get a shot off.'

'Do you think the police'll believe that?'

'Winnie, I've acquired a reputation for unusual behaviour, most of it undeserved. Why wouldn't they believe me?'

'You have a point.'

'Besides, it's not an impossible scenario, plus I'll be alive and I don't want to die without having married you.'

Winnie looked at him with a mixture of affection and annoyance. 'Are you proposing to me, Sep?'

'I don't know. What did I say?'

'Something about marrying me.'

'I thought I was talking about shooting an intruder. Let's face it, I'll be innocent until proven guilty and he'll be the intruder not me. Probably the same man who killed all the others. If he's only wounded he'll blow the whistle on who's behind it all because I think whoever it is has hired a hitman. Fiona will be the investigating officer, with a bit of—'

Winnie threw her hands up in surrender. 'OK, OK, I give in! Forget us getting married, where's this bloody gun?'

Stanley Butterbowl, aka Mr Wolf, watched from his car as Winnie helped Sep from her van into a wheelchair and into his house. Wolf knew where Sep lived and an element of guesswork plus regular drive-bys had told him that Black was now living back at home. The woman staying with him might be a problem. Wives and girlfriends are always problems. Screamers, the lot of them.

Night-time was always a good time. He was guessing that Black would be sleeping downstairs, but where was the woman sleeping? Upstairs? All he had to do was keep watch at night and keep an eye on the house lights. If lights went on and off both upstairs and downstairs it would pinpoint the whereabouts of both the woman and Black. Wolf smiled at his own genius. Such deduction was as clever as he got. He looked at his huge hands and opened and closed his fat fingers. Yeah, these'd do both jobs. Highly efficient murder weapons, hands. No bangs, no blood, no screams, if the job was done right and possibly no one finding the bodies for a few days. All he had to do was break in. While Black was in hospital he'd fixed a downstairs window around the back of the house so that it didn't lock properly. He could open it in a few seconds with a screwdriver. He'd also been in the house and knew the layout well enough to go straight to whatever bedroom the woman was in. Wolf grinned and settled back in his seat. The waiting would be the hardest part of this night's work.

As he picked his gnarled teeth with a toothpick he was wondering how much trouble the woman might cause him. Black would be a sitting duck. He had no intention of using a gun on him either. His bare hands would do the job much more quietly. Silence was always a bonus in his line of work. Maybe he should do her first. He wouldn't get any extra money for it but it'd help his cause. Yeah, he'd do her first. But one scream from her would alert Black. Shit! What to do? The more he thought about it the more he thought he needed backup. He took out his mobile and stabbed in a number.

'Bazza, it's Wolf. D'yer wanna want to earn yerself a monkey ternight? Cash money. It's in me skyrocket right now.'

'Doin' what?'

'I want yer ter fix a whore with yer hands and I want it done quietly. She'll be sleepin', so all you have ter do is go in, put yer mitts around 'er neck and stop 'er breathin'. She'll probably be naked so there's that in it for you as well. I've known you strangle naked tarts for fun.'

'Maybe I'll do it fer a grand.'

'Piss off, Bazza! A grand's all I'm gerin' fer killing Sep Black who'll be downstairs. I'm giving you 'alf me bleedin' take and you get the easy job.'

'Sep Black? The copper?'

'Yeah.'

'Bloody hell! I thought he was in 'ospital. Was it you what ran 'im down?'

'Bazza, d'yer want this fuckin' job or not?'

'Who's the tart?'

'Her name's Winnie O'Toole.'

'Yeah, I know 'er. Still a whore, is she? I thought she'd stopped sellin' it and opened a clothes shop. Very tasty. Yer think she'll be naked?'

'I reckon so. Tarts like her allus sleep naked. This is a job with fringe benefits.'

'And yer've got the monkey on you?'

'I have. You go home tonight five hundred notes richer and, knowing you, yer'll be skint right now.'

'OK. You'd better pick me up.'

'I'll be round in ten. Be ready.'

'Do I get tooled up?'

'It's a hands-on job. I don't want ter wake the neighbours up, but bring what yer like. I'm on me way.'

THIRTEEN

Sep made himself comfortable in his new chair with his bad leg propped up on a footstool and a small table by his side on which was a bottle of Glenfiddich and a glass.

'Do you want the telly on?' Winnie asked.

'No, just stick some sort of music on. Nothing too intrusive, I want to talk and think.'

'Is this some new multitasking skill you've acquired?'

Her banter often made him smile. To Sep, banter was important in any relationship. 'There's a classical CD in there somewhere.'

'Classical music, you?'

'Well, orchestral stuff from the shows. It's as near as I come to classical. I've often promised myself to upgrade my musical taste. You like classical, don't you?'

'Some . . . Wagner mostly. I've got his Ring Cycle on a couple of CDs. I think you'd like Wagner if you gave him a chance.'

'You have a similar taste in music to Adolf Hitler. It's us who should have similar tastes if we're to get married.'

'There you go again, Sep. Are you serious about this marriage business?'

Sep was quiet for a few moments, then he said, 'According to the surgeon I nearly died back there. I know I've been through stuff like this in the past but I think I'm getting too old for it all. I'm going to go back into uniform and packing this strong arm detective stuff in. The hours are steady in uniform. Detectives work all hours. What I need is a normal life.'

'So, you want us to get married?'

'Don't press me, Winnie. We're engaged, so I have got it in mind, but *when* is another question altogether. I need to get myself ready for it.'

'That would be great, Sep, but I know you're at your weakest right now. What are you going to feel like when you get your strength back?'

'Winnie, right now I'm thinking clearly. The stronger I get the dafter I get.'

'Yeah, that's what bothers me.'

'I thought about it a lot back at the hospital. Do you know how many times I've been taken into Casualty?'

'Seventeen.'

He smiled. 'Ah, you've been talking to Fiona. What else did she talk to you about?'

'Such as?'

'Such as she thinks I'm an idiot for not marrying you and I have to agree with her. How about you?'

'How about me what?'

'Do you agree with her?'

'If you must know, yes.'

'When I get back I'll be plain old Inspector Black and you'll become Mrs Winnie Black . . . at erm, at some stage.'

'I accept your latest proposal, but don't keep me hanging on too long. I have other admirers, you know.'

'I'm not surprised. Do I get an engagement kiss?'

'Yes, but that's *all* you get.'

'With this leg it's all I can manage.'

They kissed, passionately, then Winnie asked, 'Does this mean you're not going after the person who's trying to kill you?'

Sep gave this some thought. 'What I'm going to do is wangle an interview with the *Yorkshire Post*. They've always chased me for stories. This time I'll give them what they want. I'll tell them I've had enough and that I'll apply for a transfer to uniform and leave it to the CID people to follow up on the James Boswell case . . . and the Santiago case . . . and my case for that matter. I'm having nothing to do with it, so whoever's paying a hitman is wasting their money and I need them to know that. Having said all that, I don't know if I'll get a transfer any time soon.'

'Of course you will,' said Winnie. 'A man who's been knocked about as much as you have, they can't expect you to go on forever. The *Post*'ll love it. I bet the paper'll be running Sep Black stories for weeks. You'll need to start a scrapbook.'

'They're not all memories I cherish. The bottom line is I definitely want to marry you because I know I love you.'

'You definitely know that, do you, because I did wonder?'

Sep looked at her and smiled. 'Yes, I do love you and I know you love me, and I know we'll always get on, and I know you'll always look out for me, and me for you, which is a lot more than I can say for my first wife.'

'Sep, if you go back on your word about this I'll leave you for good. I promise you that. This also goes for you packing the bloody detective job in. I want a husband who comes home in one piece every night.'

'Sounds good to me so, are we engaged at the moment? I've lost track of where we are.'

'If you need a clue, I haven't got a ring.'

'You'd better wheel me to a jewellers tomorrow then.'

'Sep, I hope you're serious about this. Loving you is as a much a curse as a blessing. I wouldn't be able to stand it if you let me down. For you to let me down would break me to the extent that

I'd have to disappear from your life completely. I know exactly where I'd go and it wouldn't even be in this country, in fact it wouldn't be in this hemisphere.'

'Your long lost aunt Maude's in New Zealand?'

'Maude died last year but she left me a place out there, with me being her only living relative. There's a house and a job out there with the family business if I want it . . . and I've got the money to get there.'

'Blimey!' said Sep. 'You've really given this some thought, haven't you?'

'So, are you able to mend your ways?'

'The way I feel right now I don't think I've got any ways to mend.'

'No more wild oats to sow?'

'All sown and forgotten. You're the only wild oat I'll ever need.'

She tilted his chin up with a finger and saw a tear in his eye. A rare occurrence for Sep Black.

'Why that?' she asked.

'I don't know – delayed shock maybe. When I was coming round from under the anaesthetic I had a sort of awareness of what was happening and what was happening was me dying. It's hard to explain but I thought I was going to die and I wasn't ready.'

'Did I come into these thoughts by any chance?'

'They weren't thoughts as such, just an awareness of my mortality, which was coming to an end. The surgeon told me they lost me for a full minute, which is a long time dead – defibrillator job and all that – maybe that was it.'

'Did you see a bright light beckoning you towards it?'

'No light. When you're that close to the exit door it's like your brain's running on fumes with not much to fire the thought processes. All I had was this . . . this vague awareness. They were about to call it when someone suggested they give the defibrillator one last go for luck and bang! The flat line on the computer screen beeped back to life, as did I.'

'Is that because you decided you weren't ready to die, so you didn't, just out of awkwardness.'

'Something like that. How do you know?'

'Oh, it was just something Fiona said when you were in theatre.'

'Oh.'

Sep wiped away another tear, embarrassed at having to do so, but it was an action that further endeared him to Winnie who put an arm around him. It was something of a stretch to reach right across his broad shoulders, but she managed it.

'We're too good together to throw this away, Sep. Look, if you want to carry on with being a detective you should be a Sherlock Holmes not a Sam Spade. Use your brain not your brawn.'

'You're assuming I've got a brain, then?'

'You're a very smart guy, I know that.'

'I don't go out looking for fights.'

'No, but you think you're indestructible. You walk into danger with your eyes shut. Maybe I should be your eyes from now on.'

'Winnie, I'll settle for your eyes any day of the week.'

'Just as long as you confine this sweet talk to me and not every skirt that passes you by.'

He took her hand and squeezed it. It was all he could do to reassure her without filling up again. Tears were alien beings to Sep Black.

'I'll put the telly on,' Winnie said. 'There's a good western on Sky.'

Sep took a sip of his whisky and settled back in his chair, determined never to let this good woman down – and to enjoy the three Ws – whisky, western and Winnie.

A short while later Wolf was picking up Bazz who got into his car with a Smith and Wesson .357 revolver in his shoulder holster and a sheath knife in his belt, just in case. He told Wolf about this because Wolf would want to know.

Wolf nodded. 'Only if needed,' he said.

The house was slightly isolated from its neighbours and was double-glazed, so a gunshot might not create too much concern, should the need arise.

FOURTEEN

There was but a slither of moon in the clear sky and Wolf was wearing black clothing so his movements in Sep's back garden wouldn't have been noticed even if there had been close neighbours watching. It was 11.45 when he prised open the window to the kitchen. A full hour after the upstairs light had gone out. An hour is plenty of time for people to fall asleep. He opened the window and the two of them climbed through, dropping to the tiled floor silently. There was enough light coming through the window for him to make his way to the door, beyond which was the hall. He knew the layout well and gave Bazz whispered directions. Up the stairs and into the door opposite. There would be a double bed facing him, a window to his right and built-in wardrobes running the full length of the wall to his left. A dressing table would be under the window and in the bed a sleeping woman.

Bazz raised a thumb to say he understood. He didn't hear his own footsteps as he mounted the carpeted stairs. When he got to the top he checked the Smith in its holster and the knife in its sheath; neither of which he was planning to use, but there just in case. If he had to shoot the woman, he'd fly down the stairs. Wolf should have finished his own piece of business by then. He pushed open the bedroom door and saw the bed in front of him. In the gloom he picked out the vague shape of the sleeping person.

Downstairs Wolf approached Black, who was snoring gently. As the hitman leaned over him, Sep kicked up with his good leg and caught Wolf in the groin, causing him to shout out. Sep rolled out of bed, the pain in his right leg masked by the rush of adrenalin surging through him. This would be the man who had run him down, come to finish him off. Wolf, partially recovered, had pulled out a knife and was standing in a knife-fighter's pose. Sep took a quick step towards him and batted the knife away with a swinging left hand, sending it spinning across the room.

There was enough dim light penetrating the curtain for Sep to see what, if not exactly who, he was up against. Wolf was a powerful man but much smaller than Sep who was six three and sixteen stones of solid muscle. As an ex-special forces soldier Sep Black always had the edge in close combat. In the same move as he batted the knife away he threw a heavy punch at Wolf's nose that made excellent contact and this, plus the pain in his groin made the hitman scream even louder with a combination of pain and rage. He stuck his hand inside his coat and took out a pistol which he pointed at Sep's face, holding it two inches from his nose, screaming with rage.

'Know any prayers, pig?'

A more experienced assassin would have stood back to take the shot but Wolf was holding the gun well within Sep's reach. In one swift movement Sep jabbed his right hand up beneath the gun, which fired a round into the ceiling, at which point Sep went straight into part two of a much-practiced move and twisted the weapon from Wolf's hand, causing it to fall to the floor.

Just these few moves had taken a lot out of Sep after his long hospitalization. He felt he hadn't a good punch left in him. Wolf sensed this and hurled himself at Sep, knocking him to the floor. As he fell back, Sep grabbed at Wolf's clothing and pulled him down with him so they both fell together and as they landed Sep proceeded to head butt Wolf on his already damaged nose. He held the hitman's head firmly in position so he couldn't avoid the rain of blows Sep was landing on him. Eventually Sep's strength deserted him completely and he fell back on the floor, breathing heavily and raucously and completely done in, awaiting whatever Wolf could throw at him, but Wolf was in no state to do anything. The centre of his face demolished, he could scarcely see for all the blood and the pain too intense for him to carry on with the fight. All he wanted was to get out of here. He struggled to his feet and staggered away, moaning loudly as Sep, soaked in Wolf's blood, tried to regain his breath.

Upstairs, Winnie, awakened by the commotion downstairs, was watching the menacing figure of Bazz approaching her. She screamed for Sep.

A shot and the scream from upstairs didn't immediately register with Sep who had struggled to his knees, still breathing heavily and immensely grateful that Wolf had left him alone.

Dripping blood from his demolished nose, Wolf climbed out through the same window he'd arrived through and made for his car, forgetting all about his crony. Downstairs, the memory of the shot and the scream now registered with Sep who could do little more than gasp, 'Winnie? What is it, Winnie?'

The room light was out but he had an elbow crutch leaning against his chair. It was a skill he hadn't fully mastered but the urgency of the moment spurred him on despite the pain in his right leg. He arrived at the bottom of the stairs and switched on the hall light.

'Winnie, what is it? What's wrong?'

His voice was just a croak. Perhaps she couldn't hear him. On the stairs there was a balustrade to Sep's left and a handrail to his right. He abandoned the crutch and attempted to climb the stairs by holding on both sides and hopping up from step to step using his good leg. Step by step he hopped slowly up using his good leg, increasingly exhausted by the effort. After all those weeks in hospital the fight had taken a lot out of him.

'Winnie. I'm coming up, are you OK?'

No answer. Sep looked back at the crutch, thinking he'd been foolish leaving it behind; maybe he should have thrown it up on to the half-landing. Two more steps, then rest, then two more. Silence. Jesus, what had happened? He got to the half-landing and leaned against the wall to regain his strength, breathing heavily. His injured leg was giving him pain, his good leg ached with the effort. Three steps to go. After his breather he did them all in one burst. Then he hopped over to the bedroom door. It was half open. He pushed it fully open and peered inside. The light was still out but there was enough light coming from outside for him to see Winnie standing by the bed and a dark shape on the floor. He reached around for the light switch and turned it on. His exhaustion made speaking difficult but he managed a wheeze.

'Bloody hell, Winnie! Who's that?'

'I don't know, Sep. I shot him. I think he's dead.'

'Shot him? What did you shoot him with?'

She pointed to the gun lying on the floor, having dropped it out of her frozen hand.

'My gun, where did you get it?'

'It was in the drawer. I . . . I took it out w-when I heard noises downstairs. Are you all right? You've got blood on your face, what happened to you?'

'It's not my blood, Winnie. Bloody hell! You shot him, did you? I thought someone had shot you.'

He sat on a chair with great relief, still breathing heavily. This was a situation that needed some clear thought.

'Am I in trouble, Sep?'

'Not if we get our story straight, Winnie.'

'You mean we lie, do we?'

'We certainly do. There's a time and place for the truth, Winnie, and this is neither. Right . . . you – you shot an intruder . . . There – there was one downstairs after me, but I fought him off.'

'You fought him off? How could you fi . . . fight anyone off in your state?'

Their voices were stilted and strained. It was more a series of groans than a conversation.'

'He was here to kill me. Look, do you . . . do you . . . think you could go downstairs and bring me that elbow crutch up. I left it at the bottom of the stairs.'

'I shot him with your ill-illegal gun, Sep. I killed him.'

'I know, Winnie, but you're alive, which is more important. Just get me the crutch, we – we just need to make our story fit what's here.'

Two minutes later Sep was leaning heavily on the crutch, standing over Bazz's body. Winnie was standing in the doorway, with a hand over her mouth, still in floods of tears.

'Winnie, can you come over here, please?'

She complied, cautiously.

'Look, I want you to open his coat. I want to see where he was shot.'

Winnie bent down and opened Bazz's coat. The bullet had entered straight through the heart, so there was no doubt that he was dead.

'What's that under his left armpit?' Sep asked.

Winnie took a closer look, then she looked up at Sep. 'It's a gun in a holster.'

'That could be helpful. Can you take it out?'

Gingerly, Winnie took the bloodied gun from the holster and gave it to Sep, who now noticed something else. 'Is that a sheath knife in his belt?'

'It is, yes.'

'He's a hitman,' said Sep. 'Winnie, you've just shot a hitman who was here to kill us both no doubt. Well done.'

'Sep, I don't think the police will be saying "well done" when they find out I shot him with an illegal gun.'

'But you shot him with his own gun.'

'Did I?'

'That's our story.'

'Sep, it's not even the same type of gun as yours.'

'No, but it's a small handgun, as is the Webley you've just shot him with, which is a stroke of luck.'

'Luck? Really?'

Sep put his Webley in the hitman's holster. It fitted perfectly

'See? Made to measure for my gun.'

'So what?'

'So, I want you to pick my gun up, get a facecloth from the bathroom, rub all the prints off it and dry it off. Then put it in his right hand and squeeze it tight, to get his prints on it, then put your prints on top of his, then drop it on the floor, exactly where it was when you first dropped it.'

'How do we know he's right-handed?'

'Because the holster's under his left armpit. He'd have a job getting it out with his left hand. My Webley is going to be the gun he brought in his shoulder holster. It's a gun I picked up on a job some time ago; they can't trace it to me. We'll have to hide his gun.'

'But how did I come to shoot him?'

Sep looked around. On the bedside table was a heavy brass travelling clock. He picked it up and weighed it in his hand. 'This'll do,' he said.

'Do for what?'

Sep held it over Bazz's body and dropped it in his eye. Then he looked at Winnie.

'This is what happened Winnie. You heard a noise outside the door and you knew it couldn't be me. You picked up the clock and held it in your hand as a weapon, scared to death you were.

'Then he came into the room, all big and ugly in the dark. He came up to the bed and you saw a gun in his hand. You threw the clock at him as hard as you could. It hit him in the face – in the eye, even. It made him drop the gun on the bed right next to you – you picked it up and shot him.'

'That's it, is it?' said Winnie.

'Yep. What's wrong with it? Unless you went to bed with your own gun, which is highly unlikely. We know he was armed because he had a holster that the gun fits in. He was also carrying a knife and it might well be that he's the man who killed Graham Feather.'

'Couldn't he have been the man who tried to kill you?'

'Possibly. I'd lay good money it was one of them and there's enough DNA around to identify both of them if they've ever been arrested in the past. Forensics definitely found some DNA at Feather's crime scene. It's perfect, Winnie.'

'Shouldn't we get rid of his gun?'

'No, it's a .357 Smith and Wesson, not a bad weapon. I'll clean his prints off it and hide it somewhere.'

'But won't the police find it?'

'Why would they even look for it? They have his weapon here. Everything else fits. You were the right distance from him when you shot him. The bullet went right through him and hit the wall.'

Winnie turned to look at the wall behind her. There was a single bullet hole in it, surrounded by hairline cracks.

'The bullet will obviously match the Webley which he brought in his holster,' Sep said.

'I feel sick,' Winnie said.

'Natural reaction for a human being,' said Sep. 'I threw up the first time I killed a man and that was also in self-defence.'

'This guy one might well have raped you before he killed you. Had you not acted as swiftly as you did you'd be dead by now, so might I, had he gone back down and saw me struggling with my man. Take a look at his hands, Winnie, like bunches of bananas. Did you ever see such deadly murder weapons? Strangulation is the method of choice for many hitmen. I reckon that's what he had in mind for you.' He paused and added, 'that and worse.'

'You mean rape? Why would a hitman waste time raping me?'

'Because that's what they do to attractive naked women. They're evil men, Winnie.'

'I'm naked! Oh my God, Sep! Why didn't you tell me before?'

'I thought you knew.'

'Fiona, it's Sep. Are you on shift?'

'Yeah, ten till six. Why?'

'Well, I know I should have reported this through more official channels but I'm hoping for Winnie's sake that you'll be dealing with it.'

'Dealing with what?'

'Winnie's just shot a hitman. He's dead in my bedroom. Is Hawkins on shift?'

'Not until tomorrow.'

'Excellent. Best not disturb her beauty sleep. This means I'm the Cold Case senior officer on duty.'

'*Are* you on duty, sir?'

'I am now.'

'Winnie OK?'

'She's in shock, but she saved both my life and hers. There were two of them. I was attacked as well.'

'Are you OK?'

'Not too bad, considering.'

'We'll have to bring her in for questioning.'

'I know what we have to do, sergeant. I can tell you pretty much what happened.'

'Why, were you there?'

'No, it happened upstairs, I was downstairs fighting off my man. What she managed to do was amazing.'

'I hope it's not too amazing, sir.'

'Now then, Fiona. She saved the life of your best pal. Just remember that. Bring a uniformed officer with you. Is Inspector Renholm on duty?'

'I'll check, sir.'

Fiona and Inspector Renholm looked at the evidence presented to them by Sep. Winnie was downstairs, drinking sweet tea and rehearsing the answers to the questions Sep had prepped her on. What actually happened was so near the truth that she had no problem mentally substituting the hitman's gun for Sep's. It was a better story and one she wanted to believe herself. It was the very story Sep was telling the two policemen:

'Winnie heard the noise we were making downstairs. I reckon one of them will have killed James Boswell and Graham Feather and the old woman in the Grimshawe Hotel.'

'So, how did Winnie get hold of his gun?' asked Fiona.

'Well, the noise we were making downstairs woke her up. She saw her bedroom door opening and she picked up the travel clock off the bedside table as a weapon. It's quite a heavy thing.'

'She armed herself?' said Renholm. 'Most women would hide under the bedclothes.'

'Believe me, Winnie's not most women.'

'True,' confirmed Fiona, who felt obliged to back Sep's story. 'It's definitely what Winnie would have done.'

'She saw the man come into the room,' said Sep, 'and she was terrified. Then she saw he was pointing a gun at her and she threw the clock at him. It hit him in the face and he dropped the gun on the bed. Winnie picked it up and shot him, all in one movement by the sound of it. End of story.'

'She threw a clock at him?' said Renholm.

'She has a good right arm on her when provoked. She once threw a cup at me. Luckily she missed by half an inch otherwise she'd have taken my head off.'

'Is she used to guns?'

'She's been on a firing range with me a few times, so she knows how to pull a trigger, that's about all.'

'I assume you heard all this. What did you do then?' asked Renholm.

'Well, I heard the gunshot when I was still occupied fighting my man off. He ran away. I heard Winnie scream but I didn't know what was going on. I grabbed my crutch and got myself out to the hall and shouted up to her but I couldn't hear anything so I thought the worst. Anyway I somehow managed to get to the top of the stairs and I still didn't know what had happened. I was knackered when I got up there. Winnie was standing in the bedroom, absolutely frozen with shock. Then I saw the body and she told me what I've just told you. I took a look at him and noticed he'd obviously come armed and ready to kill, with a gun in a shoulder holster and a sheath knife. The gun was on the floor where Winnie had dropped it. We left the scene as it was, so forensics can take a good look at it all. There's a bullet in that wall. It obviously went straight through the man, which it would at such short range.'

'I see,' said Renholm, trying to assimilate all he was hearing. 'Do you think one of them might be the man who ran you down?'

'I didn't see who ran me down but I'd put money on it being one of them. Probably the one who attacked me. He'll have been sent to finish the job.'

'Well, we need to find out who they are for a start,' Renholm said.

'I'm aware of that,' said Sep, thus reminding Renholm that he wasn't the senior man on this case.

'Either of you recognize the body?'

Both Fiona and Renholm shook their heads.

'The one who attacked me has a very smashed-up nose,' said Sep. 'This is mainly his blood. Forensic are welcome to as much DNA as they like.'

'We'll certainly be doing that,' said Renholm. 'Hopefully the dead man's body will identity itself, which might give our Cold Case Unit a decent lead in the case.'

Fiona looked at Sep's face. 'Did you nut him or something?' she asked.

'I did, many times. He was badly hurt when he left, probably needing hospital treatment.'

'I'll get the station to check all Leeds and district hospitals for a patient with a badly damaged nose,' said Renholm.

'Oh,' remembered Sep. 'The one who attacked me had a knife and a gun. I managed to knock them out of his hands. I don't think he took them with him. If he'd found the gun I reckon he'd have shot me before he left. I did him a lot of damage. They should be downstairs somewhere with his prints on them. He wasn't wearing gloves. Plenty of his DNA splashed about the room as well.'

'Good, anything else?'

'Well, we don't really need to take Winnie in for questioning tonight. Her mind's all over the place,' Sep told him. 'What she did took guts but she's still in shock. Killing someone does that to you, no matter who they are.'

'I think we can leave that until tomorrow,' Renholm conceded. 'It seems to me that we've probably got the sequence of events as they actually happened. I'll get a forensic team here right away, see what they make of it. What do you say, Fiona?'

'I agree, sir.'

Renholm had asked a question that met with Sep's approval. No way would DCI Wood have asked for the opinion of a mere sergeant.

'Just one thing,' added Renholm to Sep. 'This house is now a crime scene. I'm afraid you won't be able to stay here tonight.'

'Right,' said Sep, now wishing he'd got rid of the hitman's gun. 'I'll, er, need to change my shirt and grab a jacket, which are in the back bedroom.'

'DI Black, we'll need all your clothes for forensics; Miss O'Toole's nightclothes as well.'

'She, er, wasn't actually wearing anything,' said Sep.

'In that case we'll need the clothes she's wearing now,' said Renholm.

Sep looked at Fiona. 'Ask Winnie to come up. I'd prefer her to help me change than you.'

'So would I.'

'There's some of her stuff in the back bedroom as well,' added Sep.

Winnie joined Sep in the back bedroom and helped him undress. She glanced at the wardrobe on top of which was the incriminating gun. The shock she was still suffering was etched into her face.

'Don't worry about that,' Sep said. 'I should have got rid of it properly, which I could have done had I thought about it. I think I kept it because it's a gun I really like – a stainless-steel Smith & Wesson, three-inch barrel .357 revolver. A handy thing to have for personal protection. Mind you, it's not exactly a hitman's weapon. It's like a pea-shooter compared to something really useful like the .44 Magnum Clint Eastwood had in the *Dirty Harry* films.'

'I see. So what are we going to do? Try and smuggle it past them?'

Sep smiled and shook his head. 'After I bought the house I fitted some hidey-holes, for want of a better word. One of them's down there.' She followed his gazed to the skirting board in the corner.

'That corner moulding comes away if you prise it up with a screwdriver.'

'Where do I get a screwdriver?'

Sep grinned. 'There's one on top of the wardrobe.'

Within two minutes Winnie had pulled up the corner moulding to reveal a small gap behind it, big enough to hide a gun.

'Don't get your prints on anything,' Sep warned her. 'If it's ever found, it's my problem not yours. In fact, if it's ever found I'll deny all knowledge of it. This gun's not a recent model. It could have been there ten years or more.'

'Sep, you really are a devious bugger.'

'I play to my strengths.'

After carefully wiping it free of all prints she put the gun in the hole and replaced the moulding, examining it with a critical eye. There was no clue as to it being anything other than a continuous part of the skirting board.

'Very good, Mr Black. How many more of these are there?'

'Four altogether, some bigger than others. Some even more ingenious than that.' He studied her face and asked, 'How're you feeling?'

'Not good.'

'It'll wear off, especially when you get to realize that you've rid the world of a bad man who was out to kill us both.'

'I know, Sep. I'm trying. But he was alive and now he's dead because of me.'

'It takes some getting used to.'

'It's not something I want to get used to.'

'Fair enough. Now help me on with these trousers or they'll think we're up to no good in here.'

They emerged, respectably dressed, with Sep struggling on the elbow crutch. 'Is there any reason why I shouldn't stay at Winnie's tonight?' he asked of the two police officers.

'None at all,' said Renholm.

'In that case, we'll need some help carting my wheelchair over there and my medications and stuff. Plus another change of clothes that I've left in the bedroom.'

'I'll sort that out, Sep,' said Fiona.

'Will you be searching the house for any reason, because if you are, I want it leaving as you found it. I'm a very tidy man.'

'I see no reason to have the house searched,' said Renholm, now thinking it would do no harm to have a cursory look round the place, which didn't look all that tidy to him. He'd heard about this Sep Black character and it would do no harm to see how the man lived. Sep read his mind.

'You won't be able to resist taking a look round. Just don't leave a mess. I'm not in a position to tidy up after you.'

In Sep's mind this was as good as telling Renholm that there was nothing incriminating to find in the house – apart from a killer's gun, which they already had, if his story was to be believed.

The man killed by Winnie was identified as Bernard Armstrong Zermansky, better known as Bazz, a known felon with a lengthy crime sheet. He had too many associates for the Cold Case Unit to zero in on anyone in particular, although Sep thought that Stanley Butterbowl might be worth looking at. The dead man was a known associate of Butterbowl's. According to Winnie, who felt she had every right to ask around about her would-be murderer, he was a man with whom Zermansky had been seen in a certain pub and a man suspected of being a hitman for several West Yorkshire gang bosses.

FIFTEEN

S ep looked up at the unimposing council block and commented,
'I hope the lift doesn't stink.'
'I just hope it works.'
'If it doesn't, I'll just hobble up on my crutches.'

His hope was optimistic. The lifts in many such council flats were ingrained with urine, both animal and human. Sep was in a wheelchair, which he'd now upgraded to a motorized one. The entrance to the block of council flats was up one step which did not have a ramp, so he took out a thirty inch wide wooden wedge from the wire basket beneath the chair and handed it to Winnie who positioned it in front of the step, giving Sep his own personal ramp. It required quite a run at it to mount the step without falling backwards. However, it was a skill Sep had perfected and he managed it first time.

Winnie pressed for the fourth floor and pressed the other end of Sep's scarf over her nose. They looked at one another, each with an end of the scarf over their mouths and with smiling eyes that said, *Together we can handle whatever the world throws at us.*

The lift worked, which Sep considered to be a bonus. It stopped at the fourth floor and the door slid open. Another bonus. Sep steered his chair out and took a breath of fresher air coming through a broken window.

'Flat 42,' Winnie said. 'I'm guessing it's not far from the lift door.'

Within seconds she was knocking on the flat door. Adam opened it and stood there as if he never got visitors and didn't really know what to say.

'Mr Piper?'

'Adam Piper, yes.'

'My name's Winnie O'Toole and this is Detective Inspector Black of the West Yorkshire Police.'

Sep held up his warrant card but he might as well have been holding up the Jack of Clubs. Adam wasn't impressed. His eyes switched from the card back to Winnie.

'He's a detective . . . in a wheelchair?'

He asked the question as if detectives shouldn't be allowed to go round in wheelchairs.

'Yeah,' said Sep. 'I took the wheelchair job over when Ironside packed in.'

'He's joking,' said Winnie.

'Oh,' said Adam.

'We're investigating a series of crimes that began with the murder of Mr Santiago and we wonder if you might be able to help us with our enquiries.'

'It's only because you worked for Mr Santiago at the time of his death,' Sep added. 'We'll be talking to everyone who worked there. May we come in?'

'Why do you wanna come in?'

'Well, I think it might be better than talking out here on the landing. Hey, you have an American accent. What part of the States are you from?'

'Erm, we're from Brooklyn, which is a New York borough.'

'Really?'

'You may come in,' said Adam. 'My brother's inside but he might be scared of you. He's not very good at talking to people he doesn't know.'

'What's his name?' Sep asked.

'Simeon. He has a social anxiety disorder.'

'Ah,' said Sep, '*Now there was a man in Jerusalem, whose name was Simeon and this man was righteous and devout . . .*'

Adam stared at him in amazement, as did Winnie.

'I was quoting from the book of Luke in the Bible,' explained Sep. 'Simeon was a Catholic saint. Are you Catholic, Adam?'

'No.'

'Well, whatever you are, you look like a good man to me. I bet Simeon's a good man.'

'He's my brother and you don't need to patronize him, or me for that matter.'

'May we come in?'

Adam stood aside to allow them access. Sep led the way in his wheelchair. Simeon was sitting at a table on which there was a series of picture cards laid out in jagged lines which he was trying to neaten, but the job was seemingly too much for him.

'Hi, Simeon,' said Sep cheerily.

Simeon didn't seem to hear him. He proceeded to move the cards around.

'He just collects the baseball cards and watches games on TV,' Adam told him.

'I'm Sep and this is Winnie. We don't have baseball in England.'

'I know,' said Simeon, to the cards. 'Can't get none here.'

'I bet Winnie could get you some more cards. Have you got Clayton Kershaw and Mike Trout?'

'No.'

'I bet Winnie could get them for you.'

Simeon glanced up at Winnie, who had never heard of Clayton Kershaw or Mike Trout. She was looking daggers at Sep.

'We don't know why you're here,' said Adam.

'Ah, well, Mrs Santiago said you and Simeon might be able to help us.'

He accidentally bumped his wheelchair into a table and had to go backwards to get past it. 'Sorry about the wheelchair but I'm new to this thing. It's not permanent. I was in an accident.'

Simeon said nothing. He just gazed down at his three uneven rows of baseball cards, shifting them into different positions and humming tunelessly.

'I was run over by a van,' added Sep.

'It wasn't me who ran you over, muttered Simeon, just loud enough for Sep to hear'

'No, no, I know it wasn't you, but I think we might have a photo of the man who did run me over. Trouble is, we don't know who he is and we need to catch him before he runs someone else over.'

Fiona had compared a photo of the dead man to the police mugshot file and had identified him as Bernard Zermansky who had served time for GBH and other violent crimes. He also found out that Zermansky had still been in prison when Santiago was murdered so at least one murder was as yet unsolved. Fiona had scanned a copy of the mugshot photo and had given it to Sep, who now produced it for Adam to look at.

Sep's eyes were on Adam at the instant he saw the photo and what Sep saw was instant recognition before Adam looked away and said, quickly, 'I don't know him.'

'Really?' said Sep, eyebrows raised.

He steered his chair around the room so that he was facing

Simeon, who now had his back to his brother. Winnie had twigged what Sep was doing and proceeded to show Adam another set of photographs which had nothing to do with the case and which had Adam shaking his head as Sep showed Wolf's photo to Simeon.

'I bet *you* know who this is, Simeon. Smart lad like you. I bet you recognize him.'

Simeon did indeed recognize him and gave a startled cry. Adam looked up and said, 'Simeon, don't tell them.'

'Your brother doesn't want you to tell us you recognize the man,' said Sep. 'But it's a bit too late for that because you both know very well who he is . . . and we know you know. That's why we're here.'

'He frightened me,' said Simeon.

'Well, he won't be frightening you anymore because he's dead,' Sep told him.

'So he can't get us?' said Simeon.

'He can't get anyone,' said Sep. 'Tell me what you know about him.'

'I told you, he's not very talkative,' said Adam.

'He frightened me,' said Simeon.

'How did he frighten you?' asked Winnie.

'He shot me.'

'What?'

'Only with his fingers,' said Adam. 'He didn't have a gun or nuthin'.'

'What was he doing at your work?'

'He came with a woman,' said Simeon.

'What woman? What was the woman's name?'

'Mrs Hardacre,' said Adam. 'I'm not sure she was actually with him. They just came at the same time.'

Sep closed his eyes at the introduction of yet another name to the list of people he'd have to investigate. He'd almost forgotten about Mrs Hardacre whose name had come up on James Boswell's computer.

'Who's Mrs Hardacre, what does she do?'

'Dunno,' said Adam, 'we didn't ask. We were told not to ask too many bloody questions is what Mr Santiago said.'

'What does Mrs Hardacre look like?'

'She's a bit of all right.'

Simeon grinned at his brother's description. 'She is as well,' he said.

'You mean she's pretty?'

'Yeah.'

'How old?'

'Not as old as you.'

Simeon was speaking to Winnie who scowled at him.

'He doesn't mean to insult you,' said Adam.

'Well, Winnie's not very old,' Sep said, 'so this Mrs Hardacre must be quite young, is she?'

'Yeah. I bet she's as young as Simeon.'

'And how old is Simeon?'

'Twenty-four and a half.'

'How many times have you seen her?'

'Once, I think,' said Adam.

'She smoked cigarettes inside and you're not supposed to do that,' said Simeon, all in one breath. It was the longest speech they'd heard from him.

'I agree,' said Sep. He looked at Winnie and inclined his head back to Simeon. 'I like this feller,' he said.

'She's taller than me,' said Simeon, who was becoming more loquacious by the minute. Sep thought it might be the prospect of Winnie getting him some baseball cards. This was something he needed to look into. Would they sell such things on eBay?

'How tall are you?' asked Sep, assessing Simeon's height, 'five foot nine?'

'I bet I am.'

'So she must be quite tall then, to be taller than you.'

'Bottle-black hair,' said Simeon.

Sep looked to Adam for confirmation. Adam shrugged. 'If Simeon says it was bottle-black, it was bottle-black.'

'You mean dyed black?'

'Didn't like her,' said Simeon.

'Nor me,' said Adam. 'She was very haughty.'

'Haughty?' said Sep. 'Now that's a term you don't hear much nowadays.'

'They say it a lot in Brooklyn,' said Adam, 'about women from Queens – hoity-toity, if you know what I mean.'

'Yes, I know hoity-toity. Anything else?'

'No.'

'And that man,' said Sep, indicating the photo of Bazza Winnie was holding, 'did you hear him speak?'

'Talk like Auntie Deck,' said Simeon.

'Auntie Deck? Who's Auntie Deck?'

'In the jungle,' said Simeon.

Sep was giving this some thought when Winnie beat him to it. 'Ant and Dec,' she said.

'Ah,' said Sep, 'they talked like Ant and Dec. So the man was a Geordie. That's more than we got from Fiona.'

'Well, he did his time in Durham Prison,' said Winnie, 'so his accent wouldn't have stood out. He'd have been normal to them.'

'She had a brown mark,' said Simeon, jabbing a finger in his left temple.

'You mean like a birthmark?' Winnie asked.

Adam shrugged. 'I didn't notice that, but if Simeon said she had a brown mark, I believe him. He has a problem, but he knows stuff like that.'

'Only a very little mark,' said Simeon, looking at his hands. 'Like my little fingernail.' He waggled the aforesaid nail to illustrate his point. Sep looked at his hands which were large and pale and very clean.

'What is it you do at work?' Sep asked him.

'I sweep and mop and polish.'

'I bet you're good at that.'

'I'm very good, aren't I, Adam?'

'Very good indeed.'

'You must be to do work like that and keep your hands so clean,' observed Winnie.

'Wear gloveses on my hands and I wash them all the time—after toileting and stuff.' Another mini-speech.

'Gloves,' corrected Adam.

'Auntie Deck man. Don't like him,' said Simeon.

'You'll never see him again,' Sep assured him.

'He's dead, Simeon,' said Adam.

'I'm very glad,' said Simeon.

'So am I,' said Sep. 'Did either of you have much to do with Mr Santiago?'

'I work at clean and tidy,' said Simeon. 'Adam work on his televisions.'

'He means computers,' explained Adam. 'I work in IT, which

is how we both came to work there. I worked for a firm that serviced the computers at the New York Stock Exchange, in fact I was the one who serviced them.' Now that he was on a familiar subject his conversation became more articulate, even boastful. 'I'm very good with computers.'

'You mean he valued your services so much he gave Simeon a job as well?'

'Simeon's very good at what he does, best they've ever had, according to Mr Santiago.'

'And do you both still work there?'

'Yes, we do.'

'Doing the same sort of work as before?'

'As before, yes.'

'What sort of IT work do you do?' Sep asked Adam.

'I work mainly in software design.'

'Anything in particular? By that I mean a piece of software that a rival company might want to get their hands on.'

Adam was ahead of him. 'You mean kill Mr Santiago for?'

'I do, yes.'

Sep spotted a hint of anxiety in Adam's eyes and wondered why. 'Killing Mr Santiago wouldn't do anyone any good,' said Adam. 'All our work is highly protected. No hacker could get into our systems.'

'I imagine you're a valued employee.'

Adam became immediately defensive. 'Both Simeon and I are valued employees. We both do the best we can.'

'I'm sure you do,' Sep said. 'Anyway, thank you for your co-operation. You've been most helpful.'

'Blimey, they were hard work,' said Winnie. 'How come you knew all that Bible stuff? And where will I get those bloody baseball cards from?'

'Winnie, I've got no idea but it's what you're good at.'

'Sep, don't patronize me like you patronized them.'

'I wasn't trying to. I was just trying to put us all on a level playing field. As far as the bible stuff's concerned, we were about to interview a lad called Simeon, so I looked it up. It's the only quotation I could give you. I figured it would give him confidence, knowing that I knew he was named after a famous saint.'

'Famous? I've never heard of him.'

'Neither had Simeon, but he has now. I just gave the lad a leg-up in life and he'll remember that and he'll remember who gave him that leg up.'

'I think we need to understand a bit more about his mental problem if Simeon's going to be part of the investigation,' said Winnie. 'Anyway, how do you think it went?' she asked, over her left shoulder. They were driving home in her van which she'd had converted to accommodate his wheelchair. He was sitting diagonally behind her.

'Like you said, they were hard work and we need to pay them at least one more visit,' said Sep. 'They were running out of steam back there. Next time we go they'll know us as friends and they'll be more cooperative.'

'I thought they did OK. Adam seemed pretty grounded to me.'

'I agree, but I think they can do better,' said Sep. 'Adam was hiding something when I asked him about the software he was designing. I might have pressed him on it but I know bugger-all about software, or hardware come to think of it. Mrs Hardacre was mentioned in James Boswell's notes. Her name's Olivia Hardacre and as far as I know she never worked for Santiago.'

'Really?' said Winnie. 'So, all we know about her is that she's tall and pretty with a birthmark on her face.'

'And she's hoity-toity,' added Sep.

'Did you get the impression that Adam was a little bit . . . er . . .' she twirled a finger around her temple, '. . . you know, as well as his brother?'

'Sandwich short of a picnic you mean?'

'Well, half a sandwich, but not quite full shilling.'

'I think so, but not when he talked about computers and suchlike, otherwise he wasn't quite your normal Jack the Lad I'll grant you that.'

'Well, it could be,' said Winnie, 'that Adam's an ultra-bright, high-functioning bloke, who prefers to channel all his enormous brainpower along the very narrow IT pathway, to the exclusion of all the interesting other stuff— well, interesting to us, but not to them. Some academics despise such stuff as being a waste of brainpower. Such a combination would make him a computer genius, would it not?'

'You mean and therefore indispensable to Santiago TechSys?'

'I think he's got something inside his noggin that Santiago valued highly.'

'Winnie, you might be on to something. The Piper brothers might be the key to everything. Maybe we should check their backgrounds.'

'I'm guessing their background is back in Brooklyn – you'd have to check with the NYPD which might mean giving them what you have on Snowball.'

'NYPD? Is that the North Yorkshire Police Department? If it's the American NYPD I'm giving them nothing on Snowball. That'll open a real can-of-worms.'

'I think you know which NYPD I mean.'

'I do and that's a complication too far. I'll give that a miss, unless it becomes absolutely necessary. You know, James Boswell might have been killed by his girlfriend's husband, likewise Charlie Santiago. Bloody hell! Why can't men be more faithful?'

'Why indeed?' said Winnie too wholeheartedly for Sep's liking.

'There is another alternative,' he said.

'What's that?'

'All I do is concentrate on proving that James Boswell wasn't involved with a prostitute, which is all his wife really wants. Then I step down and apply for my transfer. That's all Mrs Boswell wants out of this.'

'I thought you'd already proved that to her.'

'To her, yes, but she's going to need more. I haven't proved it to her friends and family and not to the parents of her daughter's friends when she starts school. All I've given her is my very strong opinion, with which she agreed most gratefully.

'Whoever killed Santiago and attacked us is of no interest to her. OK, whoever murdered him is a job for the police but not for me. Personally I'm happy to believe it's this Bazz character, even though we know he can't have killed Santiago, with him being banged up at the time.'

'Doesn't Bazz being dead make life easier for you?' Winnie asked him.

'No, it's the person who hired Bazz who's the danger, which is why it's probably a good idea to broadcast the news that Sep Black is off the case.' He smiled and added, 'It might be interesting to see who goes to Bazz's funeral.'

'It might be more interesting to find out who's paying for it.'

'The police in his case. If only to make sure he has a funeral, just to see who turns up. It won't be a lavish affair.'

'Well, I think we should go,' Winnie said. 'Phone cameras at the ready.'

'Didn't I just tell you that I'm off the case?'

'You did, but I don't believe you. You'll be looking out for a tall, beautiful lady with a birthmark on her face. You'll take the tracker and you'll stick it on her car.'

'In this chair? That's Fiona's job. You're not coming. Anything else we'll be doing?'

'Yes, you'll both stay in the background, with hats on and you'll be looking out for Mrs Santiago and the Piper brothers and anyone else you've come across in the course of your investigation.'

'Why's that?'

'Because none of them have any reason to be there.'

'That's very good, Detective O'Toole.'

'Does that mean I can come to the funeral?'

SIXTEEN

'Have you had this valeted, Sep?'

'Yep, washed, polished, valeted inside and out, vacuumed, even polished up the tyres. Forty quid, which includes picking up from the house and bringing it back when the job's done.'

'And all for a killer's funeral?'

'No, I have it done every month. Where's the car park by the way?'

'There's an overspill park behind some bushes. I'll drop you off and park your car there, away from prying eyes.'

'Good. Officially, I'm not supposed to be here. I'm still on sick leave. They don't know I can get about on a crutch nowadays. Apart from us, there'll be three coppers there, Fiona definitely. More coppers than mourners, I should think. They stand out like . . . like . . .' he tried to think of suitable simile. Winnie helped him out.

'Like bollocks on a starving dog.'

'Winnie! Do you have to be so crude? This is a funeral, which is a religious ceremony.'

'Sorry, vicar.'

'Let's just say they stand out, all coppers do at funerals. We should stay in the background as if we aren't actually with the coppers or his funeral party. Just take a few photos with that telephoto lens of yours. Make sure you get the ones first out of the chapel. They tend to be the ones closet to the deceased. I doubt there'll be many – if any. I'll be interested to see who's talking to whom as well.'

Winnie got into the driver's seat of Sep's shiny Jaguar, his pride and joy, which he looked after like a baby. 'I often wish I got looked after as well as this car,' she commented. 'Can you press a button or something to bring the hood up? My hat's going to blow off.'

Sep pressed the required button, the hood came up and clicked into place as Winnie started the engine and roared off with unnecessary wheelspin.

'Bloody hell, Winnie! You've just worn twenty quid's worth of rubber off the tyres.'

The funeral was much more sparsely attended than they had hoped. Of the non-coppers, maybe three men and one woman, all of whom looked to be from Bazza's strata of society and three other men, all in dark coats and black ties – the traditional garb of the under-cover copper at a funeral. There was no social chatter outside the chapel. The four, possibly genuine, mourners headed for a nearby car park, followed by the three men in black coats, plus Fiona, who had a GPS tracker in her pocket.

'Just a thought,' said Winnie. 'With Bazza's name being Zermansky, shouldn't this be a Jewish funeral?'

'I doubt if Bazza was the devout type. Maybe he was corpus-non-grata at the Jewish cemetery'

'Your lot are a bit conspicuous for undercover coppers,' commented Winnie, standing beside Sep on the steps of the crematorium. They'd viewed the service from a room next to the chapel which ran a CCTV relay of the service, usually for when the chapel couldn't hold all the mourners, which was hardly the case here. Winnie had already photographed all the mourners as they left

'There's no one more conspicuous than an undercover copper at a funeral,' said Sep.

'Not like when *you* were an undercover copper, Mr Jimmy Lennon.'

This raised a half-smile from Sep. In a previous undercover case in his guise as Scottish ne-er-do-well, Jimmy Lennon, he had scarcely recognized himself in a mirror. Maybe one day he'd use it again, but now was too soon after that momentous time – a time that had turned his life completely around, including bringing Winnie into it.

'Did you get any decent pictures?' he asked.

'Yeah, I got everyone.'

'What about the woman?'

'Yeah, I got her . . . and the one who came out later.'

'Really? I didn't spot her.'

'I know, that's why you brought me. I got a decent profile which should show if she's the one with a birthmark.'

'Left side?'

'Yes.'

'Is she quite tall?'

'She is.'

'Let me have a look.'

Winnie brought up the screen and handed the camera to him. 'This other woman— do you know who she is?' he asked her.

'I don't, no.'

'It's Mrs Santiago. We need to know why she's at the funeral of the man who broke into my house and tried to kill us.'

He was scrolling across the various shots when they heard the explosion. The shock wave shook the bushes like a sudden gust of wind. A large pall of smoke appeared, followed by darting flames. Everyone, including the police and mourners, turned to look. The three mourners looked but chose to carry on, as if the incident came as no surprise to them. The police ran towards the explosion.

'It came from our car park,' said Winnie, taking Sep's arm and encouraging him into a hurried hobble on his crutch towards the explosion. They rounded the line of bushes and saw an upturned car blazing amid a cloud of black smoke. It had obviously been blown into the air and had landed on a small Vauxhall. Sep stopped and swore, violently.

'It's my bloody car! The bastards have blown up my bloody car!'

Winnie helped Sep towards where they stood among the group
of policemen. No point concealing their presence now.

'Is that your car, sir?' called out Fiona, without taking her eyes
off the blaze.

'Yeah. Who else?'

'Thought so. Mine's the one underneath it. Bloody hell! I can't
even *park* next to you in safety.'

'There was someone in it,' called out a policeman. 'He's been
blown out the far side.'

The group ran round to the far side of the blazing Jaguar to
where a man's body was lying with his legs half out of the car.
A policeman made a wild rush for him and made a grab at his
feet before abandoning the attempt and retreating back through
the flames, setting himself on fire in the process. Sep and Winnie
arrived just as his colleagues were rolling him on the ground,
trying to smother the flames with their coats. Sep shook his head
in disapproval.

'That wasn't very clever. The man's obviously dead.'

'Why obviously?' asked Winnie.

Sep nodded his head to his left. 'Because his head's over there'
He pointed at a human head lying on the ground on its side and
facing them. 'The explosion will have blown the hood off my car
and his head with it.'

A policeman produced a fire extinguisher from the police car
with which he sprayed the burning copper, whose flames had been
all but extinguished and who was screaming curses at his latest
saviour.

'Just get me a fucking ambulance!'

Sep went over to take a closer look at the dead man's head and
noticed the strange, jagged pattern cut into his shaven hair and,
more noticeable, the large, round hole in his left earlobe filled
with a black plastic disc with a skull pattern on it. Sep had seen
all this before. He stared at the dead face and nodded to himself.
Yes, it was him all right – couldn't be anyone else. He called back
to Winnie.

'Yeah, I know him.'

'What? You recognize a dead man's head?'

'I recognize his haircut and that thing in his ear. He's that East
European guy who works at the valeting place – poor lad. When
they brought the car back I mentioned that I was coming here to

a funeral. Wish I'd kept my big mouth shut now. If he'd been done for stealing my car, he'd have got three months or maybe a slap on the wrist and community service. They wouldn't have chopped the poor sod's head off.'

'It's hardly your fault, Sep. Can someone cover that poor man's head up?'

A policeman took off his coat and covered up the severed head. Muted curses were still coming from his foam-covered, but now extinguished colleague, DC Dickinson.

'Well, the dead man won't have planted the bomb,' said Sep. 'The bomb was for me. It was just his hard luck to try to steal my car.'

'Why would anyone want to kill you? You can't even walk and they should know by now that you're giving the detective game up.'

'Winnie, this is big-time criminal behaviour, not just someone wanting to take the "fun" out of funeral. They won't stop until they've got me – or until I get them.'

'So your detective career isn't over yet?'

'It would appear not.'

'You could always leave it to the West Yorkshire Police.'

'You mean Cock Robin Wood and his Merry Men?' Sep looked at her, then across at Fiona and his colleagues, then back at her. She got the message, as did Fiona.

'I'll arrange for a guard to be put on your house, sir,' called out Fiona.

'Thanks, Fiona, but I think I'd need an army to keep this lot at bay. I reckon it's all to do with the Charlie Santiago killing. This isn't the work of a wronged husband. This is bigger than that. By the way, I'm guessing that the bomber is watching us right now. He'll certainly know he didn't get me.'

'I'll get the plain-clothes people to have a scout round to see if there's anyone acting suspiciously.'

Sep nodded his agreement to this. People trying not to act suspiciously usually overdid it to a degree that made them obvious to an experienced policeman.

'We're checking the mourners out right now,' Fiona added.

'I doubt if any of them was involved, although one of them might have been paid just to pass information on to whoever did it. I'm a real sitting duck – can't even walk. I'd like you to take us back to my house to collect some stuff, then I'm leaving town for a while.'

'In that case both of us are,' added Winnie.

The bell of a fire engine was sounding in the distance as he wheeled away from the fire and the mayhem, accompanied by Fiona who was saying, 'DC Dickinson will be all right once the ambulance sorts him out. It's his life's ambition to be a hero, no one told him it might be painful.'

'By the way, Fiona,' said Sep. 'The car thief worked at the car wash on Bentley Lane.'

'Recognized the head, did you?'

'I did, yes.'

'Only you would recognize a severed head, sir. I suppose you suggest I take it along to the car wash in a Tesco's bag for formal identification?'

'Whatever works for you. If you're wondering how he got my car started, he'll have used a key. You can't start a car like that by hot-wiring. He'll have taken the key I gave him to some dodgy key-cutting place where they can make a record of the transponder chip that goes in the key fob. They're not supposed to, but the dodgy ones might if it's a valuable car. He'll be in league with someone from the key cutter's. They've most likely nicked dozens of cars using that ruse.'

'But why would a car thief plant a bomb in the car?'

'He didn't. The bomb was planted by the guys who are after me. They'll have got there before the thief to plant the bomb. They'll have known I was coming here, because he'll have told them as they wanted to keep tabs on me or something. The thief double-crossed them by stealing the car. He didn't tell them that – perhaps he should have mentioned it.'

'Well, he was hardly going to tell them that,' said Fiona. Sep was a pain in the arse but he was also a source of useful information.

'There's a key place not far from Bentley Lane,' Fiona mused. 'He cut me one for my Vauxhall. Eastern European bloke, nice chap.'

'That's an Eastern European head under your mate's coat,' Sep pointed out. 'Is Cock Robin on today?'

'No, he's on one of his many courses . . . probably a golf course.' Fiona smiled at her own barb, as did Sep, who rarely let a colleague's wit go unrewarded.

'Then I suggest,' said Sep, 'that you tell this story to DI Renholm. Tell him you want a warrant to confiscate the key shop's computers. Take my key. If my transponder's recorded on there, which it shouldn't be, you've broken a car thief gang. If not, do the same with all the key places in the area. You could clear up a lot of car crime in one go – which'd be one in the eye for Wood. Fiona, are you listening to me? You're looking worried, what's the problem?'

Fiona was staring at his destroyed car. 'I'm wondering how to word my insurance claim. Do I say it was damaged by a car falling on it from above?'

'If you tell them it was Sep Black's car, they'll believe it.'

Fiona nodded. 'It'll certainly add credence to the story.'

'Did you hear what I just said about a warrant for the computer? And you'll need to take a computer expert with you.'

'Yes, I'll do that, thanks. I really liked that car you know . . . sixty-five miles a gallon. I only filled up once a month.'

'I quite liked mine as well, Fiona. By the way, Mrs Santiago was at the funeral, did you notice her? We got a photograph. We'll send you a copy of her photo to your phone.'

He turned to Winnie. 'We can do that, can't we?'

'If she gives me her phone number, I can do it now.'

'Also,' said Sep, 'this crutch thing's a bit tiring. What I need is a car that's converted to carry a wheelchair with me sitting in it, preferably a four-by-four. Where could we hire one of those?'

'I'll make enquiries.'

'Let Fiona know what you find. The police can pay for it.'

'I assume I'm doing the driving?'

'Correct.'

'It's nice to be wanted. I'm hoping we're going abroad. Nice villa somewhere hot. Is it near the sea?'

'Quite near.'

'Do us both good, a bit of sunshine. Are we going through the tunnel? I've never been through the tunnel, or the ferry. I don't mind the ferry. Where are we going?'

'Scarborough.'

SEVENTEEN

Sep parked his wheelchair next to Fiona's desk in the police station. 'They're bound to have followed us here and they'll be keeping a watch on my house as well. So, how do I get my stuff?'

'You don't. I get it for you,' said Fiona. 'Just give me a list of what you need and where it all is. I'll bring it back here in a holdall.'

Fiona was on her mobile, tracking down a mobility vehicle. She covered the receiver with her palm and said to Sep, 'I'm on to that mobility place in Crossgates that Winnie mentioned. They've got a Mercedes Sprinter van converted to carry a wheelchair without collapsing it. It has a wheelchair lift and everything. Do you know if you qualify for a mobility allowance?'

'No idea. How much to hire it for a month?'

'At least a thousand, I should think.'

'We'll take it. If I don't get that allowance I'll claim it back on expenses.'

'I wouldn't hold your breath.'

'Or from Mrs Boswell,' added Sep.

'It strikes me she's the main reason you're sticking with this.'

'I'm sticking with it because it's my job, just as it's your job.'

Fifteen minutes later the Mercedes had been ordered and paid for courtesy of the Cold Case Unit, much to Fiona's amazement.

'They think like I do,' Sep had explained to her. 'This could end up being a serious result for the unit. I've been offered two detective constables to join our team.'

'Are you going to take them?'

'That's not actually up to me. I've just said I'd like to carry on for a bit on my own, along with you and Winnie.'

'Winnie? Is she being paid or something?'

'Two hundred a week in the hand, as a consultant/informer/carer, call it what you like. She may well be worth it, if only for one piece of information. All I need to do now is for me and Winnie to get away in the Merc without them knowing I'm in it.'

'In that case, it'll be as well if the Merc doesn't come anywhere near this station.'

'If the police can get me and Winnie to the mobility place, say, in a vid van,' suggested Sep, 'without us being followed, we can pick up the Merc and get straight off.'

'OK, sounds like a plan. Yes, I'll arrange that.'

Fiona enjoyed being part of such subterfuge. 'I'll drive to your house to pick up your stuff with a big copper in the car wearing your coat and hat and using a crutch. They'll think that's you.'

'I never wear hats.'

'You would today, it's raining.'

'We both go in, but only I come out, so they'll think you're in the house. By that time we have the video van waiting back here with you and Winnie already in it. I'll throw you your bag of stuff, then you both shoot straight off in the video van to pick up the Merc. No one in their right mind's going to tail a video van. In any case, you'll be followed by an unmarked car keeping an eye out just in case.'

Two hours later they were around the back of the mobility shop in Leeds, where Winnie had done all the paperwork and Sep was figuring out how to work the lift by using a remote control.

'This is just brilliant,' he was saying. 'I was thinking it might be an enclosed van but it has windows in the back and even some parking brackets for the chair so I don't roll around when we're moving. You just have to adjust them to suit the chair.'

'I'll do that, sir,' said the man from the shop. 'Are you going far in it?'

'Yes, we're heading up north to the Scottish Highlands.'

'Beautiful part of the world, sir. Fair old journey though.'

'Yeah, three hundred and fifty miles, give or take.'

'Well, this is the ideal vehicle for such a journey. We have branches in Glasgow and Inverness, if you have any problems.'

Winnie made no comment. Tactical lies are necessary when people are trying to track you down. Scarborough was on the coast, sixty-five miles due east at that end of the A64 – an excellent road which starts and finishes in Yorkshire. Exactly *where* they were staying she had no idea. Sep's mobile buzzed. Fiona's name showed on the screen.

'Hiya.'

'You were followed up to the cop shop on York Road. That's why the vid van pulled in there for five minutes. The tail car drove on.'

'Yeah, we did wonder.'

'We had two cars with you. One car on him and one with you. We tailed his car but ended up in a pub car park on the Wetherby Road. The driver's still in the pub. Silly sod's drinking pints of strong lager. When he gets going again we're going to pull him for drink driving.'

'So we pick up a live one. That'll be really handy, especially if he's over the limit and we can hold him.'

'The way he's putting it away it won't be a problem, unless someone else picks him up. We've got a backup car on its way to help us follow any car that comes to pick him up.'

'You'll need to think of a reason to stop both cars and apprehend everyone in them.'

'If only I had your imagination, sir.'

'Just tell them you've got both cars reported as stolen. You can always apologize a few hours later when you find out the computer's on the blink, by which time you'll have checked their mugshots and maybe held them on suspicion of something else. Let's face it, we already know they're villains.'

'Is that what you'd do, sir?'

'Of course. Always take full advantage of the power invested in you. So, we're clear to leave here right now, are we?'

'Oh yes. I'm parked just up the road from you. I'll be following you for a few miles to keep an eye out for further villains. I'm in a white Astra.'

'Thanks, Fiona.'

'By the way, sir. I'm back on the Cold Case Unit, if only to look after you.'

'Well, you're doing a good job of that so far.'

Newby Cottage was in open country a mile and a half west of Scarborough and about half a mile off the A171. Winnie had no idea where they were headed. She'd been given a postcode for the satnav and had followed its instructions right up to them leaving a paved road when the satnav lady said, '*You have now reached your destination.*'

She drove through a gate that seemed to open and close for

their convenience and drove along what was little more than a cart track.

'Is it me or has the satnav told me wrong?'

'No, this is the way, not far now.'

The track was running through a wood that opened out into fields. To their right, on a hillside, was an old cottage in a state of disrepair.

'Please tell me that's not it.'

'That's it,' said Sep.

'Really? Well, has it got all mod cons?'

'It's got water and electricity, a telephone and proper plumbing and it's got a Sky dish around the back and Internet connection.'

'Whose is it?'

'Mine. I bought it blind for a real knockdown price. I own all these fields as well. There's an old guy called Elijah living there – a real handyman. He looks after the place. Believe it or not it's in much better condition now than when I bought it. Hopefully he'll have made a start on the roof before the winter sets in.'

'Elijah?'

'That's right. I call him Eli.'

'Is Eli trustworthy?'

'Yeah, he's a reformed burglar, but I'd trust him with my life. He was a jobbing builder before he took to burglary. His trouble was he used to go back and burgle the houses he'd worked on. I never had any problem finding him. Lucky for me he's a much better builder than he was a burglar.'

'Burglar? Bloody hell, Sep! How old is he?'

'In his seventies I should think. Very active man for his age.'

'If he gets active with me, he won't reach his eighties.'

'No, he's past all that, but don't play cards with him, not for money. He'll clean you out in ten minutes.'

'Well, I can't imagine anyone tracking you down here.'

'If they do, we'll see them coming, Winnie. Eli will have seen this car as soon as it left the main road. Right now he'll be standing at the door watching out for us.'

'How will he know?'

'I told him we were coming. I had a few CCTV cameras positioned in the trees and linked to a monitor in the cottage.

Whenever there's a movement big enough for it to be a vehicle or even a person the monitor beeps. Eli rigged it all up for me.'

'Why? Is he on the run or something?'

'No, he's as clean as a whistle now. It's for me. There've been times in the past when I've needed somewhere to hole up without travelling halfway round the world; I'm not very popular with the villains on my patch, so when I get leave I like to go to ground. This is ideal because I'm near enough to home to get back quickly and I can stay in contact through a computer – Skype and all that stuff.'

'Contact with who?'

'With Fiona and my daughter, Phoebe – with you, if I'd come on my own.'

'Fiona and Phoebe know about this place, do they?'

'No, but they know I won't be far away. Winnie, these bastards have tried to run me down, stab me in my sleep and blow me up. I need to keep on their backs, but from a safe place.'

'If you do see anyone approaching, what do you do?'

'First of all they have to stop at the locked gate where we can see them. I have a wireless connection to a speaker set in the gatepost. I ask them their business.'

'I wondered how we got through there with no trouble.'

'I'd already told Eli we'd be arriving about now and what vehicle to expect us in. If we see trouble arriving, there's another track at the back leading to the road. We can be clear before they get here.'

'What if they come at night and we can't see them clearly?'

'We have lights out there as well as cameras. The beauty of it is, Winnie, that only three people in the whole world know I own this this place. You, me and Eli. How is anyone going to find out where I am?'

'What if Eli blabs?'

'I've told him not to and, unlike you, he does as he's told. Eli's a loner. People around here think he lives here on his own like some sort of hermit. He goes shopping once a week on an old track bike. If he has any problems, he can ring me.'

'Does he ring you often?'

'He never rings me. I always ring him. He owes me a big favour, Winnie. He'll never let me down. Plus, I let him live there for nothing in exchange for him maintaining the place.'

'How long have you had the place?'

'A few years.'

'God, you're a secretive bugger, Black.'

'And yet still alive.'

EIGHTEEN

Eli was indeed standing in the doorway with a loaded shotgun. Sep slid open the side door of the van and shouted at him. 'Who the hell do you think you are, Davy Crockett?'

'Just protecting the old homestead.'

'If the police find you with that gun, you'll need protecting.'

'I've got a licence for it for clay pigeon shooting.'

'They gave you a licence with your record?'

'My sheet's been clean for eighteen years, which is better than some of the guys in that shooting club. What's with the wheelchair? You a full-time cripple now?'

'No, I just help them out when they're busy.'

Sep pressed the switch on his remote that sent out the lift platform. He began to ease his chair out on to it when Winnie yelled at him.

'Sep, you idiot! Stop!'

She had appeared by his side to make sure he got down safely, with it being his first time.

'Why?'

'The lift's not quite lined up yet and you're a foot from the edge – you've got to wait for it to click into position. Another turn of the wheel and you'd have been over. Then we'd have had a broken wheelchair and you might have had a broken leg!'

'OK, calm down. I get the message.'

'Turn the motor off and turn the wheel with your hands. That's what you're supposed to do for fine manoeuvring. Did you not listen to the man at the mobility place?'

'Is that what he said?'

'Yes, I assume that's Eli pointing a gun at me?'

'That's Eli but his gun's broken and pointing down, so don't worry.' Sep looked up at the house that appeared derelict and unloved.

'Does the roof still leak?' He asked.

'Nope. The only thing that leaks around here is me,' Eli said. 'Don't let the look of the place fool you. It's as watertight as a duck's arse and draught proof. You told me to make it look uninhabitable.'

'Well, you've certainly done a good job with that. I just hope it's habitable inside.'

'Of course it is. I inhabit the place myself. Who's this you've brought to see me?'

'Ah, sorry. This is Winnie O'Toole.'

'Pleased to meet you, Winnie O'Toole. I'm Elijah McMurphy, but you can call me Eli.'

Winnie held out a hand of greeting that Eli shook.

Winnie laughed. 'We have a right collection of names between us, Septimus, Elijah and Winnie O'Toole.'

Eli saw the funny side and gave a loud cackle that displayed a mouthful of teeth that were too white and even to be the originals. He was a small, bow-legged man with pink cheeks, twinkling blue eyes, a purple nose and long hair which was wild and white and uncombed. Winnie took an instant liking to him.

'Eli,' said Sep, 'I'll need you to fix me a ramp up to the front door.'

Eli was ahead of him. 'I've got a sheet of half-inch ply that'll get you in and out. How long 're yer stayin'?'

'Depends . . . days, weeks, maybe months if things get nasty.'

'Somebody after you?'

'Yes.'

He looked at the wheelchair. 'Looks like somebody caught up with you.'

'Somebody did. But I'm hoping they won't find this place.'

'If they do, that somebody'll get a warm reception.'

'I'll need to sleep downstairs,' Sep said. 'That OK?'

'Yeah. I got a room upstairs that I can sleep in.'

'Is there a room for me?' Winnie asked.

Eli looked from one to the other and said nothing.

'In my state I probably need you with me,' said Sep. 'Eli, could you put another bed in my room?'

'Well, if you need another bed, I've got one.'

'That'll do. I'm not safe to be left on my own.'

'What's new?' said Winnie.

Within minutes Eli had rigged up a ramp that enabled Sep to drive into the house. Winnie was in before him, intent on investigating the home they'd share for the immediate future. Sep took a glance around the living room that was as a tidy as could be expected of an elderly man living on his own.

'Well, you've kept it spick and span,' remarked Winnie, 'I'll give you that. Can you show me where we'll be sleeping?'

Eli led them to a short hallway and opened a door at the end. Sep steered his chair inside. It was a large room, the largest of the three bedrooms and it was tidy but tired. It had a double bed which was still unmade, a large old-fashioned wooden wardrobe, a dressing table, a three-tier chest of drawers and two chairs.

'Where's the bathroom?' Sep asked.

Eli pointed to a door in the corner. 'I made one of them en-suite bogs, with me needing to pee during the night. Saved me many a trip upstairs that has.'

Sep took a look inside and almost gasped with amazement. 'Eli, you've put a bidet in there.'

'I know, it came with the set. There was plenty of room for it, so I stuck it in. Great for washing me feet. I sometimes fill it with warm water and sit with me feet in it and yes I do know what it's for, only I don't find the need ter wash meself downstairs as often as some.'

Winnie was now standing behind them, looking around with equal amazement. 'Bath,' she said, 'shower, washbasin, WC and a bidet.'

'That's for soaking his feet,' said Sep.

'What else?' said Winnie.

'Do you think there's room for another bed in the room?' Sep said.

'It'll be a squeeze,' said Eli.

'I'm forced to agree,' said Sep.

'You'll have to make room,' said Winnie, 'and we need to fix Sep up with some handrails.'

'I can do that,' said Eli, but yer might have to make do with sleepin' with yer man ternight.' Before she could complain he added, 'Let me show yer me office.'

The room next door might have belonged to another building. It had new carpet wall-to-wall, Venetian blinds at the window, two smart, modern desks and two equally smart office chairs. On the desks were three computer monitors, two telephones, two computers, three keyboards and an expensive printer. On one wall was what might have been another monitor or a large screen television.

'I'm seriously impressed,' Sep said. 'At least I might be once you've explained it all to me.'

'Inside each machine,' said Eli, 'I've overclocked Intel eighteen core processors, all running a hundred and twenty-eight megabytes. There's not much commercially available that can beat these in benchmark tests.'

'Am I supposed to understand all that?'

'All you need to understand is that in this room we can hack into any computer in the world, including police computers and, combined with my expertise, I can hack into military-grade computers no matter what the strength of their security encryption and firewalls. I've rerouted our IP addresses through a loop of dummy servers in Finland. Nobody can trace us here.'

Sep turned to Winnie. 'Is he speaking English?'

'He sure is. I'd love to mess with this stuff.'

'She's a computer nut like you,' Sep explained to a bemused Eli, 'only she's actually studying it properly.'

'I studied it properly.' He pointed to a fully-laden book case. 'See all them books? They're all about computers. I've read and studied every one of 'em.'

Eli flicked a switch that brought the wall-mounted TV to life. The screen was split into four quadrants, each one showing a different CCTV view of the track from the main road to the house; the last one gave a picture of the path leading up to the house, including the front door. Eli pressed a key that zoomed the camera in to a point where the face of any visitor would be easily recognized.

'We can take stills of any picture we want,' Eli told them. 'No one can get near this house without us knowing. There are sensors that beep when anything bigger than a fox goes by and at night I have an infrared switch so we can see in the dark.'

'I'm impressed,' said Sep, 'but I'd be more impressed if we knew how you'd come about all this equipment.'

'It was all bought as a security system for a big-time villain, only it did him no good with him doing life on Dartmoor right now and not expected out any time soon.'

'Does he know you've got it?'

'Actually, Sep, no one knows I've got it. It's all bought and paid for, but by him not me. I doubt if he knows he even bought it.'

Sep stared at him as a dozen questions came to mind but he decided to ask only one. 'How long have you had it all?'

'It came into my possession about four years ago. I was working legit for the computer firm that sold it to him, which is why I know how it all works. It was an order paid for in cash and waiting to be delivered, so when he got banged up I had it delivered to my house for safekeeping. It's not stolen or anything, just being looked after until your man comes out.'

'How long's he in for?'

'Thirty-five years.'

'How old is he?'

'Seventy-three and he's got real bad emphysema.'

Sep gave the matter more thought and cast his mind back four years. Such a major villain he'd surely have heard of. 'Eli, are we talking about a gypsy gangster from Doncaster called Jack Scully?'

'Er, yes. I thinks that's him.'

'Jesus, Eli! He's a real bad man. He's doing major time on the block in Wakefield prison. He's already killed a prison officer which has added a life sentence to his tariff.'

'Well, I'm not in there so why would I worry? I never met him so he wouldn't know me from a cow's arse. I worked for the same computer place for six months after he got sent down and no one came asking after the stuff. The shop will have thought it had been delivered but they'd never know by who. The bloke who paid the cash over went down as well. Ten stretch, I think. He's up in Durham Prison.'

In a hotel room in Leeds three men sat at a table: Carl Redman, Roscoe Briggs and Stanley Butterbowl, Stanley preferred his street name – Wolf. All wore expensive suits and mean faces.

The boss, Carl Redman spoke: 'Black has to be eliminated. I don't know how much he knows and that's a major fucking problem.'

'Maybe we should just fix the feller yer workin' for,' said Roscoe Briggs, who was completely bald. 'At least you know where he is.'

'No, we need him. This whole scam came from him. He's got one of them computer brains. He can do stuff a normal brain wouldn't think possible, which is why it's never been done before.'

'I bet Santiago wished he'd never brought us in on the deal,' said Roscoe.

'He brought us in so he'd have a scapegoat if things went wrong. Santiago'd still be dead whether or not we were part of it.'

'Who killed him then?' asked Wolf.

'Not us and that's also a problem,' said Redman. 'According to my source, they've tied it in with another two murders. A bloke called Boswell and an old woman who worked at the dump where he was killed.

'So we're bein' chased by the pigs for three murders we didn't do? Not sure I like that.'

'What's not to like? It'll throw the pigs off our track. They can't tie us in for any for them three jobs.'

'Bollocks! I done bird for stuff I ain't done before now,' said Roscoe.' Anyway, what about this guy yer workin' for? Will he have killed Santiago?'

'Nah, that don't make sense. Santiago was obviously killed by someone who knew the scam and wanted in on it. My man was *already* in on it.'

'Yeah, but he don't have ter share with Santiago anymore.'

'He needed Santiago's business ter work from and I'll tell yer somethin'. *We* don't need Santiago's business. I can set up a business what'll do us nicely and we can work the scam ourselves, along with my man.'

'Whose name you won't tell us.'

'Not yet. I spent a long time building up contacts all over the place – contacts what trust me and I'm not gonna to give any of 'em ter you, unless I have to. And if yer want out, yer can fuck off right now!' Having delivered this ultimatum he cast them all a challenging glare.

'OK, OK,' muttered Wolf. 'So, what do we do? Now that Black's left town? Do we leave him where he is? He's prob'ly too shit-scared ter come back.'

'No, we track the bastard down and blow him away. He's in a wheelchair so he'll most likely be in some kind of mobility vehicle. Where would he go for one of those? With all his interfering in police affairs Black ain't the most popular man down at his nick.

I've got a pig in me pocket who can take a look at CCTV to see which way he went. My information is that he left the cop shop in a video van. We find out where that went and take it from there. He'll think he's in the clear but we can track him down. My guess is he won't have left Yorkshire. Pigs like him don't like to be too far away from the action. With my contacts he should be easy ter track down.'

'This seems all very complicated,' said Wolf. 'Why don't we just forget him and carry on as if he knows nuthin' – which is a fairly strong possibility.'

Redman shook his head. 'Nah, I'm not interested in possibilities, I deal in certainties. If Black knows anythin' at all, we could walk straight into a police trap. Don't forget we'll be wanted for murders various, some of which we ain't even done. Life without parole for all of us.'

'OK,' said Roscoe, 'you're the boss. We track Black down and eliminate the fuck out of him.'

NINETEEN

Winnie climbed into bed next to Sep. He'd already been there twenty minutes while she took a shower. He had his back to her when he said, 'I don't want you taking advantage of me, young lady. It's a serious crime taking sexual advantage of a disabled policeman.'

'If you weren't disabled, I'd be sleeping on the floor. I was supposed to have a bed of my own.'

'I can't turn over to kiss you goodnight, this is the only side I can sleep on,' said Sep. 'Even then it'll be bloody painful every time you turn over.'

'I'll try and keep still.'

'Thank you. By the way, I'd like to inform you that I've just acquired my first erection since the accident, which is good news in its own way but, right now, it's of no use to me whatsoever. Still, it bodes well for the future, eh?'

'Have you had any thoughts about the people who are after you?'

'Yes, with it being to do with stocks and shares and I think there's someone really big behind all this.'

'Well, there's nothing bigger in the world than the stock market. Sep, if it's that dangerous shouldn't the Cold Case Unit just take the whole thing to the West Yorkshire Police Organized Crime Unit? Or this new lot—the NCA or whatever they're called?'

'Maybe, maybe not. Trouble is, right now these villains are targeting *me* and if we bring in the NCA their first interest won't be to protect me. They'll be viewing the bigger picture, of which I form an insignificant but irritating part – Woody'll make sure of that.'

'Surely he won't be involved in it?'

'I think it's a strong possibility he will. If not him, someone else at least as senior. He's a senior officer and if he's bent and I think that's a strong possibility, the bad guys will have bought him and will definitely use him.'

'And he'll blacken your name and leave you as a sitting duck.'

'Something like that,' said Sep. 'I need to work this on my own for a while before I hand it over to the big boys. The trouble is that Santiago had no record for criminality. Clean as a whistle. The cops keep records of everyone suspected of anything. They'll definitely have one on me – and one on you for assisting me.'

'What? They can't do that.'

'Winnie, there's no law against keeping records. I have records of hundreds of people I have reservations about. If one of their names crops up in an investigation, it quite often gives me a head start – known associates and all that.'

'I'd like to know what they think they've got on me. Can you find out from Fiona?'

'I don't need Fiona. You do have a fair old sheet, you know.'

'I know and you're responsible for most of it.'

'It'll also say that you're the lover of DI Black and that won't be my doing.'

'Lover? How would they know that?'

'It's true, isn't it?'

'Well, yes, but I hope you don't go around broadcasting it.'

'Of course not, but going back to the mystery of why Santiago was murdered, it's unlikely that he'd be willingly mixed up with a criminal gang who resort to wholesale murder. There's a lot more to this than we know.'

'Maybe he didn't realize who he was mixed up with. If what he was doing was so profitable it'd attract the attention of major gangsters, would it not?'

'It would,' said Sep, 'and like you say, Santiago might well have been a relative innocent among serious villains – it happens.'

'And these serious villains are after you because they think you might be on to them?'

'Yeah, which means the quicker I do get on to them the better.'

'I need to get onto this ASAP,' Winnie suggested. 'I think this is as much to do with computers as the stock market and I'm the only expert we know.'

'Apart from Eli.'

'I think Eli's more of an expert in putting the hardware together. What to do with it all is more my area of expertise. I should have a field day with the stuff in the room next door. Is there anything else I should know?'

'Yes, you've missed your chance. My erection's gone down.'

'They don't last long at your age. You might get another one next week.'

'If I do I'll smuggle it down to the village rather than trouble you.'

'Thank you. I was thinking more about our safety here. Are you absolutely sure no one other than us three knows about you owning this cottage? What about the person you bought the place from?'

'That was years ago. I've no idea who the previous owner was and I don't imagine he knows who bought it. It was all done through an estate agency.'

DCI Wood opened the door of the Cold Case Unit office and stood there long enough to alert them to the presence of a senior officer, but his presence didn't impress anyone. No one in the room took any notice; none of them liked him. He knew that and thought he'd open with a joke.

'Is Ironside in today?'

'If you mean DI Black, no, he's not,' said Fiona without looking up from a file she was examining.

'Any idea where he is?'

'Right now he's on sick leave and wants to keep his whereabouts a secret and who can blame him, sir?'

'Quite right. It's just that I heard he was back at work and using a wheelchair.'

'Well, he's using a wheelchair but he's not back at work yet.'

'So he's lying low, is he?'

'Something like that.'

'Right. The next time you speak to him, would you tell him I'd like a word?'

'Yes, sir.'

Wood stood there, perhaps hoping someone else might decide to be more helpful than the Burnside woman. Everyone carried on with what they were doing, including conversing with each other as if he didn't exist. He went back to his office in a dark mood, enraged by the dismissive way his subordinates in the Cold Case Unit had treated him – no doubt influenced by that bastard DI Black.

Back in his office, Wood was trying to think of a way of tracking Sep down. Out of the blue a thought struck him and brought a smile to his face. He picked up the phone and dialled the switchboard.

'Becky, I'd like you to get me a Mr John Dunhill of Dunhill and Broome estate agents in York.'

'Yes, sir.'

'Five minutes later his phone rang. 'I've got Mr Dunhill for you, sir.'

'Ah, good . . . Mr Dunhill, this is DCI Wood of the West Yorkshire Police. I was invited to speak at your Lodge dinner a couple of years ago.'

'Yes, I remember you. And a jolly good speech you gave, I must say.'

'Thank you, but in our conversation just before the dinner the talk got around to our Detective Inspector Septimus Black.'

'Oh yes, I remember the name.'

'Not a name you can forget in a hurry.'

'Yes, a loose cannon if ever there was one, by the sound of him. Not the sort of man we'd have as a member. I do hope you're not proposing him?'

'No, no, nothing like that. It's just that I remember you mentioning that a man of that very name had bought a property from you some years ago and it's aroused my curiosity as we're trying to track him down right now and it's very much to his benefit that we find him.'

'He bought a property, did he? Erm, yes, I believe he did. That's right. It was the unusual name that rang a bell with me and when you spoke of a Septimus Black I wondered if it might be the same man.'

'Do you know where it is?' Wood asked.

'You mean the property he bought? Not offhand but I can soon do a check and ring you back. You do realize that normally we keep our transactions confidential, but with you being a senior policeman I imagine all is in order.'

Ten minutes later Dunhill rang him back. 'Yes, I've tracked down the sale and it was indeed to Mr Septimus Black who worked for the West Yorkshire Police. The property was near Scarborough. Mainly three hectares of fairly useless land which was neither arable nor development land. We were glad do get rid of it, to be honest. He was the only prospective buyer and got it for three thousand five hundred pounds, which was as low as we dare go without giving it away.'

'Just land, there was no house on it?'

'Actually, there was. A derelict property known as Newby Cottage.'

'Would you be able to tell me exactly where it is?'

'Of course, we have a location map in our file. I'll scan it and send it through to you if you give me an email address.'

'Would this include the postcode?'

'Yes, we can give you that.'

'Thank you. I'm very much obliged.'

TWENTY

Sep was bored. He and Winnie had been holed up in Newby Cottage for three days. He'd spent most of his days chopping up wood with Eli and improving his skill at walking with and without a crutch to the extent that he could now walk several yards crutch free – completely unaided. He'd brought with him the .357 Smith revolver he'd acquired from Winnie's attacker. It was fully loaded with five rounds which meant he couldn't practise with it but he was well acquainted with small arms and didn't need to. If trouble arrived, five shots would be all he'd get, but out here he didn't expect trouble. No one knew where he was, not even Fiona.

Where the track to the cottage joined the main road was a lay-by and in that lay-by was parked a car in which sat two men, Roscoe Briggs and Wolf. On the evening of the third day, Winnie took the Mercedes van out to buy supplies from the nearby village of Seamer. The car followed her to a convenience store where she bought milk, bread, tea and various other requirements, including pipe tobacco for herself. The men in the car didn't approach her, but as she left the shop they did take her photograph which they emailed to Redman. The word came back that this was indeed Black's woman and that they had found where he was hiding. A second car left Leeds carrying Carl Redman, a thug known as Animal and several weapons, including improvised firebombs, better known as Molotov cocktails. The two men already out there had been instructed to take a look at the cottage and its surrounding area in the fading daylight, as the attack was planned for night-time.

'We've got visitors,' said Eli, coming out of his computer room. Sep and Winnie followed him back in. One of the screens showed two men walking down the track: Roscoe Briggs and Wolf. Neither of them were dressed casually enough to look like local country folk and both of them walked with aggressive determination.

'Don't like the look of them,' commented Sep. 'They look like a couple of handy lads looking for trouble.'

'They won't know we've clocked 'em,' said Eli. 'They must have climbed over the gate.'

'If they're looking for me,' said Sep, 'how the hell did they know to come here?'

'When I went out in the van there was a car parked in a lay-by out on the main road,' Winnie told him.

'Anybody in it?' Sep asked her

'Not sure. I didn't think it was important, in fact I turned the other way.'

'Winnie, in our situation everything's important.'

'OK, I'm sorry.'

'Did it follow you?'

'Sep, I wasn't watching out for anyone following me. I thought we were safe out here.'

'One of those guys is holding a gun,' observed Sep, moving closer to the screen. 'Can you zoom in on him, Eli?'

Eli zoomed the camera in and picked out the intruder who was holding a handgun. Both of them were looking all around as if trying to acquaint themselves with the area.

'One of them's got plasters on his face,' said Winnie.

'Yeah, so I notice,' said Sep. 'I think I might have bumped into him before.'

They disappeared from the screen quadrant and appeared in the one next to it. The two men took cover behind some trees, eventually reappearing on a third screen.

'We should be able to see them through a bedroom window in a minute,' said Eli.

He and Winnie ran upstairs, with Sep trailing behind. He joined them in Eli's bedroom, standing back from the window in the shadows to avoid being seen. The two men appeared two hundred yards away and stopped walking, just looking at the cottage and talking to each other.

'We're being cased in readiness for the big event,' Sep told them.

'Jesus! When's that?'

'Tonight I would think, after dark. It wouldn't surprise me if they were just the advance party. How the hell did they find this place?'

Sep looked at Eli as he said this. The old man held up his palms in protest. 'Hey, don't look at me. I've said nothing to no one ever since I came here. Most people round here don't even know who *I* am, never mind you.'

'Well, they've tracked me down somehow, which makes this place useless to me.'

'We can leave by the back road if needs be,' said Eli.

'If they're casing the place the odds are they already know about the back road,' said Sep. 'In fact, it could be that they're all here already. What we don't know is, how many.'

'It could be they're the only ones,' Winnie pointed out.

'I hope so, but I doubt it.' Then he added, 'No, two's not enough. The last time they sent two they lost one and I gave the other a bloody nose.'

Sep looked at his watch. The two men on the screen were now walking away. 'They'll all be meeting up somewhere.' He looked at Eli. 'Have you still got those two shotguns here?'

'I have, yeah, but they're not much good after about a hundred yards. The scatter gets too wide after that. A few pellets might bring a partridge down, but not a man at that distance.'

'I know,' said Sep, 'but I'm thinking about closer than that. Get them, would you, Eli? And as much ammo as you've got.'

Darkness was falling as Sep checked over the two shotguns. He had his Smith with him, fully loaded. It was a small revolver but by far the most potent of the weapons they had at their disposal. Under normal circumstances, were he not crippled, Sep would face this challenge on his own, but in this case he used common sense and rang Jane Hawkins.

'Ma'am, I've got a problem. I'm holed up in a cottage I own near Scarborough and the bad guys have found out where I am.'

'They've done better than us. I hadn't a clue where you were – other than not here.'

'I'll give you directions and the postcode, ma'am. These people are armed so I think we'll need an armed unit to help us.'

'Us? Who's us?'

'I'm here with Winnie and an old friend called Elijah McMurphy. He looks after the cottage when I'm not here. Elijah has a couple of shotguns but they won't be much use against real guns shooting at us from a distance.'

'OK, Sep, give me your location. I'll contact the Scarborough Police and see what help they can give us. An armed unit might take a while to muster. Keep your heads down until they arrive.'

'Thanks, ma'am.'

'Take care, Sep.'

'I always do, ma'am.'

'Yes, I've noticed.'

Sep turned the situation over in his mind then turned to his two companions, saying, 'Look, it might be a while before we get help so I think in the meantime I'll have a look round outside and see exactly what we're up against.'

'Have a look round?' said Winnie. 'Sep, you can hardly walk!'

'I can move fairly quickly on crutches and I can walk a bit. I don't have to go far to get around the back of them and I've got the Smith.'

'Sep Black, you're a genuine lunatic.'

'Winnie, we need to find out what we're up against and who's more capable out there, me on crutches . . . or you?'

'Ooh, I suppose you are, big head. But we really need you in here.'

'I'll get back here soon enough and when I do I'll know what we're up against . . . and I might have done them some damage.'

Now on their own in the cottage, Eli and Winnie watched the screens. In the fading daylight Eli had turned the cameras on to infrared. The picture turned monochrome but bright images of two moving people were plain to see. Eli left the room and came back with two shotguns. He handed one to Winnie.

'Ever fired one of these?'

'Yep, I used to go clay-pigeon shooting.'

'So you'll know how to load it.'

'I do. I also know they have a very limited range and accuracy, with them being smooth bore. They can bring a piece of clay down at a hundred yards but they can't bring a man down at that distance.'

'True, but they can sting a bit at that range and they're all we've got.'

Eli placed a box of cartridges on the table. Winnie took two out and loaded them into one of the shotguns.

'Like you said, they'll do decent damage to anything a hundred yards away but the effective range is about half of that,' Eli told her, 'although by the time the shot's travelled a hundred yards the spread's pretty wide and it'll hurt like hell, even if it doesn't penetrate.'

'If they're all we have, they'll have to do,' said Winnie, holding hers to shoulder to get the feel of it. 'Single trigger. The last one I used had two triggers. One for each barrel.'

'These are fairly modern. You need to pull the trigger and pull it again, one pull for each barrel.'

'How do you think we should play this, Eli?' Winnie asked. 'It seems to me that they need to be at the end of the garden path for these to be of any use.'

'I think we should keep the lights turned off so they think we're asleep and keep a lookout on the monitors. As soon as they get to the end of the path we let 'em, have both barrels.'

'You mean, kill them?'

'I doubt if we'll kill them, but we'll certainly stop them. We should shoot through the upstairs windows. Aim at their legs. That should slow 'em down.'

They both went upstairs to a room with a large, sliding sash window. Eli opened it about nine inches and they both knelt behind it with weapons at the ready. It was a clear night with enough moonlight for them to make out the end of the garden path quite clearly. Out of the dark appeared the two men, both holding hand-guns. Weapons with far greater range and accuracy than the guns Winnie and Eli had. The intruders stopped before they got to the gate. The smaller of the two men appeared to be giving instructions.

'The little one's the boss,' decided Winnie. 'I'll take him.'

'Why you?'

'Because I'm a bloody good shot with one of these things and I won't be blowing his head off.'

'OK. I'll take the big feller.'

They heard breaking glass from below, followed by a shot.

'Could that be Sep shooting?' Winnie asked, hopefully.

'Could be.'

There was another shot. Winnie made no comment about this, like Eli she was concentrating on the job in hand. The approaching men had now reached the front gate. Winnie and Eli silently poked their gun barrels out of the window and took aim. 'Count of three,' said Winnie. 'One . . . two . . . three.'

Four bangs were followed by loud screeches of pain from the two men down below, who now began to fire their handguns, indiscriminately, at the cottage. Winnie and Eli reloaded and fired again. This time bringing the smaller man down. The bigger man hauled him to his feet and proceeded to drag him away until they both disappeared into the gloom. Winnie couldn't wipe the grin off her face. Eli did it for her.

'I reckon they'll be back and firing from out of our range,' he said.

'Only if they're capable,' said Winnie. 'I think we did them a lot of damage. Do you think we should get in the van and drive off?'

'I don't know, Winnie. Sep's out there. I don't want to leave him.'

'He'll have heard the shooting,' said Winnie, 'and there should be an armed police unit on the way.'

'The bad guys won't know that, so they won't be scared off. They'll most probably know about the Merc and have it covered.'

Now out of range of the shotguns, two intruders, Carl Redman and Animal, took cover behind trees. Animal was annoyed.

'They were ready for us!'

'I'm aware of that. I've got an arse full of buckshot to remind me!'

'I took a few pellets meself,' growled Animal. 'Where the fuck's Wolf and Roscoe?'

'Comin' up behind us. I want you to get round the back of the house and torch the fuckin' place,' said Redman. 'I'll follow on as best I can. After that you can get me to a hospital before I bleed ter death.'

'Will it be all right if I gerrem ter patch me up as well?'

'How many bottles have yer brought?'

'Five.'

'Right. We'll skirt around the back out of sight and burn the bastards out. You go first, I'll cover you and keep an eye on the front door in case they try and make a run for it. If they get past me, Roscoe and Wolf'll get the bastards. Remember, Black's the one we want.'

Sep's plan had been to get himself behind a pile of logs about a hundred yards away from the back of the cottage. He and Eli had put them there after chopping down an unwanted sycamore and cutting its trunk and branches into logs ready for winter burning. His aim was to take cover behind them and see if anyone was approaching the house or already in the vicinity. If not, it meant the back road was clear and they could all escape in the Mercedes which was parked at the back of the house.

If there was someone there and he could get a clear shot at them, he was prepared to take it and to hell with police gun regulations. Precious lives were at stake here, especially Winnie's. He opened the back door and swung out on two crutches, heading for the log pile. Already in position was Animal, although he hadn't seen Sep, who was struggling over the uneven ground. Sep was only halfway to the log pile when Animal went into action.

He had a rucksack filled with Molotov cocktails – bottles filled with petrol with a petrol-soaked rag stuck in the neck as a fuse. He lit one bottle and hurled it at a downstairs window where it broke the glass and smashed into pieces inside, spreading its burning contents all around the room. He had followed this with two more through different windows before Sep managed to bring him down with a single shot. By this time the ground floor of the house was completely on fire and Redman was firing random shots at the front door as he stumbled Sep's way, following Animal.

Redman cursed as he saw Animal go down. He saw the flash of Sep's gun and fired a shot which missed and caused Sep to duck behind the logs. Redman fired twice more but his shots were all misses with Sep having taken good cover and Redman now in pain from his wounds, courtesy of Winnie.

Sep crawled away from the logs, keeping the broad trunk of a nearby tree between him and the gang boss. He could hear shots coming from the house now; Wolf and Roscoe had arrived on the scene. The unmistakeable boom of a shotgun mixed in with the sharper crack of powerful handguns and he knew that more men were advancing behind Redman; although he had no idea who they all were. Sep felt he needed to get back to the blazing house to help, but he also knew it wasn't an ideal place for him to be right now. It wasn't an ideal place for anyone to be and yet he'd left Winnie in there. Her parting words had been, . . . *but we really need you in here.*

He peeped around the side of the trunk and saw Redman taking aim at where he'd just come from. Sep fired his second shot of the night, but as he was standing and still unsteady on his feet, missed. From the flash of Sep's gun, Redman now knew exactly where Sep was and adjusted his aim accordingly.

The cottage had a stone, garden wall to one side which would give Sep cover if he could reach it. He fired two more shots at Redman and immediately set off for the wall, hoping his shots might keep the gunman's head down for sufficient time for him to get there. Sep reached the wall and more or less threw himself over it. Shots were being fired at the house but weren't being returned, which gave Sep cause to worry. He could see the front gate where two men were firing handguns at the house and not seeking cover. Why not? he was asking himself.

Sep then turned his attention back to Redman who was unaware that Sep was no longer behind a tree. Sep took careful aim at the man's body, resting his gun on his left forearm to steady it and brought the gang boss down with his last shot. Two down, how many more? Two at least and him with an empty gun. The pain in his leg was now intense and making it difficult for him to think clearly, just when clarity of thought was essential. His feeling of guilt for leaving Winnie and Eli in the house didn't help matters.

Shots were still being fired at the front of the house and Sep was back on the wrong side of the wall for this – a sitting target. He needed to have the wall between him and the shooters, so he threw himself back over and almost passed out as he landed on his leg. He lay there for a short while as the house blazed. Dense smoke was pouring out of the door. Jesus! How could anyone be alive in there?

He managed to take a look back over the wall and saw two men advancing on the house with guns blazing. No one in the house was shooting back. Why was that? There was an obvious, worst-case scenario here that he didn't want to think about. He was just hoping that the Scarborough Police had got their fingers out and sent an armed-response unit double quick. Right now would be a good time for them to arrive.

His prayers were answered as he heard shouts behind him and the sound of running footsteps, warning shouts and more gunshots; heavier gunshots he recognized as coming from the Heckler and Koch 17 rifle, used by armed police. He was brought to the ground by a man from behind and his hands cuffed within seconds. *Very efficient*, Sep thought.

'Well done, but I'm a copper!' he shouted, 'same as you, I hope!'

'Name?'

'DI Black, West Yorkshire Police, and you're an armed unit sent by Superintendent Hawkins in Leeds. The bad guys are over there, shooting at the house. There are two people inside who we need to keep alive if possible – *that's if they're not already dead.*' He added the last sentence in a defeated tone, as he was almost certain they would be. The cuffs were unlocked. The gunfire increased, all shots being aimed at Redman's men.

'OK, sir,' said the officer. 'My apologies. We have no way of knowing who's who.'

'Well, everyone else who was shooting, apart from you, are the bad guys. I think there are four of them. The two people in the house have shotguns, but they seem to have stopped shooting.'

Explosions were now coming from the cottage, blasting out of the upstairs windows. Gas explosions probably, at some point the main pipe would catch a spark and the whole building would blow up. A police officer arrived carrying a megaphone. Sep took it off him and ran towards the house. The assailants were now all down and the police had stopped shooting. Sep stood at the end of the path and held the megaphone to his mouth, calling out Winnie's name.

TWENTY-ONE

'WINNIE . . . WINNIE O'TOOLE!'

No answer, just smoke pouring out of the building. 'Winnie, you need to get out. There's gas in the building, you need to get out before the whole place blows up. Winnie, the police are out here. It's safe!'

He took a few steps forwards and tried to see through the smoke.

'Don't go any nearer, sir,' called out a voice behind him. Sep took another two steps forward and tried to peer through the smoke, which had him choking. He took three steps back. No way could Winnie and Eli be alive through there. But no way was he going to give up hope on this woman.

'Winnie, it's me, Sep. If you come out, you're safe.'

Another explosion blew out a bedroom window, causing him to turn and shield himself from the glass splinters. The inside of the cottage was a raging inferno. He dropped to his knees and screamed at the ground as if he wanted it to swallow him up. Then he shook his head to clear the smoke from it and forced himself to take a last look at this bloody house that was taking Winnie's life. In the whirling smoke he made out a vague face, or was it his imagination at work forming a face in the smoke? No, it was two faces. One of them was saying something. A word hoarsely spoken in a voice he could barely hear.

'Sep!'

'Winnie?'

'Yeah.'

The relief he felt was a sensation he'd never felt before. She was still alive, no doubt about that, but for how long?

'Get out, Winnie! It's safe out here. There's gas in the house. It's going to go up!'

'Help us, Sep. Eli's been shot.'

He tried to go towards her but he'd already inhaled too much smoke. Any more and he'd pass out and be no use to anyone. He was at the end of both the path and his tether, on crutches and holding the megaphone, which he dropped to the ground. His bleary eyes were trying to fix on her as she moved towards him. Her face was blackened and clothes wreathed in curls of smoke, as was her hair. She had one arm linked under Eli's armpit, staggering under his weight. At the sight of Sep she managed a smile, her teeth glowing white amidst their sooty surrounds.

Two policemen, with fresh lungs, ran past Sep and were with Eli and Winnie in an instant, hurrying them away from the blazing cottage. When Winnie reached Sep she threw her arms around him with such vigour that she knocked him off balance. They fell to the ground, wrapped in each other's arms as the policemen carried Eli past them. They picked themselves up and took a minute to stagger a good hundred yards from the house; Sep on crutches, with Winnie helping him. Once clear, he threw down the crutches, leaned against her for support and kissed her.

'Winnie! Thank God you're OK. Jesus! I thought you were dead in there. I thought I'd lost you. I didn't want to lose you.'

At that point the fire reached the gas main and the whole house exploded in flame as if a huge bomb had been dropped on it, blowing the roof clean off, scattering dangerous debris to within a few feet of them and smothering them with dust.

Winnie's words came out in fits and starts. 'Bloody hell, Sep . . . I – I . . . thought we were dead as well. We had to get our heads right down to the floor below the smoke. They . . . they set the cottage on fire then . . . then . . . they were shooting at us, so we couldn't get out.'

'I know, I saw them. Two more turned up. I thought they might.'

'Did you – did you get them?'

'I brought two of them down, but I think they've all been got. Unfortunately I think at least a couple of them might be dead.'

'Why unfortunately?'

'Because I needed to talk to one of them.'

'Bloody hell! Ever the copper! You mean Redman?'

'Yeah – well, if he's one of them – and the bloke who set fire to the cottage. I winged two of them but when they started firing at us, the police finished them off good and proper.'

'We tried to fight them off using the shotguns, Sep. I think I hit one man's arse, but they had real guns, so we had no chance.'

Winnie now saw a group of heavily armed policemen milling about. 'Thank you,' she shouted, hoarsely.

'Has anyone rung for the fire brigade?' Sep was asking. 'This is my cottage.'

Winnie looked at the blazing embers and said, 'Bit late for that, Sep – it *was* your cottage. I hope it was, er . . . insured.'

'I think it was.'

'You only think?'

'Well, it was never worth insuring.'

'All that computer stuff of Eli's must have been worth a bomb.'

'I think the least said about that stuff the better.'

Sep saw Winnie's wounded arm.

'Winnie, you're bleeding. Are you hurt or is that Eli's blood?'

'Bit of both, Sep. I got shot in the arm.'

'We need an ambulance!' Sep shouted to anyone who might hear. 'We need fire and ambulance.'

Miraculously they heard an ambulance approaching. Hawkins had anticipated such a need.

'Jesus!' said Sep. 'I should never have left you two back here. How bad is Eli?'

'He's not good, Sep.'

'Shit! I should have stayed.'

'Sep, if you'd stayed the two you winged might have done us more damage, maybe even killed us both. The first two did enough damage on their own. You put the second two out of action when it counted. I'm glad we didn't have four of them shooting at us.'

'Yeah, I suppose you could be right.'

They headed towards where the police had laid Eli on the ground. A police medic was taking a look at his wounds.

'How is he?' Sep asked.

'Bad stomach wound. He needs to get to hospital straight away.

What about the woman?' asked the medic, seeing the blood on Winnie's arm.

'Don't worry about me. Just take care of Eli. You need to get him to hospital *right fucking now!*'

The ambulance people heard and responded in a flash by loading Eli onto a stretcher and putting him into the ambulance. As the driver got in Sep called out to him. 'Quick as you can. Blues and twos all the way.'

'No problem.'

As the ambulance sped off, Sep said to Winnie, 'Let's take a look at that arm. They should have a first-aid kit in the police van.'

'It's not too bad, Sep. In fact, I think it just went in and out. I don't think it broke a bone.'

'That's what you think, is it, Dr O'Toole? I think we'd better get it bandaged and you to the hospital.'

'Thanks. Did it really worry you when you thought I was dead?'

'If you must know, I was sick to the stomach at the thought, yes.'

'Because you thought you'd lost me?'

Sep said nothing. Arguing would have been just wrong and he knew it. The relief he'd felt when he saw she was alive was the most powerful emotion he'd ever felt about anyone. In fact the remnants of that sickness were still with him and the memory of it painfully etched into his mind.

'I need to get some sleep,' he said. 'I'm going to interview the other two men later today. They're both wounded but they'll live. Lucky them, eh?'

'Do you know who they are?'

'Well, I certainly know who one of them is – Stanley Butterbowl, otherwise known as Wolf. I recognize him from the state of his face. Not sure who the other one is, but I'll find out soon enough. I'm hoping it's the boss man.'

'Right then,' said Winnie. 'Get me fixed up at the hospital and we'll find a hotel for the night. I'm thinking the Grand Hotel and you can get the police to pay for it.'

'No problem. Look, there's another ambulance just arriving. You take that one. I hope Eli's all right.'

TWENTY-TWO

Scarborough Hospital

E li was in Intensive Care with a less than fifty/fifty chance of survival. Winnie's wound had been dressed. She had discharged herself and was spending the day in the Grand Hotel. Sep had had a few hours' sleep at the Grand Hotel and, still on crutches, had gone to Butterbowl's ward. He and Roscoe were the two survivors. Redman and Animal were both dead, having foolishly taken the armed police on in a fire fight. A uniformed officer was sitting by the bed to which Butterbowl was attached by a long chain and a handcuff.

'So, Mr Wolf. Do you have anything for me? If you want reduced jail time it'd better be good.'

Butterbowl looked a sorry sight. His face was still bandaged up from the wound Sep had previously inflicted on it and now the rest of his upper body was wrapped up in a plaster cast. Lucky for Sep he could still talk.

'Reduced jail time? Am I supposed to believe that?'

'You can please yourself. Exactly what have you been charged with?'

'Nothin' yet. They've been mendin' me leg ever since I got here. It were your lot what did that ter me, yer bastard!'

'There you go then. You haven't been charged with anything and I'm the senior copper around here, so what I say goes As far as I'm concerned you've paid for what you did to me by what we've done to you. It could be that your leg is so badly broken that you'll never be able to walk properly again, which could well put you out of the hitman business. No one hires a cripple for a hitman.'

'They've not told me that.'

'Well, they don't know for certain yet – it's only wishful thinking on my part, but I've seen your X-rays and I know a bit about broken bones, so I think I'm on a winner.'

Sep was lying about seeing the X-rays, but in essence he was telling a truth, albeit by lucky guesswork, which would stand him in good stead for when the doctor came and confirmed his prognosis.

'So, do you have anything for me?'

'I think yer lyin' ter me.'

'Aw, come off it, man! What have I got to gain by lying? If you don't know anything, you don't know anything. Me lying isn't going to make you know what you don't know.'

It was a statement that had Wolf confused. Sep was an expert at such convoluted language. A doctor arrived. Sep and the uniformed officer stood back as he drew the curtains around Butterbowl's bed. Sep stood close enough to the curtains to be able to hear the doctor confirm the prognosis that Sep has already given.

'I've been in consultation with the surgeon who's going to fix your leg, but the prognosis isn't good, I'm afraid. It's so badly damaged by bullets that he was considering amputation, but he's giving you the option of him operating and putting it back together as best he can. If he's successful, you just might be able to walk on it after several weeks of fairly intensive physiotherapy but it's unlikely that you'll ever be able to walk properly again. Unless of course you agree to amputation and having a prosthetic leg fitted. I know it sounds drastic but sometimes it's the best option. There are some excellent prosthetics available nowad—'

'How much of me leg are yer talkin' about?'

'All of it unfortunately. It would be taken off just below the hip and a full prosthetic leg fitted.'

'You what? Have all me leg chopped off! Bollocks ter that! I want it put right.'

'I see. I'll inform the surgeon. He'll need to operate as soon as possible. It's just a question of how soon we can get a theatre slot.'

Sep and the constable stepped back as the doctor opened the curtains and left the ward. Sep then moved back to the bed.

'So what's the story with the leg?'

'They were talkin' about cuttin' it off.'

'Really? In that case, me and you are straight. I won't be pressing any charges for the damage you've done to me, providing you've got something of interest for me. That leg of yours might well be the price you pay for escaping a life sentence. Not a bad swap, I'd say. A leg for a life.'

The bitter expression on Butterbowl's face wasn't one of agreement.

'I might have summat,' he said. 'But it might be summat or nowt.'

'Look, Mr Wolf, as long as I know you're on my side and not taking the piss I'll keep my side of the bargain and not press charges. I can't help your mate Roscoe. He doesn't seem to know anything, but I'm thinking you're the type who the boss would confide in.'

'Well, he did a bit, yeah.'

'You know he's dead, don't you?'

'Redman's dead?'

'Yeah, he died back there. Only you and Roscoe are still alive. Lucky boys, eh?'

Sep drew up a chair and sat down, leaning his crutches against the bed. 'OK, tell me all you know.'

'Well, it's not much, but you bein' a copper might be able to make summat of it. I know Redman were doin' jobs for a bloke who worked for Santiago.'

'Would this be the man who killed Santiago?'

'No idea who killed him, but I know after Santiago died the bloke Redman were workin' for took over some sort of scam Santiago were runnin', and Redman wanted a piece of it himself.'

'What's Redman's first name?'

'Carl . . . Hey, you don't know much about him, do yer?'

'I know enough. What do you know about the scam?'

'Nuthin'. Redman were a real secretive bastard. He only told us what we need to know. I do know it's to do with stocks and shares and all that bollocks.'

'Is there a woman involved that you know about?'

'Woman? Not that I know of.'

'What about the Piper brothers? Have you heard of them?'

'Oh, them two gormless twats? Beats me why Santiago had 'em workin' for him.'

'They told me about a woman called Mrs Hardacre who was with you that day.'

'What?'

He shook his head at first then, 'Oh yeah, I remember. No idea who she was. She weren't with us. She just turned up when we did. I thought she was one of Santiago's punters. Mind you, she were a looker, so she might have been one of his tarts.'

Sep pondered on what he'd been told as Butterbowl looked up at him.

'Well?' he said.

'Well, what?'

'Have I given you enough?'

'It depends on what I can do with it, I need to find out who this bloke is who worked for Santiago and who Redman was working for.'

'*Was* working for. I reckon he still is.'

'Jesus! Have you been listening to me? Redman died last night, along with one of his men.'

Butterbowl grinned. 'That'll be Animal. He's the one what burned your place down. Dead man Redman, eh? Serves the bastard right.'

'I agree.'

'So I've already given you enough to nail him.'

'You haven't given me anything I didn't already have.'

'Well, he had this place on Water Lane.'

'The old jam factory, I know. I assume the late Bazz worked for Redman.'

'He did. Good lad, were Bazz.'

'Not good enough. A woman took him out and you weren't good enough either, trying to take out a cripple in his bed. So far we've whipped your arses, Wolf. Bazz is dead, Animal's dead, Roscoe's laid up in another ward, you're crippled for life and now Redman's dead. He wasn't exactly Al Capone, was he? That's the sort of firm you've been working for. What the hell have you got to lose by coming over to my side?'

Butterbowl made no comment because Sep was right.

'Had he lived would Redman have helped you out in any way at all, considering your leg injury, I mean?' Sep asked.

'No chance, I reckon Redman would have blown us both out – us bein' in here, we were no use to him anymore.'

'So you wouldn't have got paid for what you did yesterday, which includes losing a leg?'

'No, he only paid for results, did Redman.'

'And now he's dead.'

'So you say.'

'Oh, he's dead all right. Burnt my cottage down trying to kill two of my friends, but I brought in an armed-response unit. Have you ever come up against one of those before? They frighten me to death and I'm on their side. I told them I'd prefer to have Redman kept alive but when a man's armed and shooting they don't piss about don't them lads. Animal tried to run for it but he didn't get far. Hmm, I wonder if the Piper brothers know who this bloke is who worked for Santiago?'

'Doubt it. Them two thick twats don't know their arses from their elbows.'

'One of them's got a mental problem,' said Sep, annoyed at the man's attitude.

'That's not my fuckin' fault.'

'No, it's not his either. Anyway, I've got more important people to see in this hospital, so I'll maybe see you later.'

'What about our deal?'

Sep had left, but not without the satisfaction that the fool Butterbowl had believed him about the deal.

Sep went to the nurse's station in the Accident and Emergency ward, where a nurse looked up at him with a questioning look on her face.

'Can I help you?'

'I hope so. Ignore the crutches. I'm a policeman, DI Black.'

'Yes, I know who you are.'

'I've come to check on my good friend Elijah McMurphy, who was brought in last night with gunshot wounds.'

'I believe Mr McMurphy's still in theatre.'

'After all this time?'

'Yes. He sustained very serious injuries, including smoke inhalation. The lady who came in just after him discharged herself. She should have stopped overnight. She had smoke inhalation injuries herself.'

'Ah, well, she's actually at the Grand Hotel. Do you think I should get her over here?'

'Don't bother. She was actually quite rude when I tried to insist she stopped here.'

'Well, she'd had quite a trying time . . . almost died, as did Eli.'

'So I've heard. Two of the men who caused it are in here as well.' She smiled at his raised eyebrows before adding, 'In the mortuary.'

'They were bad people,' said Sep. 'Had they lived they'd have spent the rest of their days in prison.'

'What about the other one? The one with the funny name?'

'You mean Stanley Butterbowl? He likes to be called Wolf.'

'I can see why. While he's in here, he'll be Stanley Butterbowl.'

'His future doesn't look too bright either,' said Sep.

'Someone needs to tell him to agree to having his leg amputated. From what I've heard it'll come off eventually anyway.'

'I'm not too concerned about his well-being, I'm afraid. So, how's it looking for Eli? He's one of the good guys.'

'I don't know. Do you want me to find out?'

'Please.'

She picked up a telephone and dialled a single number. 'I've got Detective Inspector Black here enquiring after Elijah McMurphy.'

The answer had her frowning, then saying, '. . . Oh.'

She put the phone down and paused before saying, 'I'm sorry to tell you that they lost Mr McMurphy in theatre.'

'What? He's dead?'

'I'm afraid so. His wounds were too severe. He sustained a lot of internal damage.'

The shock of losing an old and valued friend had Sep wobbling on his crutches. The nurse came around her desk and supported him.

'Here, take a chair for a few minutes.'

'Thank you.'

Sep had known Eli for years, first as a burglar whom he'd arrested several times, until, after his last stretch in prison, he eventually placed him in the cottage as a caretaker and odd-job man. As far as Sep knew, Eli had gone straight ever since and now he was dead, at the hands of Sep's adversaries. He sat there with his eyes misting with tears. Right then he only wanted one person – Winnie O'Toole. He looked up at the nurse.

'I need a taxi.'

'I'll get you one.'

'Thanks.'

Winnie was sitting at a table on a public balcony, high over the sweeping panorama of Scarborough Bay. She was looking out to sea, smoking her pipe. Her wounded arm in a sling, resting on the arm of her chair. There were two glasses of beer on the table. Sep hobbled over on his crutches and sat down opposite her, grunting with pain as he landed in the chair. She winced in sympathy.

'You OK?'

'Not really.'

'In what way?'

'Eli didn't make it.'

She stared at him as his words sank in. 'You mean . . .' She paused before she got the next words out. 'He died?'

Sep gave a single, sad nod. 'On the operating table. He was too badly injured – they couldn't save him.'

'Oh no.'

Tears welled up in her eyes. Sep reached across the table and took her good hand in his.

'He was a good man,' he said.

'I know. He had a lot of devil in him but I really liked him.'

Sep shook his head in sadness. 'Me too and it's my fault he's dead. They were after me, not him. I should never have left you two back there.'

They sat there for a while, clutching each other's hands, as they shared the pain of a friend's death.

'The cottage has gone as well,' he said, eventually. 'All that's left is a lump of useless land. No Eli, no cottage, no nothing. Why the hell did I come out here with that murderous lot on my tail? Eli was a happy man out here – happier than he'd ever been in his life and I took that life away from him. What right did I have to do that?'

Winnie tried to diffuse the unhappy subject by changing it. 'We'll have to explain to the mobility shop that their wheelchair was burned in a house fire – that's where a bit of home contents insurance would have come in handy.'

'Oh, I'm not bothered about bloody insurance, Winnie! You're still alive. That counts for a lot in my book.'

He let go of her hand and turned his head to look out to sea, where the world was calm and harmless, but it hadn't always been. On the horizon were two large tankers, heading south from the North Sea oil rigs.

'In 1914,' Sep said, 'there were two German ships out there, shelling this town. One of the shells hit this hotel. A lot of innocent people were killed that day.'

'Why do people do such terrible things?'

'It's what human beings do when they go to war; they get very destructive. History books call it the horrors of war. With me, it sometimes goes with my job.'

Winnie nodded, remembering that since she'd met Sep she'd killed twice, both in extreme situations in order to save her own life. 'I suppose some people don't deserve to be on this Earth,' she said.

'Well, the ones who killed Eli didn't . . . and two of them aren't anymore.'

'That's good,' said Winnie, 'but it won't bring Eli back. 'He told me he was seventy-eight and that's the oldest he'd ever been.'

Sep smiled. 'Yeah, that sounds like Eli.'

'He told me that when he knew we had no chance of getting out alive.'

Sep smiled. 'Probably his last joke, eh?'

'No, he told me he'd always wanted to be shot at the age of ninety-eight by a jealous husband. Mind you, he told me he was old enough to die and that this was a hell of a way to go.'

'Maybe it was,' said Sep. 'He'd lived a wayward existence, a lot of it locked up. Maybe he thought it was a fitting end. I imagine he was very pleased that you were with him at the end,' he said, looking up at the sky.

Winnie's eyes widened in amazement as she followed his heavenly gaze. 'Bloody hell, Sep! Don't tell me you're religious.'

'Not really. I suppose I'm an agnostic, but God comes in handy at times like this. We'll give Eli a decent funeral and we'll both be in the chapel, praying along with the vicar that he's gone to a better place, will we not?'

'Yes, we will.'

They both stared out to sea once more, with Winnie blowing smoke rings into the calm air. Sep watched this and asked, 'How did you manage to fill your pipe with one hand?'

'The fingers still work on both hands. Any more questions?'

'Yes, who's this other beer for?'

'You, if you turned up before I drank it.'

'In that case, we'll have a toast to our good friend Elijah McMurphy.'

They clinked glasses and called out, 'Elijah McMurphy.'

'He was a prophet, you know,' said Sep.

'Elijah McMurphy was a prophet?'

'Not our Elijah. In the Bible, Elijah was one of God's first prophets.'

'Good. Our Eli should do well up there, then. It's always handy
to be well in with the main man.'

Sep studied her and asked, 'Have you managed to wash your
hair?'

'Why, does it look OK?'

'It looks better than it did back at the cottage. There was smoke
still coming out of it back there.'

'There's a hairdresser's up the street, they washed it for me.
Like you said it was full of smoke and in a right mess.'

'Was any of it burnt?'

'Singed a bit, but they cut all that out.'

'You like to get your priorities right.'

'I always feel ten times worse when my hair's a mess.'

'Your hair's always untidy but it always suits you.'

'You mean *I'm* always untidy?'

'No.'

'If you must know it's a style of my own, I call it called tastefully dishevelled.'

'Tastefully dishevelled—that describes you.'

'Thank you, Septimus. I'll take that as a compliment.'

'My pleasure . . . Winifreda.'

'How did you know I was Winifreda?'

'I'm a copper. It's my job to know such stuff.'

Sep smiled. He felt better and he knew that was because he
was with Winnie O'Toole; she had that effect on him. He watched
her puff away on her pipe, an action that wouldn't be endearing
in most women, but in Winnie O'Toole he found it both amusing
and endearing. He looked at her face which would be better
described as handsome rather than beautiful. It was an intelligent
face, well-framed within a mass of beautiful auburn locks, which,
apart from the smoke from her pipe, was now washed clean of
fumes. Locks that were 'tastefully dishevelled'. She had beautiful
teeth that gave her a dazzling smile and her skin had a light, natural
tan and a few freckles that spoke of a mixed race somewhere in
its history, it gave her a gypsy appearance that added to her attrac-
tion. As he looked at her, an awful thought struck him. His friend
Eli had died in the carnage at the cottage but – and it was this
thought that sent a shudder up his spine – it might just as easily
have been Winnie and her loss would have been unbearable, especially with it being his fault. She became aware of his gaze.

'What?' she said.

'Nothing, it's just that . . .'

'Just what?'

'Well . . . if you'd died as well, it would have been too much for me to handle. I er . . . Oh dammit, Winnie! It's my job to look after you, not put you in danger. This is ridiculous! I'm not going to be able to do without you.'

'Now there's a coincidence.'

'What does that mean?'

'Oh, Sep, you're a detective. What the hell do you think it means? We live together, we sleep together; do you think I'm some sort of slapper who'll do that with anyone?'

In view of her past occupation as a prostitute Sep decided to say nothing but she read his mind, as she often did.

'Sep, the stuff you're thinking about, it's all in the past. On top of which I love you, which is something that's never happened to me before.'

'Right,' said Sep, 'my reaction back at the cottage tells me I love you as well and I'd really like to kiss you but you've only got one working arm and I'm on crutches.'

Winnie got to her feet. 'Oh, stop making lame excuses, you miserable bugger and get your arms around me!'

They were in their room, doing their carnal best, despite their collective injuries, when Sep's mobile rang. It was a call he'd been expecting – dreading – all day. Superintendent Jane Hawkins.

'DI Black, in the light of recent events I need you back here for a full debrief of the events of yesterday. Where are you and how soon can you get here?'

'I'm actually in bed, ma'am, trying to catch up on a night's sleep.'

'Are you injured?'

'Some smoke inhalation but otherwise fine.'

'Good. I've called a meeting here for eight o'clock this evening. I want you to attend. DCI Wood will also be here, along with one of our superiors – if you get my drift.'

'Drift well and truly got. I'll be there, ma'am. Oh, I'll need another wheelchair. Mine was destroyed in the fire.'

'OK, we'll sort you one out.'

'Maybe you could explain what happened to the hire company. It might sound better coming from you.'

'I'll, er, I'll see to it, Sep.'

Sep turned to Winnie. 'Duty calls, but not just yet. That was Jane Hawkins. I'm due at a meeting in Leeds at eight o'clock. My good friend DCI Wood will be there.'

'Do you think she's going to expose him?'

'I think she's going to try. It'd help if I had more on him.'

She sat up in bed and lit her pipe. 'Good thinking about the wheelchair,' she said. 'Do you think they'll pay for the other one?'

'It'll do no harm to ask. It was damaged in the course of my duty. By the way,' he warned her, 'you're not supposed to smoke in these rooms. I'll be getting a bill for de-fumigating the place.'

'Shut up, it helps me think. Sep, do you reckon that estate agent in York knew about the cottage?'

'He'll have known about it, yes.'

'And he might well have mentioned it to Wood?'

'There's no "might" about it. He definitely did.'

'Ah! Mystery solved then. Do you think those two thugs in hospital will know the name DCI Wood as one of Redman's contacts in the force? It could be that he mentioned it to them. You might be able to tempt it out of them in exchange for a vast reduction in sentence.'

'I must buy you some tobacco for that pipe. Keep smoking, Winnie, you're on a roll. I'll be back later. I need to get me a taxi.'

TWENTY-THREE

Back at the hospital, Sep swung into Roscoe's ward on his crutches. A police constable was sitting by the criminal's bed reading a newspaper. He got to his feet as soon as he recognized Sep. Roscoe was attached to his bed by a handcuff on a long chain, as Butterbowl had been in another ward.

'Can I take your chair, constable?'

'Of course, sir.'

Sep leaned his crutches against the bed and sat down. 'Well, you might just be in luck, Roscoe,' he said. 'Your mate Stanley Butterbowl, or Mr Wolf as he likes to be called, has given me practically nothing, which is just plain stupid, considering Redman is dead.'

Roscoe laughed out loud. 'Stanley Butterbowl? Is that his name? I didn't know that. Bloody hell!'

'My thoughts exactly. Not the name you want if you're a dangerous hitman, which he won't be when he's lost a leg.'

'Havin' a leg off, is he?'

'Very likely. Compared to him you got off lightly back there.'

'I took a bullet in me side and one in me arm. The bastards knew they'd got me in the arm, there was no need to shoot me again.'

'I know. It's a risk you take on your side of the law.'

Sep pretended to gather his thoughts and looked intently at Roscoe, as if he were about to impart some important information.

'Look, I'm only allowed to guarantee a reduced sentence for one of you and it's not going to be him, silly man. I'd actually despaired of you having anything useful to tell me . . . but there might be something that will reduce your sentence quite drastically.'

'What's that?'

'I want to know how you knew where we were last night. Who told you? And remember you don't have to worry about Redman or his knuckle-dragger, Animal, whose real name was Colin Lonsdale by the way. Both of them are dead. I'm asking you first because I think you're the best of a bad lot. If you can't tell me, I'll ask Butterbowl and if he knows anything I'll guarantee he'll tell me and leave you to rot in prison for the next twenty odd years. I've had a word in the right ear and, given good information, I can get that reduced to a five stretch, before you're in front of a parole board telling them what a good boy you've been and no longer a threat to anyone on the outside.'

Sep made the sentence slightly indefinite to make it sound more genuine. Roscoe said nothing for a while as he mulled over Sep's incredibly generous offer. Sep was wondering if he'd made it too generous, so he added, 'Like I said, I can't guarantee it'll only be five – that'll be left up to the judge, but I reckon you can do a six stretch standing on your head.' His lack of certainty helped to ensure his offer sounded valid.

'I can, yeah.'

'So what's it to be? And look, Roscoe, for me to get you off all that time I need to record your answer on this.' He took out a pocket voice recorder he'd bought in a local electrical shop in anticipation of such a need and switched it on, holding it out towards Roscoe. 'It's the way we do things when we're doing deals with people. I'll get a copy made of the tape and give it to you, so you can show it to your brief.'

It was an outright lie, but in Sep's world Roscoe was a man who didn't deserve the truth. The police constable gave a baffled frown. Sep looked round at him, saying, 'I'd like you to be witness to this, constable and to take notes.'

'Sir.'

The meeting in Leeds

The conference room was soundproofed and devoid of any distracting ephemera hanging on the walls. It was a room intended for the occupants to concentrate only on the matter in hand. The table seated five police officers, including Sep, Detective Superintendent Hawkins, DCI Wood and Superintendent Ibbotson of the uniformed branch. There was also a Deputy Chief Constable Gibbs who was seated at the head of the table with the less senior officers ranged two at each side of him. It began with Sep relating the events of the previous evening.

'And you interviewed the two surviving men in Scarborough Hospital,' said Hawkins.

'I did, ma'am, yes. With Carl Redman, their gang boss, being dead, I thought they might be more forthcoming than they actually were.'

Hawkins addressed herself to Gibbs. 'The two men killed were both involved in a firefight with our armed-response unit.'

'So I understand, but I'm curious to know how this gang got to know the exact whereabouts of Detective Inspector Black after so much trouble had been taken to conceal his destination.'

Sep looked at Wood who was shifting, uncomfortably in his seat. 'I was wondering the same thing myself, sir, so I gave Detective Superintendent Hawkins as much information as I could about who knew I owned that property, in particular the estate agent who handled the sale four years ago.'

Gibbs looked at Hawkins for an explanation.

'That's correct, sir. I rang Mr Dunhill of Dunhill and Broome, estate agents in York and asked him if anyone had been enquiring about the sale of the cottage to DI Black. It transpired that one of our officers had made a similar enquiry just before the incident.'

Sep's eyes were fixed intently on Wood who was now going pale. Wood met Sep's gaze and he knew that Sep knew it was he who had made the call. His devious brain fizzed into action as he awaited what Hawkins had to say.

'I sorry to say,' she said, 'that it was one of our own officers who made the call. In fact, it was Detective Chief Inspector Wood here. I asked him to be at this meeting so that he could explain his actions.'

'And you gave him no forewarning of this?'

'No, sir.'

All eyes were now on Wood who put on a frown of umbrage at the very thought that he might be implicated in all this. Sep broke the silence with a statement of his own.

'DCI Wood did know about the cottage. He once asked me about it after he'd met Dunhill the estate agent at a Masonic dinner. I can assure you all that no one else knew about me owning the cottage, apart from Elijah McMurphy who was killed in the attack.'

'Yes,' said Wood, 'I did know about the cottage and I did make that call, but it was merely to establish the whereabouts of DI Black who tends to be a law unto himself and fails consistently to inform his senior officers of his whereabouts. I must say I object most strongly to the insinuation that I'm in some way connected with this gang.'

Sep gave a slight nod and raised his eyebrows in appreciation of Wood's quick thinking but he knew it would never be enough. Wood wasn't up against gullible idiots.

'I understand from Mr Dunhill that you asked him for an exact location, including a postcode,' said Hawkins. 'Why did you need his whereabouts in such detail? Wouldn't a "cottage near Scarborough" have been enough? You didn't intend driving out there to pay him a visit, surely?'

'It was the gang who needed the exact location,' put in Sep. 'You can't kill a man by shooting at a postcode.'

Gibbs looked at Hawkins. 'I assume you are DI Black's immediate superior. Were *you* aware of DI Black's exact whereabouts?'

'No, sir. I knew he'd taken himself out of danger, but I didn't need to know his exact whereabouts. I simply knew he was heading out of the clutches of the gang and he would inform me of his whereabouts when he got there.'

'And did he inform you?'

'He informed me later in the day.'

'That was only after he'd had a run in with the gang,' blustered Wood, who had acquainted himself with the sequence of events. 'Black only rang her because he needed help.'

'OK, so I rang because we needed help. Standard procedure. What's wrong with that?' asked Sep.

'But you will have had an exact idea of where he was,' said Gibbs to Wood. 'Certainly as exact as the gang who went after him.'

'That doesn't mean to say I'd given them this information.'

'No, but it would certainly solve the mystery of who did,' said Sep. 'I'd like to know myself who gave me away, so that they could come and kill me. When this thing unravels this gang's been mixed up in all sorts of villainy. Murder, attempted murder, fraud and whatever crime this Snowball company's committed. If there is a mole in this force, he's due a life stretch at least. They've tried to kill me; they've killed an old friend of mine and wounded another . . .'

'The other being Winnie O'Toole, a known criminal with whom you have a close relationship,' sneered Wood.

'She's been a reformed character for many years, who's been of great help to the police, as Superintendent Ibbotson will no doubt confirm,' countered Sep, looking at the superintendent for his confirmation.

'She has indeed,' said Ibbotson.

'In fact,' Sep went on, 'she was of great help in this insofar as she advised me to do a second interview with one of the two men in hospital – the lesser injured of the two. A man called Roscoe Briggs.'

'Who couldn't possibly be of any help!' snapped Wood.

'Know him, do you?' said Hawkins, drily.

All eyes were on Wood once more. 'Yes, ma'am. He's known to the police as a petty criminal who works on the doors of disreputable clubs and hires himself out as a strong-arm man.'

'Yeah, that's him,' said Sep, 'I interviewed him because I thought his boss, Redman, might have slipped up and given him an important piece of information.' He took out his pocket voice recorder. 'In fact, I recorded my interview on this. Would anyone mind if I played it?'

He looked at Wood as he asked this question. Wood shrugged as if it were of no importance to him, but his face was pale and twitching and, to Sep, he looked as if he was about to explode. Sep switched on the recorder and placed it on the table. His own voice was the first to be heard:

'OK, Roscoe. I need you to answer one question and one question only. You help us and we'll help you. I'm recording this and I have Constable Scaife here, as witness to your answers.'

'What question's that?'

'I want to know how Redman found out where I was.'

'He rang someone.'

'What sort of someone?'

'A copper. Who d'yer fuckin' think?'

'What copper was that? Do you have a name?'

'Yeah.'

'That's the information I want, Roscoe. What's the name?'

'He's a detective called Wood. High-ranking bastard. He's in Redman's pocket. That's all I fuckin' know.'

Sep switched the tape off and looked around at his assembled colleagues for their reaction. Wood was now on his feet, screaming in protest.

'This is ridiculous! Black obviously set him up to say that.'

'I did no such thing,' said Sep, calmly. 'I can bring in the constable who witnessed this interview. You can talk to him yourself and make your own judgement, ma'am. We already know Wood checked with the estate agent as to exactly where I was and now this. I would point out that there's always been an officer by their beds listening to everything I said to both of them. In Roscoe's case it was a Constable Scaife who took notes of the conversation I recorded on this tape. If I'd set DCI Wood up, Constable Scaife would know.'

'What's the name of the other man who ended up in hospital?' asked Hawkins.

'Believe it or not his name is Stanley Butterbowl, ma'am. He likes to be known as Mr Wolf.'

'Not sure I blame him. Is there any reason why we can't ask him the same question concerning DCI Wood's involvement in all this?'

'None at all, ma'am,' said Sep. 'I'm sure he'll be most helpful.'

Hawkins folded her arms and looked at Wood, saying. 'Well, none of this is looking too good for you, DCI Wood. I'm very much inclined to have you suspended pending further investigation of all this.'

To Sep she said, 'What exactly did you promise Roscoe Briggs before you turned on the tape?'

'A reduced sentence, ma'am.'

'How reduced?'

'I said I could get it reduced to six years before he got a parole board.'

'And he believed you?'

'He did, ma'am. I can be a very believable person when I try. But we're not bound by my promises which were made very much off the record.'

Gibbs was nodding his head in agreement as were the other officers, all in full agreement, including Sep. Still on his feet, beads of sweat had now appeared on Wood's forehead. He stuck his hand in his pocket and pulled out a handgun which he pointed at Hawkins, who looked him in the eye and said calmly, 'I don't know where you got that from but you should put it away before you get in so deep you'll never get out.'

'Of course I'll never get out. Black's right. I'll be banged up for life. Well, you can forget that. I'm out of here now and don't try any heroics, Black.'

Sep held up his palms in a placating gesture. 'Hey, I don't need to do anything. You really are a stupid sod doing this with all us here. Do you honestly think you'll get away with it?'

'Try and stop me.'

'No one's going to try and stop you. You've got a gun, we haven't. If you get out of here, and it's a big "if", you'll be wanted by every force in the country. Your picture will be on the telly and in all the papers. Police will be watching out for you at all train stations, bus stations, ports and airports. What's your plan? You must have a plan or you wouldn't have brought a gun in here.'

'DI Black,' said Hawkins, calmly. 'DCI Wood is obviously suffering from stress-borne anxiety.'

'Right now, so am I,' said Sep, looking down the barrel of Wood's gun.

'It's a recognized illness, not to be laughed at,' said Hawkins, who rarely appreciated Sep's attempts at humour. As she spoke, her calm gaze had never left Wood as she tried to deflect his attention away from the gravity of the situation he'd placed himself in.

'Have you erm . . . have you been to see a doctor about this, DCI Wood?'

'About what? There's nothing wrong with me except I don't fancy spending the rest of my life banged up in a Category A prison. What's sort of life's that for a copper, eh?'

'You get what you deserve in this life,' said Sep.

'Oh, shut it, Black, you bloody idiot!' snapped Hawkins.

'I'll get away, you'll see,' said Wood, now waving his gun about, much to Sep's relief.

'Well, good luck with that,' said Sep, cheerfully.

His manner annoyed Wood to an extent that he aimed the gun at Sep once again. Sep's cheerful smile vanished immediately. Having a mentally disturbed man pointing a loaded gun at your head tends to wipe the smile off any face. Wood's finger tightened on the trigger. Sep's eyes were glued to that finger as he prepared to throw himself sideways. His damaged leg would hinder that action so he had both hands on the chair-arms, muscles flexed and ready for action and his good leg braced against the floor, ready for the precise instant he needed to move.

Jane Hawkins had her hand on the handle of a heavy water jug and her eyes on the same trigger finger; as it twitched she hurled the water, with some force, at Wood, causing him to shoot but lose his aim as Sep, who had also spotted the twitching finger, threw himself to one side and avoided the bullet by an inch. He was on the floor, struggling to get back on his feet, when Wood stood over him, dripping with water, with the gun still in his hand and aimed at Sep's head.

'You've done all this to me, Black! Now you're gonna die, you bastard!'

The now empty water jug came down heavily on Wood's head. This time in the hands of Superintendent Ibbotson. The large, heavy, cut-glass jug didn't break as it knocked Wood to the floor, senseless. Sep rolled away to avoid him. Hawkins came round the table to help him to his feet. He sat down in his chair, breathing heavily from his near-death experience.

'Bloody hell! I thought I was a goner there. What the hell got into him?'

'*You* got into him, you damned idiot!' snapped Hawkins. 'In future, when I tell you to shut it, you do as you're damn well told! You have an unhealthy knack of getting up people's noses. Especially unbalanced people like DCI Wood, who obviously needs psychiatric help.'

'I believe they do that in Broadmoor,' said Sep.

'He might well end up in there, if he's lucky. As for you, you need a lesson in how to deal with a hysterical man who's pointing a loaded gun at you. Rule number one: "Don't take the piss out of him!"'

'That's definitely a good rule, ma'am. I'm only glad I didn't call him Cock Robin.'

'Oh, Jesus, Sep! Tell me you didn't even think about that.'

'Well, I was tempted for a minute.'

'Thank God you didn't.'

'Cock Robin? What's this about?' asked Gibb.

'Oh, DCI Wood's first name is Robin,' said Hawkins.

'And his computer password is Cock,' said Sep, 'with him thinking he's some sort of sex machine.'

'Oh dear. That man really is self-delusional,' said Gibb.

There was an embarrassed silence, broken by Sep. 'Erm, thanks for saving my life, ma'am . . . and I apologize for my stupid behaviour . . . and thank you, sir,' he added, looking at Ibbotson.

'It was my pleasure,' said Ibbotson. 'Never took to the man – Cock Robin indeed!'

'Quite,' said Gibb.

Wood was still unconscious on the floor, his hair soaked in blood. A uniformed sergeant and two constables had piled into the room, having heard the gunshot.

'Pick DCI Wood up, take him into custody and keep a constant eye on him until he comes round,' said Hawkins to them. 'As soon as he does come round, read him his rights and put him under arrest for attempted murder . . . and put that gun in an evidence bag. Better get the duty doctor to look at his head – both outside and in.'

'Good Lord! What's happened, ma'am?' the sergeant asked Hawkins.

'We found a rotten apple in our barrel, sergeant. Best get the FME to look him over as well. It could be that his mind's not in the right place.'

'He was never very popular, ma'am—even when he was a sergeant, like me.'

'He never was a sergeant like you,' said Sep.

The sergeant looked at Sep, who was still looking a bit dazed. 'Are you OK, sir?'

'When was he ever OK?' said Hawkins.

'I'm still alive,' said Sep, 'thanks to our two superintendents.'

As Wood was being carried unceremoniously from the room, Gibbs said, 'Well, the media will make a meal of this when they hear about it, which they will when Wood is charged with the attempted murder of a fellow police officer. This is a matter which will be dealt with as much in-house as possible. I want word put about the station that no one is to talk to the media about this without the express permission of an officer above the rank of chief inspector and all such officers will be instructed to refuse that permission. Have I made myself clear?'

He was talking mainly to the sergeant and the two constables who were carrying Wood. They all confirmed that they understood. Gibbs looked at Sep and said, 'DI Black, I understand you were up for promotion to DCI last year, but the promotion procedure was withheld to pacify the CPS after the kidnapping case.'

'That's correct, sir,' interjected Superintendent Ibbotson. 'DI Black has, erm, unusual methods of working, which were not to the approval of the CPS.'

'I believe he got a remarkable result due to his unusual methods. Quite the hero according to the newspapers.'

'Er . . . yes, that's true, but his actions didn't do us any favours,'

'We're not here to seek favours,' said Gibbs. 'In fact I recommend that he applies to the Selection Board for a promotion to DCI and I'll give his application my full backing.'

'Are you, erm . . . are you absolutely sure about that, sir?' asked Hawkins.

'Quite sure. It seems to me that it's all down to his unusual methods that Wood has been exposed for the corrupt officer that he is. I'm aware that DI Black is something of a maverick but I feel there's room for a maverick among the upper ranks . . . Keeps us old fogies on our toes, so to speak.'

'Old fogies?' said Hawkins. 'Excuse me, sir, but I'll have you know that I'm younger than DI Black!'

'I can see that,' said Gibbs. 'You made your way very quickly up the promotion ladder. I was referring to *us* old fogies.'

'I was a late starter,' said Sep. 'I didn't join the force until I was in my mid-thirties.' Then he snapped his fingers in exasperation with himself at how childish this must have sounded.

'It's not a bloody race, Black!' snapped Hawkins, 'It's a career.' She gave Sep a narrow-eyed glance that told him not to be too complacent about this potential promotion.

'Yeah, I know and it's a race I'd have no doubt lost to you,' conceded Sep, graciously. 'Anyway, I'd like to say thanks for the recommendation, sir and for my life, ma'am. I value both equally, but I wish to remain on the Cold Case team as number two to my saviour, Detective Superintendent Hawkins, who was remarkably cool under pressure back then. Good shot with the water jug as well.'

'She was indeed,' said Gibbs. 'Should he get the promotion would you want to keep him with you as your number two?' he asked Hawkins.

'Oh God! Do I have a choice? Sir, I think he'll take advantage of his maverick methods which you appear to condone.'

'Perhaps so, but I think he's an excellent choice.'

This raised a smile from Sep, although Hawkins knew she'd have to bring him into line as soon as possible.

Back in Sep's house, Winnie's face varied between shocked and smiling when Sep told her about the incident and his possible promotion, but the smile left her face when he added, 'Trouble is, we're still no nearer to finding out who killed Charlie Santiago and James Boswell. I'm fairly certain it wasn't any of Redman's mob, although he was definitely in on this Snowball scam.'

'Sep, why don't you leave that to people who can get about without crutches?'

'This is my case,' said Sep. 'I'm going to follow it through to the end, unless Hawkins takes me off it. I think I might hobble round to Mrs Boswell's house tomorrow and bring her up to speed.

My leg's getting better by the day. It's Eli's funeral tomorrow and right now I'm going to bed. I'm knackered.'

Sep felt out of place standing at the lectern in the crematorium. He'd prepared a eulogy for Eli which glossed over the old man's life; he simply mentioned that he'd met him through work; a mention that raised a few wry smiles in the congregation among those who had known Eli of old. Outside, after the ceremony, a man of around Sep's age came over to talk to him.

'I'd like to thank you for the eulogy you gave my dad and for not mentioning his time as a burglar.'

'Your dad? I didn't know Eli had any children. Although I have to say, you have a look of him around the eyes,'

'There's just me, my name's Peter. I was brought up by my Auntie Jean, Dad's sister.'

'What about your mother?'

'She left me with Dad just after I was born. No idea where she is or even who she is. Dad never talks about her, nor does my Auntie Jean, who's over there.'

He pointed to a woman in her late forties, talking to a younger man, perhaps in his early twenties.

'She's talking to my son, Benjamin.'

'Good grief! Eli had a grandson. Did he know?'

'I'm afraid not. In fact Benjamin knows nothing about his granddad. You see, he's a bright lad and would have found out all about him, which wouldn't have done Dad's reputation much good in Ben's eyes. I built Dad up to be a paragon of virtue so I couldn't really afford to have them meet. Ben thinks I was deserted by both my parents. What else could I tell him?'

'How long is it since you last saw your dad?'

'Oh, that was six years ago on my fortieth birthday. To be honest I thought he might have been banged up for something or other. He was living in Bradford when I saw him last, working as a jobbing builder.'

'As far as I know' said Sep, 'he'd been going straight for eighteen years.'

'Well, I figured as much, although he never boasted about it. Let's face it, most people go straight all their lives without boasting about it. Before that we met from time to time. He had my phone number and we'd meet in some pub or other. Dad told me about you and I've read bits about you so I know he wasn't exaggerating. He thought a lot about you despite you always arresting him. If he turned his back on crime I reckon it was down to your influence. I gather he lived in your cottage.'

'Lived and died in it, I'm afraid,' said Sep. 'But he died a brave death. My fiancée was with him when he was shot, she's over there.' He pointed to where Winnie was talking to some people from both her and Eli's past.

'This son of yours, what does he do?'

'He's at university, studying English.'

'Did Eli recommend this?'

'Actually, yes. Why do you ask?'

'It's what I studied at Uni.'

'Well, I think he told me that. The problem Ben has is the same as all students have nowadays – he's perpetually skint and he doesn't have a wealthy dad to support him.'

'What is it you do?'

'I'm an engineering draughtsman.'

'Sounds like a good job.'

'It's not bad. It pays the mortgage and keeps the wolf from the door, but no more. We don't have money for foreign holidays or anything, but I have a lovely wife and we all get on well together.'

'That's more important than money. What year is Ben in?'

'He got his BA last year and stayed on to do a Masters, only I don't think the money will spin out that long and I'm not in a position to help him much. He intends becoming a teacher. That would have made Dad really proud. I assume it was you who put the notice in the *Yorkshire Post*?'

'It was, yes.'

Peter's face took on the sort of guilty look that Sep had only ever seen in interview rooms. 'Is there something on your mind?' he asked.

'To be honest, yes. It sounds awful but I was half hoping that Dad had left a will that might have funded Ben through to his Masters.'

'I'm afraid Eli left nothing that I know about.'

Peter's guilty look was replaced by a bright smile. 'Ah well, I needed to ask someone, although I think I was being over-optimistic. Ben works part-time pulling pints in a local pub. He's a happy lad and there's no shortage of girlfriends.'

Sep grinned. 'Were you thinking Eli might have left a hoard of loot somewhere?'

'Not exactly.'

'Well, he did have a hoard of IT stuff which he acquired through unusual circumstances.'

'You mean he didn't pay for them?'

'Erm . . . no he didn't. But all that lot went up in the fire. I'd make an insurance claim on it but it might open a very dangerous can of worms.'

'Oh, no. I wasn't thinking along those lines.'

'If you give me your address I'll contact you if anything comes to light, although I think it's a long shot.'

'That's very good of you.'

TWENTY-FOUR

'Ah, the very man I was hoping to see. Come in.'

Sandra Boswell had a big smile on her face as she opened the door to Sep's knock.

Swinging on his crutches he followed her through into her living room where they both sat down.

'How are you doing? You seem to be healing well.'

'It's taking its time. But I've come to bring you up to date on what's been happening,' he told her.

'Well, I know already that James wasn't meeting a prostitute and that he was just having an affair, which is marginally less seedy.'

'Actually, he wasn't even having an affair.'

'Are you sure? I need to hear this, Sep.'

'Yes, you do.'

Sep gave her Julie's version of what had happened to James and added, 'I thought I'd bring you the story before the papers get hold of it.'

'Oh, Sep, that's wonderful. So, it'll be in the papers will it? When will that be?'

'When we release the details to the press.'

Sandra smiled. 'I suppose that's good. That repairs James's

reputation and it might stop me getting funny looks from some of
the women around here. My poor James. He wasn't a man
of violence, so why did he have a violent death?' She looked at
Sep and added, 'Now you're a man of violence and I bet you die
in bed in your sleep.'

'Hopefully, but my girlfriend thinks the odds are against it.'

'Anyway,' she smiled, 'you've done everything I asked of you
and my insurance money has come through, so I insist you take
the fifty thousand I promised.'

'As it happens, I will. If only to compensate me for a couple
of near-death experiences I've had recently and to pay for my Jag
that was destroyed.'

'Wasn't it insured?'

'It was but the payout won't cover its actual value, nowhere
near.'

'Well, hopefully the fifty grand will help.'

'It will, but it would be better if my employers didn't find out
about it.'

'You mean the police?' she said scornfully. 'Apart from you,
they did nothing to clear James's name. Your people will certainly
get nothing from me. Sep, I need to pay you for this as it will
give me complete closure and I'm sure James would approve of
us clearing his name.'

She got to her feet. 'I'll write you a cheque right now, then it's
done and dusted.'

'A cheque for fifty grand? I won't know whether to bank it or
get it framed.'

Sep was at home with Winnie, opening a letter from his insurance
company. He'd given himself a week's further convalescence before
he ventured out on the trail of Santiago's and Boswell's killer. It
had been a week of contemplation and of turning ideas over with
Winnie. His hasty proposal of marriage was still hanging in the
air and, although he didn't have the heart to retract it, he wasn't
opposed to the idea, but he didn't want to commit himself to it
either. The horror of her being possibly dead was still with him.
He certainly didn't want to be without her . . . ever. Was this why
he'd proposed? Was this what marriage was all about? Was he an
idiot not knowing the answers to these questions? He needed
advice here, but who to ask? Fiona, or Hawkins, or Phoebe, his

daughter who got on well with Winnie. He was favouring Phoebe when his mind turned to a more immediate problem: the job.

From what Butterbowl had told him, the man Redman had been working for had stepped into Santiago's shoes to run the scam. It was therefore a reasonable assumption that he was the one who killed Santiago. But with Redman dead, his lead to that man was also dead. Butterbowl and Roscoe had known next to nothing, as had Wood, who'd been forced to submit himself to a humiliating interview by Sep and Fiona. Sep shook himself out of his thoughts and read the letter.

'They're allowing me a hire car until my claim's settled. I'll give them your details as driver. I don't expect there's a clause in my policy that covers my Jag being blown up by a bomb, but it seems they're going to make me an offer. Mind you. I don't think the offer will buy me a decent Jag. I loved that car.'

'Buy yourself another.'

His wandering thoughts turned back to the job again. 'It might help if we knew exactly how this Snowball scheme worked. Considering who wanted a piece of it, it must be some sort of scam,' Sep said to Winnie over the breakfast table.

'It could be legal,' she said.

'Yes, it could, but there are no easy ways of making easy money legally, so I'll take that with a pinch of salt.'

'Maybe you should hand it over to your own fraud people.'

Sep allowed his mind to chew this over as he chewed on his bacon. 'I would, but this is a lot bigger than that. This involves historical murder and that's our job. I could ask for advice, but right now I don't even know what questions to ask, apart from the name Snowball, which is supposed to be a dormant company.'

'And do you believe that?'

'I don't know. I've actually asked an inspector who deals in fraud cases if he's heard of Snowball and he said he hadn't, which leads me to believe that it never got off the ground. He was going to ring me back if he did hear anything; so far he hasn't rung. What I need to do is track down some of these punters who profited from the trial run of the scam,' he said. 'They might give me some idea of how it works. Then I can start asking intelligent questions.'

'I know, but how do you track them down? Put an advert in the paper?'

'Hardly. I imagine they'll know it's bordering on illegal and they'll therefore be suspicious of such an advert as being linked to the police. On top of which they'll know Santiago was murdered. That alone'll put the wind up them.'

'What about the Hardacre woman?' Winnie asked.

'What about her?'

'She's involved in this and yet you seem to know nothing about her. It was Adam Piper who mentioned her. She might be worth following up. She might have been a punter and have you ever wondered that if Adam Piper was of value to Santiago it might well be that he's the brains behind Snowball.'

'It's crossed my mind, but if it is a scam it'd take a real criminal mind, which I don't think Adam has.'

'Who knows how his mind works? Up on the intellectual level where he lives he might have a different set of values from the rest of us.'

'True,' said Sep. 'He's certainly a one-off.'

'So, you track down Mrs Hardacre then.'

Sep gave this some though, then said, 'No point asking either of the brothers about her.'

'True, but who could we ask?'

'Santiago's wife. Hardacre might have been a punter, or she might have been one of his bits on the side. The brothers said she was a bit of all right.'

'I wouldn't put too much faith in their judgement of women,' said Winnie.

'All the same, it seems Mrs Santiago's our next lead. Do I give her a ring or do I go round to see her?'

'If you go to see her, I'm coming with you.'

'Why?'

'Because you told me she fancies you and that they had an open marriage. It sounded to me as if she was offering it to you on a plate and a standing willy has no conscience, even if it's attached to a cripple.'

'I didn't say she fancied me. She just asked me if I was married.'

'Same thing.'

'OK, we both go round. Do we take her by surprise or should I ring her first?'

'You're the copper. Why are you asking me?'

'OK, no phone call, just a copper's knock. No point letting a witness prepare for a visit.'

'Good. I thought you were going soft for a minute. You must always seek a disadvantage in a woman. Go early, before she's had a chance to do her hair and put her slap on. She'll be more concerned about her appearance than making up lies to tell you. Especially if she fancies you.'

'And especially if I've got you with me.'

'Why so?'

Sep knew she was fishing for a compliment and he saw no reason to disappoint her.

'OK . . . because you're a lot younger and you're very good-looking.'

'Not beautiful, then?'

'Same thing.'

'I prefer beautiful. Can I be beautiful?'

'Why not? Anyway, what am I saying? I shouldn't be involving you in any of this. You're not a copper and I've already got one of my friends involved and killed. I'm not losing you.'

'I thought I was a paid informant.'

'True, but informants only inform. They don't get involved in any of the legwork.'

'Sep, if anyone needs help with legwork right now it's you and I wouldn't have thought it too dangerous for me to come with you to talk to Mrs Santiago. It might put her off her guard, me, a civilian, being with you.'

'OK, you might have a point. Right, I think maybe we should go there with the assumption that Mrs Hardacre was her husband's mistress. One less hurdle to clear.'

'And if she's not?'

'If she's not, she'll put us right and tell us exactly who she is.'

'Your mind works in a very devious way, Sep.'

'I just like to take shortcuts to the truth; even if it takes a lie to get there. Some witnesses'll have you going round in circles before they tell the truth.'

'Yeah, I used to be good at that.'

Sep smiled at some distant memory. 'So you did.'

'I wonder if there's a *Mr* Hardacre on the scene, who doesn't know about his wife and Santiago?'

'One step at a time, Winnie but it's worth looking into.'

'It could be Mr Hardacre who killed Santiago.'

'At the moment it could be any number of people. It might even have been Woody, but he had nothing to do with Snowball. He's heading for Broadmoor, is that man.'

'He's certainly gone off his rocker since you got him banged up. They had him locked in a rubber room for three days for his own safety. Are you sure he had nothing to do with Snowball, Sep? From what you tell me he was in a hurry to take charge of the murder investigation when it wasn't really his job and he was all set to declare it a suicide at first, was he not?'

'He was, yeah.' Sep thought about this and shook his head in despair. 'Now you come to mention it, Winnie, I'm not sure of anything or anybody.'

'Not even me?'

'Yeah, I'm definitely sure of you.'

TWENTY-FIVE

Sep's knock was authoritative and loud enough to make Winnie cringe as she stood beside him at the door. It was seven o'clock in the morning and quite a while before Mrs Santiago opened it. She was indeed without make-up and wearing a dressing gown.

'Ah, I heard you'd been in an accident,' she observed, looking at his crutches.

'It was no more an accident than your husband falling out of a window, Mrs Santiago. I was injured in a criminal incident with a man called Redman. Did you know him, Mrs Santiago?' He studied her face carefully as she answered.

'No, it's not a name I'm familiar with. Why do you ask?'

'No reason, other than to tell you he's dead.'

His eyes were on hers as he said this, but she gave nothing away. 'There's a couple of questions you might be able to help us with,' Sep added.

'Who's us?' asked Mrs Santiago, looking at Winnie.

'Oh sorry, this is my associate Winifred O'Toole. She's not a police officer, more of a . . . consultant, so if you'd rather she wait in the car that's fine.'

Winnie treated Mrs Santiago to what she thought was a winning smile. She was smartly dressed in a dark, two-piece suit, sensible shoes and her hair tied back in a ponytail; looking for all the world like a plainclothes policewoman. Mrs Santiago looked her up and down and conceded, 'I suppose it's OK for her to come in as well.'

They followed her through to her living room and sat down. 'So, what're these questions I can help you with?'

'Well, actually there's only one question and it concerns a sensitive subject, but you told me you had an open marriage. Was a Mrs Hardacre part of this arrangement?'

Mrs Santiago smiled. 'You're asking if she was one of Charlie's bits on the side?'

'I wouldn't have put it quite so bluntly as that, but I believe she was involved with him in some way.'

'I thought the same myself. She certainly looked like Charlie's type, but she wasn't.'

'So you met her?'

'Yes, I saw her in his office one day. He told me she was purely a client of his new business venture and I believed him. We had no secrets from each other. Had she been a girlfriend, he'd have told me. I have a few gentleman friends of my own.'

'This new business venture – would that have been Snowball?'

'It was, yes. That seems to have died a death, along with Charles. No one seems to know anything about it, apart from the two backward lads. I couldn't get much sense out of them, so I gave up. There was a bit of money in the Snowball bank account which I've managed to get my hands on. I'm happy to let it die a death, to be honest.'

'By backward lads, you mean Simeon Piper whom we believe to have a social anxiety disorder, or some such condition?' said Sep, reprovingly.

'I do, yes.'

'His brother's not backward, quite the opposite in fact.'

'Really?'

'Yes. Do you have an address for Mrs Hardacre?'

'Well, not an address as such.'

'As such? What do you mean by that?'

'I mean I know what car she drives. It's a gold Lexus with the number plate OH 100 . . . flash bugger! I imagine you can get her address from that.'

'I can indeed, Mrs Santiago. Tell me, is Charlie's computer systems company still in business?'

'You mean Santiago TechSys? Oh yes. I'm actually running it myself, better than he ever ran it. I have an honours degree in Accounting and Finance which I've never used.'

'Have you really? That's interesting?'

'Why would it be interesting – because I'm a mere woman, running a man's business? I was always a better businessman than Charlie. He didn't even get a maths O level.'

'No. I didn't mean that at all. Winnie here can lose me on a computer, so can you, I don't doubt. The only degree I've got is in English, which has nothing to do with computers – or business for that matter.'

'A copper with an arts degree? Now that really *is* interesting,' said Mrs Santiago, looking at Winnie, who gave her a conspiratorial smile, in an effort to enlist her on their side.

'Touché,' grinned Sep. 'Right, so Mrs Hardacre drives a gold Lexus, registration OH 100. Do you know anything else about her . . . about her husband for example?'

'Ah, I see where you're coming from. Did her husband kill Charlie because he didn't like being cuckolded? Who knows? I don't. Never seen the man. I suppose I could have killed her for the same reason, but it never occurred to me. Maybe I'm just not one of life's criminals.'

'Or maybe Charlie wasn't worth you doing life for,' put in Winnie.

'No, he definitely wasn't. He was good looking and a good breadwinner and he didn't knock me about, but that's about all. Well-respected as a businessman, but as a life companion he'd bore the balls off a buffalo.'

Winnie smiled and memorized that one.

Sep threw his crutches in the back, sat on the passenger seat and heaved his right leg inside, Winnie, sitting in the driver's seat, asked, 'What was so interesting about her having a degree?'

Sep considered this as he got settled in his seat.

'It wasn't so much the degree, it was that she knew enough to take over the business. Which means she'd be able to run Snowball with no help from Charlie, albeit while pretending that it's dormant.'

'Who would know?' said Winnie.

'Companies House would know,' said Sep, 'and she could be the one that Redman was trying to muscle in on. That's why I asked if she knew him.'

'If that's the case, she should be really grateful to you that he's dead.'

'If she is grateful, she never let on,' said Sep.

'Maybe she's just a good liar,' said Winnie. 'Some women are, you know.'

'It seems to me that no one wants to own up to the truth in this case.'

'The truth often gets you into trouble, I've found.'

'Winnie, in the long run, it's lies that get you into the most trouble.'

'Oh dear, listen who's talking? She also told you she's not one of life's criminals.'

'That woman's made me suspicious of her and she might well come to regret it.'

'Ain't *that* the truth,' said Winnie.

Tracey Briggs knew exactly where her brother was as she took the lift up to level two of Scarborough Hospital. A police constable was sitting in a chair at the entrance to a one bed ward. He was reading a book which he put down when he saw her approaching.

'Which bed is Roscoe Briggs in? I need to speak to him.'

He looked at her carrier bag. 'Who are you?'

'A very good friend of his. You need to search my bag. He's in there on his own is he?'

'He is. It's a one bed ward for security reasons and I will need to search you.'

'I know the drill. I've visited the silly sod in hospital before. Do you want me to take my coat off?'

Being disparaging about whom she was visiting often had the coppers dropping their guard. This one searched her bag and found only cigarettes and two large bars of chocolate. Tracey held out her arms and said, 'I know you need to pat me down but don't make a meal of it like most of you lot do or there'll be a complaint and I know exactly who to go to.'

'I don't think that'll be necessary.'

It was a decision that would earn the officer a severe reprimand

and curtail his progress up the promotion ladder. She opened the door, turned towards Roscoe and said, 'Hiya, Ross.'

She spoke in a low voice as the policeman on the door had left it ajar.

'Hiya, Trace. Didn't think yer'd come all the way out here. Have yer got wheels?'

'Yeah, an old van. What's it this time?'

'Oh, got tangled up with Redman in some scam he had runnin'.'

'What're yer likely ter go down for?'

'Normally it'd be a life job but if I turn grass I could be out in five or six.'

'Who told yer that?'

'Black.'

'And yer trust that lyin' bastard do yer? From what I've heard of him yer can't trust a fuckin' word he says.'

'Trace – it's either trust him or I'm due a life stretch.'

Her voice was now down to a whisper. 'Fuck that! Believe me, Ross, the only way yer'll escape a life stretch is by gerrin' yerself out of here.'

'How do I do that? There's a copper on the door.'

'Yer can use what I've got up me armpit.'

She wore a coat with voluminous sleeves. The height of current fashion and also handy for concealing small handguns. With her free hand she took out a small gun from a shoulder holster and slid it under his bedclothes.

'What is it?'

'It's a Taurus P 111. It's a small gun but it's as good as a Smith & Wesson any day. I bought it fer me own protection when I'm workin' the streets. It carries thirteen 9-mills and it's fully loaded. No one can trace it ter me, by the way, so yer don't have to worry about that – as if yer would.'

'Have yer used it on anyone who might have reported it?'

'Just once. I were down in the Smoke sleepin' rough when this geezer thought he'd have a go at rapin' me. I stuck it in his gob and was gonna shoot the filthy bastard when he pulled himself away. He saved both his life and me a shedload of trouble. Anyway he ran away and I shot 'im up the arse. That slowed him down a bit – speeded me up as well. I shot out of there like shit off a shovel!'

'He's prob'ly gorra wife who dunt understand him,' said Roscoe.

'I bet she didn't understand how he got a bullet up his arse, either. Anyway yer tell that scuffer on the door yer need ter go fer a shit and need yer cuffs off.'

'Not sure he'll do that.'

'Well, yer can tell him it's contrary to the European Human Rights Act to expect a man ter shit while he's wearin' handcuffs. It's called an affront ter yer human dignity.'

'Is that right?'

'Yeah, I read it in the paper.' She whispered a few further instructions to him under her breath. He nodded that he understood.

With that, she turned and left. With the gun still under the bedclothes, Roscoe unclipped the magazine and checked for bullets – thirteen, plus one in the chamber, no doubt – that should be more than plenty. All he had to do was get past the copper on the door and get out of the hospital before the alarm was raised. Tracey had outlined a plan to him that seemed workable.

In his bedside cupboard was a bag of his clothes. Maybe if he could get dressed surreptitiously and walk out at visiting time. No, it'd be better if he could get himself and his clothes to the gents public toilet where he could get properly dressed. There was a dressing gown in the cupboard. He could roll up his trousers so that he looked to be bare legged with no shoes or socks, put the dressing gown on and tell the copper he was going to the toilet, as he had many times before. Mostly the copper would accompany him and stand outside the door. So if he came out properly dressed in street clothes, maybe the copper wouldn't know it was him, especially if he took the bandages off his bald head. Worth a try, that. In any case, he had a loaded gun to handle the copper with, if things got tricky. Christ! After what Tracey had just told him, things couldn't get much trickier. He was looking at a life sentence.

He opened his bedside cupboard and took out the bag. Ten minutes later, despite the difficulty presented by having one hand cuffed, underneath his dressing gown, he was wearing trousers and one sleeve of a shirt and jacket. The other sleeve of each hung loose over his shoulder. He stuck a shoe in each of his jacket pockets and likewise his socks, then swung his legs out of bed, rolled up his trousers and stood up. The gun was in his dressing gown pocket which also had a loose-hanging sleeve—only to be expected. He needed to keep the gun handy. His head was swathed in bandages and he looked for all the world like a patient taking a walk around the ward. He went to the door, which was just within reach of his handcuff chain and popped his head around.

'I need the bog, mate.'

He had always used such familiarity with whatever policeman was on the door, as it threw them off their guard a bit.

The policeman gave his request a moment's consideration and got to his feet. 'OK, no funny business,' he said, putting his book down on his chair. He accompanied Roscoe down the corridor to the patients' toilet which had a notice on the door saying: OUT OF ORDER PLEASE USE PUBLIC TOILET and an arrow pointing the way. Roscoe smiled as he recognized this as his sister's handiwork.

'Public toilet it is then,' said the policeman. 'Will you manage in there?'

'I'll have to.'

At the door to the public toilets Roscoe stopped and said, 'I, erm, I need a crap. Could yer take the cuff off, please?' He was ready to spout the European Court of Human Rights ruling but it wasn't necessary. The policeman uncuffed him without a word of protest. Another black mark on his record.

'This might take me a few minutes,' Roscoe told him, 'I'd prefer it if you waited out here.'

The policeman went inside the toilets and checked that there was no other way out. Inside were three cubicles, three wash basins and no other door.

'Right,' he said, 'I'll wait out here. Don't take too long.'

It was a decision that saved him serious injury, if not his life, but it earned him a future bollocking, which he would consider to be a fair exchange when he later learned that his prisoner was carrying a gun. Roscoe went inside a cubicle and unwound the bandage from his head, revealing a bald head which the policeman had never seen. There was a stitched-up wound just above his right ear, but his head was completely hairless. He removed his dressing gown, rolled down his trouser legs and put on his shoes and socks. There was a plaster on his hand that was covering a wound to his palm that could be easily hidden from view. He then waited for someone else to come in and use another cubicle. With the patients' toilet being out of order he knew this wouldn't take long and he was correct. It mattered not whether it was a patient or a member of the public, all he wanted was for one of the cubicles to be showing an 'engaged' sign and it wasn't a long wait. As soon as he heard another cubicle door open and close, he came out of his own cubicle, stood in front of the mirror, took the plaster off his hand and covered his head wound with it. Fully clad in his day clothes, he looked like any other hospital visitor. When the now impatient policeman came through the door he paid no attention to the bald man standing in front of the mirror, whose face obscured by the hands that were washing it. He just studied which of the three cubicles was engaged. Roscoe was leaving when the policeman tapped on the engaged cubicle door and asked, 'Will you be long?'

Roscoe didn't wait to hear the answer. He was walking away as swiftly as he could without arousing suspicion. At the end of the corridor two people were entering a waiting lift. He picked up speed and just got in behind them. Two minutes later, as the constable was now panicking about the disappearance of his prisoner, Roscoe was walking out of the hospital main door. A taxi had drawn up to pick up a passenger who'd booked him. Roscoe tapped on his window.

'What name are you for?'

'Robinson.'

'That's me, thanks. Train station, please.'

Roscoe sat behind the driver until they pulled into a station parking area, then he put his arm around the driver's neck, displaying the gun.

'Put every penny you've got on the passenger seat or I'll blow yer fuckin' head off!'

'OK, OK.'

The driver produced an expansive money bag and put it on the front passenger seat.

'Good man. Now turn left and keep drivin' till I tell yer ter stop.'

He had the driver take him to a place almost devoid traffic and pedestrians; a place where help wouldn't be immediately available. Then Roscoe leaned forward, grabbed the taxi's intercom and pulled until it disconnected.

'Gimme yer mobile phone!' he snapped.

The driver took out a mobile phone and handed it over his shoulder. 'Now get out of the car.'

It was the instruction the driver had been waiting for. He was out of the car in seconds and walking quickly away, looking for a phone box. Roscoe climbed over to the front and drove away. He stopped half a mile up the road and checked the contents of the purse – fifty-three pounds and change. It was enough to keep him going for a while, but he knew a place where he had access to much more. He dialled a number on the phone.

'Tracey, it's Ross. I'm on me toes. Where are yer?'

'Bloody hell, Ross! I'm in the van. On me way back ter Leeds. I'm just going through Seamer. Have yer nicked wheels?'

'Yeah, but it's a marked taxi and I need ter ditch it.'

'Look, I'm on the A64 just passing a big pub called the Londesborough Arms. I'll wait fer yer in the car park.'

'Good girl.'

Sep was at home when the phone rang. Winnie was cooking him a meal, his first home-cooked meal for some time. The screen told him it was Fiona.

'Hi, Fiona.'

He'd often thought of using the greeting 'Hi, Fi' but that might be a bit too familiar.

'Roscoe Briggs has escaped from the hospital.'

'What? How?'

'Apparently he went to a public toilet and just disappeared. A constable was waiting outside the door and when he got fed up of waiting and went inside. Roscoe wasn't there.'

'That copper needs a bloody good roasting. He shouldn't have let Roscoe out of his sight.'

'Sep, Briggs didn't go in just for a pee.'

'I know, he went in to change his appearance. He'll have walked out past the copper at some stage. I'd have gone in with him and handcuffed his chain to the door handle. I bet there were some clothes left in one of the bogs.'

'Just a dressing gown and some bandages, that's all.'

'That's enough. I bet he unbandaged his bald head to make himself less recognizable and walked out wearing the street clothes he had on under his dressing gown.'

'I don't know what he did.'

'Couldn't be anything else, Fiona. We've got to be one step ahead of these people all the time. Going to the bog is an obvious time to make an escape. We need to give police guards proper training for things such as this.'

'There's something else, sir.'

'What's that?'

'A taxi driver was robbed after picking up a fare from the hospital around the time Roscoe escaped. He fits Briggs's description and he had a gun.'

'He's got a gun? Where did he get that?'

'A woman came to visit him. She must have given him it.'

'Surely she was searched.'

'Not properly, obviously.'

'Bloody hell, Fiona! Somebody wants sacking here!'

'Could be he comes after you, sir.'

'Don't I bloody know it!'

Sep looked at Winnie, who was standing at the kitchen door, having worked out that Roscoe Briggs had escaped and that he had a gun. She didn't need telling who Briggs would be after next.

'Briggs has escaped?' she guessed.

'He has. Looks like he didn't believe me when I said I could get him a reduced sentence.'

'What're you gonna do?' she asked, after Sep had put the phone down.

'I don't know, Winnie. Briggs'll definitely have it in for me after I lied about his sentence . . . and now he's on the loose, well, who knows?'

'You think he'll come after you?'

'Probably. Who knows what goes on in these people's minds? I think he will, yes. I need to be on my guard . . . again.'

'Sep, in your life, will there always be another Roscoe Briggs?'

'It would seem so, Winnie.'

TWENTY-SIX

'My name's Winnie O'Toole, do you know who I am?'

'Of course I do. You're DI Black's, erm . . .' Detective Superintendent Hawkins paused as she sought the appropriate title, '. . . his lady friend.'

'I'm more than just a friend. I'm someone who cares very much for his welfare.'

'Miss O'Toole. DI Black is a fellow officer and we also care very much for his welfare.'

'I know, but he doesn't care enough for his own welfare and I think he's going after Roscoe Briggs on his own.'

'I won't allow him to do that, Miss O'Toole. He's too senior to be playing the Lone Ranger, with further seniority heading his way.'

'That's what I hoped you'd say. Has he told you that we're engaged to be married?'

'Erm, no he hasn't. Congratulations. I now understand your concern for him.'

'Thank you. Would it be possible for you to keep an eye on him and keep him out of trouble?'

'He's a police officer, Miss O'Toole and trouble is a large part of our business.'

'I know that, but Sep seems to get more than his fair share of it.'

'I'll do what I can.'

'Thank you. It would help if you didn't tell him I rang you.'

'I'm sure it would.'

As Hawkins rang off, Winnie looked down at her phone and muttered, 'What the hell is that supposed to mean?'

Sep knocked and entered Jane Hawkins's office without quite knowing why he'd been summoned there. He wasn't aware of the phone call that his boss had received from Winnie an hour previously.

'Sit down, Sep.'

Friendly use of his first name put Sep at ease as he sat down.

'You're still limping a bit, I see.'

'It comes and goes, ma'am. Not too bad on the whole.'

'But you're still not operating at a hundred per cent.'

'Not quite. Although I've swapped the crutches for this stick.'

'Which is why I asked you here. I know you'll be straining at the leash to track down Roscoe Briggs and I don't want you doing that.'

'Why not, ma'am?' asked Sep, as respectfully as he could. 'Is it because I'm potentially too important to be doing any legwork?'

'You're certainly not fit enough to be doing any leg work, but that's not the reason. The reason is that this is the Cold Case Unit and he's not a cold case. It's only a question of time before he's picked up and once we do, the CPS have enough on him to throw the key away.'

'Santiago's murder's still a cold case. I could work on that.'

'I want you to take a week's sick leave.'

'I'm not sick, just a bit slow on my feet.'

'There's such a thing as coming back too soon, Sep. When you come back full time, I want you to be operating at one hundred per cent. I've got another case I want you to take a look at. You can hand over everything you've got to DS Burnside, who will report directly to me.'

'And cut out the middleman, eh?'

'Precisely. Do you have anything you want to tell me . . . anything of, erm . . . of a personal nature?'

Hawkins had his engagement in mind. She wanted to tell him it was his duty to keep his head down if he was to become a married man once again. Sep frowned, genuinely puzzled.

'Erm . . . no, ma'am.'

'OK. I'd like you to go home, put your feet up for a week and come back one hundred per cent fit.'

Sep sighed. 'OK, you're the boss.'

'I am and I will still be your boss, if you ever get your promotion. I don't want you to forget that.'

'Sep, why the long face?' said Winnie.

They were talking over the breakfast table. Winnie had cooked him a full English breakfast: fried eggs, bacon, tomato, sausage and fried bread. It was a breakfast that would set him up for most of the day.

'You've been grumpy ever since you got back from seeing Hawkins yesterday. Is everything all right?'

'Not really, she's put me on bloody sick leave for another week.'

'Good for her,' said Winnie.

'What the hell am I going to do for a whole week?'

'You could visit your brother, maybe take him fishing.'

'Our Clive's blind and he's only got one arm.'

'The fish don't know that – which is what you told me the last time you took him fishing.'

'Ah, right.'

His brother was in a nursing home, paid for by the government

as scant compensation for his losing his sight and an arm in the
Iraq war. Sep always felt guilty for not being able to care for
Clive himself but his job prevented that, plus it was a fine nursing
home where his brother had made many friends.

'Might just do that.'

'You're a good brother to him, Septimus.'

'Better than our five sisters who hardly know he was injured.
The name's Sep, by the way.'

'Not Septimus Ruddigore?' she teased, 'so named by your dear
mother.'

'If you insist on addressing me by my full title, it's Detective
Inspector Septimus Ruddigore Black, MM, MA. My dear mother
was expecting me to become prime minister and didn't want the
name Joe Black to stand in my way.'

'Sep, this MA of yours. Why did you take it?'

'I wanted a degree and it's what I was best at. Then when I got
my BA, I thought I'd try for a Masters.'

'For what purpose?'

'I don't know. To show people that I'm not an idiot and I quite
liked university life.'

'I don't have a degree. Do you think I'm an idiot?'

'Not at all. I think you're very bright.'

'I'm bright enough to think you're an idiot, wasting a good
degree like that. You could have been a teacher. It would have
been a lot safer.'

'I haven't got the patience to teach, Winnie.'

'It'd have made my life a lot more pleasant, not having to worry
about you every minute of the day.'

'Oh, the car insurance claim's about to be settled,' he said, 'so
we lose the hire car.'

Winnie glared at him and gave up on the previous topic of
conversation. 'Will it buy you a replacement Jag?'

'It'll barely buy a new set of tyres. The other one was in
brilliant condition for its age.'

'She's paid up, has she?'

'She has, but you keep your mouth shut about it, especially to
my colleagues in the police.'

'I got the impression that you wouldn't take her money.'

'I wasn't going to, but my near-death experience helped me
change my mind. That car was a life force in itself.'

'Good for you. I imagine she'll consider it money well spent.'

'She was very grateful,' said Sep.

'So you're taking Clive fishing, then?'

'I am, yes. But there's one thing I need to do before I pass all my information over to Fiona. I need to talk to Stanley Butterbowl.'

The name brought a smirk to Winnie's face. 'You mean Stan the Strangler?'

'The very man. I reckon he knows where Roscoe will be holed up.'

'Well, if anyone can get that from him it's you. When are you going?'

'I thought I'd call in today. I'll drive myself.'

'You sure. All the way to Scarborough?'

'He's not in Scarborough. He's been brought over to Jimmy's in Leeds where we can keep an eye on him. Anyway, driving's not a problem for me. I've driven when I've been in a much worse state than this.'

'Remind me again why you took your degree? To prove *what* to people?'

Sep was at home, enjoying a rare lie-in when his phone rang.

'Sep? It's Fiona.'

'DS Burnside. What's all this Sep, business? You'll soon be referring to me as DCI Black.'

'Really? You got your promotion . . . Detective Chief Inspector, sir?'

'Not quite. I've got to go on an improvement course to make me suitable for such a rank. God knows how Wood got there. How can I help you?'

'Are you always going to be this formal with me . . . sir?'

'I'll need to get used to my newly elevated rank, sergeant.'

'Right, well, I've got something that might just befit your elevated rank, or it might only befit a lowly sergeant.'

'It certainly won't befit anyone until I know what it is.'

'It's about Adam Piper, sir.'

'What about him?'

'He's in custody, sir. Pulled in last night for DUI. He's sobered up and is due for release, but you might want a word with him, sir.'

'Adam Piper drunk? That must be an out-of-body-experience for him. Have you spoken to him?'

'I have, sir, and I'd like to be there when you speak to him, as you've spoken to him before.'

'Why's that? I'm supposed to be on sick leave.'

'Because I don't think he has too much of a mental problem, sir. In fact, he's quite high functioning.'

'Really?'

'Yes and he was driving a Porsche 911 which is registered to him at an address we don't have for him. Didn't you once tell me he can't drive?'

'I think I did, yes.'

'And he does drive and doesn't live in a council high-rise any more. He has a house in Alwoodley – a fairly expensive house I would imagine.'

'I'm on my way down.'

Adam Piper's eyes opened wide in alarm when Sep walked into the interview room. He shifted nervously in his seat alongside the court-appointed solicitor.

'Good morning, Adam.'

'Good morning.'

'The court has given you a duty solicitor but you may bring in your own solicitor if you have one. It appears that you can afford one.'

'I'm all right as I am, thank you.'

'Has Sergeant Burnside put you under oath?'

'I have, sir,' chipped in Fiona, 'just this minute and the tape is running.'

'Excellent,' said Sep. 'So, this interview is being recorded. Present are Adam Piper, duty solicitor Peter Horner, Detective Sergeant Fiona Burnside and Detective Inspector Black.'

Sep focused his attention on Adam. 'Nice car.'

'Yes and it's legally mine.'

'Bought and paid for?'

'Yes.'

'Didn't you tell me you can't drive?'

'It was Simeon who told you that. He can't drive. I can.'

'Brand new Porsche 911 Turbo S, eh? Very impressive. All I'll be able to afford with my insurance money is another used Jaguar which won't be anywhere near as good as the one it's supposed to replace. And you live in a house in Alwoodley that's worth around half a million. No mortgage on it, so you must have paid cash for that as well.'

'What if I did?'

'Now that's a very big "what", Adam. You see, I want to know where you got the money from—well over six hundred grand in available cash. Very few people have that sort of money in liquid asserts. But you do . . . or you did.'

Sep sat back in his chair and perused Adam, who was searching his mind for an answer. Sep gave him no time to do this.

'You see, we know about the Snowball scam that Santiago was running and we know that it's resulted in several murders and attempted murders, including three attempts on my life and here you are, a young man right in the middle of Santiago's business dealings – a computer expert, no less and you have money to burn. If you're expecting to be released any time soon, you're mistaken, Adam. In fact, I'm wondering why we haven't charged you with murder yet.'

Sep looked at Fiona as if for an answer.

'We were waiting for you, sir,' she said, respectfully. 'I believe we do have enough to charge him and hold him.'

'What am I being charged with?' Adam asked. 'I was arrested on a driving charge, or was that just a ruse to get me in here?'

'Adam,' said Sep, 'No ruse, you were definitely over the legal alcohol limit and as far as these other charges are concerned, I don't need to know the specifics, right now. All I need to know is that you fall into the category of very strong suspect for a string of serious crimes. The big mistake you made was throwing all that money around. We'd be failing in our duty if we didn't find out where it came from. So, tell me where the money came from, or you'll be formally charged with aiding and abetting in the murder of Charles Santiago and put straight back into the cells and you'll stay there until you go to magistrates court for them to agree to our request that you be remanded in custody, pending a trial at Crown Court. You will probably be held on remand at Armley Prison.'

'How long for?'

'Not sure. Definitely weeks, probably months and prison's not the cushy life these bleeding-heart liberals seem to think it is. It's a depressing place to be – scary as well. It's a place where you're well and truly on your own – every man for himself. How long you're held depends on the Crown Court backlog and how long it takes us to put the case together. If you help us, it might not be too long.'

Adam looked at his solicitor, who nodded his confirmation of what Sep had just said.

'How am I supposed to help you?' Adam asked.

'By telling us all about yourself and all about Snowball. What exactly is it and how does it work? And I also want to know all you know about Carl Redman and his gang of thugs.'

'I don't know anything about Carl Redman.'

'I don't believe you, Adam, but you can begin by telling me about Snowball and don't tell me you know nothing about that.'

Adam spoke quietly into his solicitor's ear, who said, 'My client feels he may be able to help with your enquiries provided he and his brother be granted immunity from prosecution and not held in custody.'

'I'm now wondering,' said Sep, 'what crime your client thinks he might be prosecuted for.'

'I'm advising my client not to answer any more questions,' said the solicitor.

'Is your client aware that we have enough circumstantial evidence to hold him in custody until such time as he does agree to answer questions, even if those questions are asked in court?'

'I understand that,' chipped in Adam, who spoke quietly to his solicitor once more.

'The help I might be able to give you,' he said, 'is with the death of Mr Santiago, but the immunity I want is for any prosecution arising from both Snowball and the unfortunate death of Mr Santiago. I would add that I and my brother are completely innocent of his death. What worries me is that you may seek to charge us with anything at all that might strengthen the rather flimsy case you have against us. As far as my house and car are concerned, I bought them with money I made out of legitimate dealings on the stock market.'

'Well,' said Sep. 'I think I'll have to seek permission to give you the immunity you seek.'

'Then I'll reserve my statement until you receive this permission.'

TWENTY-SEVEN

'There's something I need to do,' Sep said to Winnie. He had got out of bed and was headed for the bathroom when he made a detour downstairs to the kitchen where she was cooking breakfast as a reward for a successful bout of lovemaking.

'I need to speak to Julie Rogerson and her boss at Tyke News.'

'What about the other thing?'

'What's that?'

'Tracking down Roscoe Briggs who wants to kill you.'

'Oh, did I not mention him? He's number one on the list.'

'I thought he might be.'

'Winnie, I don't want to be looking over my shoulder all the time watching out for him. I need to be able to think clearly and having a killer on your tail doesn't help at all.'

His head was buzzing with notions of what to do and why. He hadn't felt this creative for some time and he wondered if his success in bed had triggered something dormant inside him. If so, it was an excellent means of both physical and mental stimulation which he must tell her about.

'You know, none of this makes sense. I know these killings are linked but the link is very tenuous for anyone to take such risks and kill so many people.'

She turned and looked him up and down, appraisingly. He was wearing a white, towelling bathrobe that was made to fit a much smaller person.

'You know, Sep, I didn't think anything could ever make you look effeminate but I've changed my mind.'

He turned and headed upstairs for the bathroom, deep in thought and saying 'I think somehow Roscoe's played a big part in all this. Someone's gone to a lot of risk and trouble to spring him. I really need to track him down.'

He was still deep in thought when she called out to him.

'Sep?'

'What?'

'One egg or two?'

'Oh, er, two please.'

He wished she wouldn't disturb his train of thought like this. He'd had a plan in mind that might well trick Adam into giving him the information Sep knew he had. Another word with Julie might not do any harm, or would it? So much was going on inside his head.

His mobile was ringing from his coat pocket in the bedroom. Jane Hawkins was just about to ring off when he answered.

'You took your time answering.'

Many subordinates might have apologized, but not Sep. 'My mobile was in the bedroom and I wasn't,' was what he said, albeit politely.

'Oh . . . anyway, just to tell you that we've released Adam Piper. We had no proper grounds to hold him and you should have known that. We have no reason to believe that the money he bought the car and the house with was obtained illegally. He bought them with his dealings on the stock market at which he's some sort of genius and we can't lock him up for being a genius.'

'Ma'am, I did know that, but I wanted to hang on to him for as long as possible to get more information. He was playing a game with me yesterday and, given another hour with him this morning, I think I had the beating of him.'

'Perhaps you should have told me that.'

'There's something else I should have told you. He more or less challenged me to charge him with something that would hold him so I charged him with aiding and abetting the murder of Santiago. It was something I plucked out of the air, with us having no real grounds to charge him but . . .' he paused for thought.

'But what?'

'But the look on his face when I linked him to Santiago's murder. I expected a look of contempt or some such thing, but what I got was a look of shock, as if I'd found something he was confident I would never find.'

'Well, whatever it is, it seems that it's there to be found.'

'I know. The question is *What is it that's there to be found?*'

'It's a big question, Sep, and you're the man to find it. Feel free to use all the maverick trickery you have at your disposal.'

Sep left Julie's house deep in thought and more confused than ever. Apart from him being able to drive again, things were definitely not slotting into place. All she had to tell him was that she and James had not been having an affair, but she'd told him that already. So, had she told him a second time to reinforce a lie she'd told him the first time? Or had they been having an affair? Or was he reading too much into this?

The problem was that he believed her, so his theory that Martyn had killed James was shot to pieces. It had to have been either Carl Redman or one of his thugs. It would definitely do no harm to track Roscoe down. Once he did that, Sep had no doubt that he could wheedle the truth out of him. Catching Roscoe was at the top of his list of priorities. Roscoe was an experienced hitman and he would have worked out by now that Sep's offer of sentence reduction was a lie. Such lies only work when a miscreant is in custody, with no hope other than to cling on to any promise made to him. Roscoe posed a danger that was always on his mind, although this might be an advantage insofar as he might not need to find Roscoe – Roscoe might find him first.

All Sep had to do was to be ready for him. For this reason he took to carrying the .357 around with him, packed in a shoulder holster. Simply carrying an unauthorized weapon might even cost him his job in the police should he be caught, never mind him using it. But, to Sep's mind, the sack is always better than death. Only he and Winnie knew about this and Winnie hadn't been too pleased at all when he arrived home and told her.

'Why don't we just bugger off somewhere, Sep?'

'You mean like New Zealand?'

'I mean out of the way of the Roscoes of this world.'

'There's only one Roscoe Briggs and I intend tracking him down. I'm not letting him chase me out of my own bloody country.'

'There'll always be Roscoes in your life, Sep. You said so yourself.'

'Could you make us a coffee, love, I need to make a call?'

'Make a call or pay a call?'

'Make a call on the telephone.'

'A secret call, eh?'

'A private call.'

'Sep, what is this? I've got no secrets from you.'

'I wish I'd said *pay a call* now. I'm ringing Patrick Lovell about something that might well prompt you into taking the piss again.'

'Ah . . . here's me on kitchen duties again.'

She was in the kitchen when Sep rang the number of the Tyke News agency.

'Patrick Lovell.'

'Patrick, it's Sep Black here. I wonder if I might ask you what sounds like a daft question.'

'Ask away. Might give you a daft answer.'

It was a remark Sep could have done without, considering his suspicion of Julie's statement.

Although Sep had abandoned his crutches he still had a slight limp, which irritated him. He hated displaying any sign of weakness that might put him at a disadvantage under extreme circumstances. He explained his dilemma to Winnie, who made it clear that she was more worried about the possibility of him chasing after Roscoe and getting hospitalized all over again.

'I don't have to go looking for him, Winnie. He'll find me.'

'Now there's a comforting thought. What're you planning on doing, having a shoot-out? You're not Wyatt bloody Earp, you know.'

'I'm not planning on anything other than arresting him. If I can locate him, I'll alert the troops. We'll go in mob-handed and I'll be at the back of the line.'

'Sep. You need to know where the line is to be at the back of it. By the way, I think you missed a trick with Julie back there. I reckon she knows a lot more than she is saying.'

'I tend to agree, but how do you know?'

'Call it intuition. How do you know what you know?'

'I call it suspicion.'

'I suggest you send Fiona to see her tomorrow.'

Julie had obviously been crying when she opened the door to Fiona and a detective constable the following evening.

'I'm Detective Sergeant Burnside and this is Detective Constable Miller. We're just following up on DI Black's visit yesterday. Have we come at a bad time?'

Julie stared at them for several seconds, as if mulling something over in her mind. 'Possibly not,' she said, eventually. 'In fact, you might have come at a good time. Come inside.'

The constable and Fiona followed her through to the living

room where the three of them sat down. Julie looked at Fiona and said, bluntly, 'You think Martyn killed James Boswell, don't you?'

'To be honest, Ms Rogerson and I speak for DI Black, who has filled me in with the whole background concerning yourself and James Boswell, but we can think of no one else with the means and a motive.'

'Well, my husband didn't actually have a motive because James and I weren't having an affair.'

'Why did Patrick Lovell think you were?'

'Oh, Patrick knew we met now and again but it was only ever in connection with our work. I told Patrick that he was talking nonsense but he wouldn't have it. You know what men are like – they like to think the worst of you. To be honest, I think Patrick was a bit jealous – I think he fancied his chances with me himself. You see, I had some information for James about the Santiago murder which I planned to give to him. We communicated by text, which is just about the worst way anyone can communicate anything as confidential as that.'

'What was the information you had for him?' Fiona asked.

'It was to do with one of the Snowball investors.'

'Would this be Carl Redman?'

'It would, yes. I knew him to be a violent criminal and I wanted to warn James not to have anything to do with him.'

'And that's all, is it?'

Julie crossed her arms over her body and rocked back in her chair. Her lips trembled, her brow began to crease and tears welled up. Her words tumbled out amidst the sobs.

'I've kept this . . . to my . . . myself . . . b . . . but it's not fair . . . fair that I have to.'

'Life isn't fair,' said Fiona sympathetically. 'Julie, if there's something you need to get off your chest concerning this case you really need to tell us. Otherwise life will become very unfair for you.'

'Please don't threaten me.'

'I'm not threatening you, I'm trying to help you. If it transpires that you've been holding something back that will help us with the case you'll be in more trouble than you can handle.'

'Actually, no, it's not all I know.'

Fiona and the constable exchanged optimistic glances. 'I didn't think it was, Julie. Just tell us what's troubling you and it'll be our problem, not yours.'

'I didn't tell DI Black the whole story. To have told him any more would have got me into serious trouble and destroyed my marriage.'

'I see,' said Fiona, looking down at her notes. 'Julie, when you first told DI Black about Carl Redman you said all you knew about him was his name. That wasn't exactly true, was it?'

'I knew his name and that he was a dangerous man, which is what I told DI Black.'

'You told him he was a heavy.'

'Heavy – dangerous man – same thing. If I didn't say he was an investor, it's because I didn't think it was all that important.'

'Julie, were you involved in James Boswell's murder?'

Julie hesitated for quite a while, before saying, 'All I can say is that I blame myself for it and probably you will as well.'

'Julie, if you tell me anything that I need to arrest you for, all I can promise is that, in exchange for relevant information, we won't apply for you to be held on remand. You'll have to spend a night in custody before going to magistrates' court but that's all. So, once again, do you have anything you want to get off your chest?'

TWENTY-EIGHT

W innie was waiting in reception as Sep came up from the custody suites where he'd taken Julie, after Fiona had arrested her for perverting the course of justice.

'I guess the girl's in trouble,' Winnie said, 'for trying to keep herself out of trouble. I've been there myself a few times.'

'I'll do what I can for her by recommending leniency in exchange for the help she's giving us,' said Sep. 'The rest is up to the courts to decide.'

'Well, Septimus,' Winnie said. 'As far as I can see that's your job done. You can transfer over to uniform now and keep regular hours . . . and keep yourself out of trouble.'

'Job? What job's that?'

'The job you took on for Mrs Boswell. The one she's paying me fifty grand for. James is in the clear. He wasn't meeting a prostitute. He wasn't having an affair. He's as pure as the driven snow.'

'I still need to catch whoever killed Santiago and I can't do anything while Roscoe's on the loose.'

'Bloody hell, Sep! Santiago's murder's a job for the West Yorkshire Police, not just you; just as it's their job to catch Roscoe Briggs and find out who killed Graham Feather.'

Sep shook his head. 'Winnie, you know I hate not finishing a job once I've started it. A good friend is dead because I involved him and I nearly lost you. It won't seem right to turn my back on it just because things got rough for me.'

'But the people who killed Eli are either dead or locked up.'

'Roscoe Briggs isn't. He's out there and he's got a real grudge against me and who's to say he wasn't the one who put the bullet into Eli?'

'Bloody hell, Sep! You're one man, not an army. If I were you I'd go and see Mrs Boswell and tell her her late husband's completely in the clear as far as having a bit on the side's concerned, then pick up the fifty grand and bring it back to me.'

'Winnie, the money is to pay for my new Jag.'

Stanley Butterbowl wasn't in much of a mood for talking, having lost both a leg and a future as a strong-arm knuckle-dragger. He had also been brought into St James's hospital in Leeds. His injured leg had now been amputated and he was waiting for a prosthetic leg to be fitted.

'What am I supposed ter bleedin' do now, eh? I can't even work the doors anymore.'

'It didn't stop Long John Silver being a pirate,' said Sep.

'Right, I'd best go buy meself a parrot.'

'Once you get a false leg who's going to know? All you have to do on the doors is *look* the part and with an ugly mush like yours, you've still got that.'

'You're a cheeky bastard for a copper.'

'Us coppers can afford to be cheeky with such as yourself. All I want is an answer to a simple question.'

'What's in it for me?'

'I'll be blunt with you, Wolf. The offer of a reduction in sentence still stands, now that Roscoe's had it on his toes. With you losing a leg, the judge'll no doubt take your disability into consideration, especially if we tell him how cooperative you've been.'

'How much time are we talking about?'

'Not sure, what've you been charged with?'

'Two counts of attempted murder and some other minor bollocks. I forget what.'

'Have you got any money for a decent brief?'

'Some, yeah.'

'A half-decent brief'll get the attempted murder charges knocked down to GBH. I find it bloody annoying but it happens a lot.'

'Then what? And don't give me any of your lies.'

'Look, I know I stretch the truth a bit with such as yourself, but if you plead guilty on the minor charges and give us whatever info we want, the police will do a deal on a fairly short tariff, so it could be that end up doing no more than a six stretch, after time off for good behaviour.'

Butterbowl gave a slow nod in appreciation of such a short sentence for such major crimes. He'd been anticipating having to spend the rest of his life behind the door. In fact, Sep had no idea what his sentence might be, other than at least three times what he'd just suggested.

'And what is it you want to know?'

'I want to know where Roscoe's likely to be. Is there a regular place where he holes up when things get too warm? And remember if we don't catch him, the judge'll be tempted to extend your sentence to make up for him not turning up to take his. They do that do judges, you know. They're like football referees when they think they've missed giving a player a yellow card. The next time his teammate commits any sort of foul that poor sod picks up a red. How's the leg anyway?'

'How would I know? I don't even know where it is.'

'But do you know where Roscoe is?'

'Not for certain.'

'I'll take your best guess.'

'There's an old foundry down by the canal in Hunslet where he used ter work as a lad. It's rustin' ter bits but there's a wooden hut there that's not in bad nick. I've known him go there ter keep his head down. It's got its own bog and runnin' water and a stove and electricity now that Roscoe's got it wired it up ter the mains. All he needs is a few cans o' food and he can live there fer weeks while you lot are runnin' all over Yorkshire tryin' ter find him. That'd be my bet.'

'What do they call this place?'

'South Leeds Foundry. What's the score with me then? When will I be taken ter the nick?'

'As soon as the hospital discharges you, you'll be taken to the hospital wing at Armley Prison, so I wouldn't moan too much about being kept in here if I were you.'

'And you'll tell the courts that I've been helpful?'

'I will, providing you're telling me the truth. If not, I'll be back for the proper story.'

'I've told you all I know about Roscoe.'

'South Leeds Foundry, eh? That's a big place if I remember rightly. Plenty of places to hide.'

'It is, but there's only one wooden hut. It's painted black. Yer'll need ter break a padlock on the main gate to get in. Roscoe's gorra key, with him swappin' their padlock fer one of his own.'

'So, no one's got a key that works apart from Roscoe?'

'I think there's more than one entrance – other keys to other locks.'

'Is there a security guard?'

'Only Roscoe, an' maybe a dog. There's no scrap metal left ter pinch unless yer can take a big wagon in there and a load o' cuttin' gear. That's been tried by some lads from Wakefield but they got nabbed within ten minutes, thick bastards! There's allus a cop car drivin' past, lookin' fer summat a bit out of order. Silly sods had left the gate wide open.'

'It's a wonder no one's seen Roscoe on the premises.'

'Mebbe they have but he's not pinchin' nowt so why bother him? They'll most likely think he's just some old dosser who's found somewhere ter kip.'

'I wonder if our boys are aware of him squatting there?' mused Sep, fully intending to ask Fiona to put that very question to her copper colleagues.

'I should think the coppers knew about him,' said Butterbowl. 'They're not completely useless, so I'm told.'

'Us useless coppers caught you and your lot,' Sep pointed out.

'If yer goin' after him, I should go now. I reckon he'll be on his toes out of the country before long. Maybe even as we speak.'

'Right, I'd best be on my way then.'

Within a minute of Sep leaving, Stanley Butterbowl took an illicit mobile phone from his bedside drawer and called a number he had on speed dial.

'Roscoe, it's Wolf. I know yer on yer toes, are yer down at the foundry?'

'Yeah . . . why?'

'That twat Black's on his way to pay yer a visit.'

'When?'

'Now.'

'Who told him where I was?'

'I thought I'd give yer a chance ter square things with him. Are yer carryin'?'

'Yeah, I've gorra 9 mil auto. Tracey brought it to the hospital.'

'Did she now? Why would she do that?'

'She's me sister.'

'I know but it's a hell of a risk for her to take. Has she got any other reason?'

'Like what?'

'Like she's got somethin' going on that we don't know about.'

'All I know is I'm free and clear and it's all I need ter know.'

'OK, right, well, yer've also got surprise on your side. Black promised me a short sentence if I told him where y'are, as if I'd fall for that shit.'

'Yeah, he fed me some o' that bollocks. Told me I'd just get a six stretch, if I helped him.'

'Yer didn't believe that, did yer?'

'Well, he made it sound as if it were possible, but now I think about it I know he were feeding me bollocks,' said Roscoe.

'That's how he works, the lyin' bastard! When he gets there you fill him full of 'oles an' leave the fuckin' country.'

'Is he comin' on his own?'

'I reckon he will be, yeah. Have yer gorra decent passport?'

'I have yeah.'

'See yer, Roscoe.'

*   *   *

It was raining on that day when Sep went to find Roscoe. He had armed himself with the .357 Smith that he'd got from Winnie's attacker, plus a pocket full of bullets. With it only holding five rounds, he didn't want to end up with an empty gun like he had at the cottage. The entrance to the foundry was in a secluded area, once a district of busy industry but no longer so.

He parked his hired Mondeo at the gate and looked through the steel mesh fence to see if he could see the black, wooden hut, but all he could see were the rusting framework of huge buildings spreading out over many acres. He had with him a lump hammer with which he struck several heavy blows at the padlock until it broke. He pushed one half of the double gate open just enough for him to get in and closed it behind him so as not to alert any passing police car. He was bare-headed, wearing a waterproof jacket and now wishing he'd put a hat on, but Sep had never been a hat-wearer. He walked along a muddy and cracked concrete roadway that led in between a threatening mass of dark steel columns and beams that had once been the skeleton of foundry. He walked past a derelict Thames Trader truck which had been decorated with the words *MAGGY THATCHA JOB SNATCHA* written in blood red, an indication of the political leanings of the workers who had no doubt lost their jobs due to the then prime minister closing down loss-making nationalized industries, many of which had been engaged in steel production and manufacture.

Above him, steel steps led to a rusting and brutal framework of steel columns, rolled steel joists and gantries, occupying three levels. On these upper levels were a number of huge steel tanks that had once held hundreds of gallons of fuel oil to help fire the furnaces and heat the workshops, offices and storage units. On this dismal and rain-sodden afternoon, it looked to Sep to have been a grim place to work. There was a smell of rust and rotting vegetation in the damp air and smoke from somewhere but he couldn't tell where. He turned up his collar against the constant drizzle. Then he checked his right-hand pocket for the Smith. The five-shot revolver was pretty accurate up to fifty yards and had an effective range of twice that in the right hands; after that it was pot luck what it hit. He'd often scoffed at the gunmen in Wild West films who brought down men a hundred yards away by shooting from the hip with a .45 Colt. No way would he ever shoot from the hip unless his target was within ten yards of him.

However, the Smith & Wesson .357 was a gun that would put him on level terms with anyone else with a handgun. He knew that Roscoe was armed with the gun he'd threatened the taxi driver with, but he didn't have the benefit of Sep's army weapons training, nor had he ever worn on his sleeve the crossed rifles badge of a British Army marksman, as had Sep, who had supreme confidence in his fighting ability, with or without weapons.

To his left was the canal which had once transported by barge manufactured goods east and west across the north of England, but right now it was empty of all water traffic, not even a passing duck deigned to enliven its still, grey murk, animated only by splashing rain. All in all it was not a good day for a man to be putting his life at risk in the hope of hunting down an armed killer; especially a hunter with a gammy leg. He thought about Winnie and how he hadn't followed up on his proposal and how he would feel if she left him for another man. 'Gutted' was the word. With all this in mind it occurred to him to turn and go back to her and tell her that they should get married as soon as possible and to hell with Roscoe Briggs. All he had to do was tell Hawkins where Roscoe might be and the troops would descend on this place and smoke the man out. So why was he doing this himself? Because the moment was right and he was Sep bloody Black, that's why.

High above him, Roscoe had spotted Sep. He figured he had a range of about a hundred yards – too far for certainty. He knew little about effective gun ranges but he knew his own capability. He looked back towards the gate. It could be that Black was being backed up by an armed-response unit, but he saw no sign of that. Black was on his own, as Wolf said he would be. Good. He had a fully loaded twelve-round magazine in his semi-automatic pistol and, if he played it right, most would end up in Black's body. That'd teach the bastard! Then off to Canada with the twenty-two grand Tracey had stashed away for him. Good girl, Tracey; a sister he could trust. Pity Redman was dead; working for him had been fairly profitable. He'd had a fake passport made and that had cost two grand because of the new digital passports that had come in a few years ago. He'd tried it once on a trip to Spain and it had worked a treat. No problem there then. *Come on, Black. What the fuck have yer stopped for? Bad leg giving yer some stick, is it? Well, I'll be giving yer some stick when yer get walkin' again.*

He trained his weapon on Sep's body and gave pulling the trigger a lot of thought. The two bullets he'd taken back at the cottage had both been removed, but the wounds were giving him too much pain for him to concentrate properly. If he missed, he knew that Sep would find cover in an instant, despite his limp. There was plenty of cover about and that would make the job ten times harder. *Just think, Roscoe, think. Be patient and wait for a definite killing shot.*

Sep lit a cigarette to calm his thoughts. The rain showed no sign of abating and was dripping down his face and inside his coat. He pulled his collar close to his neck to make himself more waterproof. Rain was hitting his cigarette and his leg was beginning to play up now, perhaps exacerbated by the damp weather. He threw away his cigarette, sat down on a low wall and bent his injured leg at the knee and straightened it a few times, then got to his feet to give it a try. Bloody painful. Wherever he went now he'd be limping. This is no doubt why Jane Hawkins had insisted on him taking a week's sick leave. He smiled to himself. Some sick leave this. God! He'd be in some trouble if Hawkins could see him now. He'd be in trouble if Winnie could see him now. He hadn't told her of his plan to capture Roscoe Briggs, only to find out where he might be from Stanley Butterbowl.

OK, off we go, DI Black. He'd taken exactly twenty steps when Roscoe lost patience and pulled the trigger from a distance of over a hundred yards. The thug had aimed for the central mass of Sep's body but hadn't allowed for the slight downward curve in trajectory as the bullet lost speed, nor for the pain in his wounded, gun arm. All the same, Sep went down. He rolled over several times towards a break in the low wall. Roscoe kept firing and kept missing but not by much. The range was too great for accurate shooting with a handgun. His bullets kicked up concrete splinters from the road, which hit Sep like shrapnel, bruising him but not penetrating his skin. He managed to get the low wall between him and the shooter whom he assumed would be Roscoe.

He looked down at the bullet wound in his right leg; it was the same leg that had been previously damaged. Well, that's not such a bad thing. At least he'd have one undamaged leg to get about on. Using his hands and arms he dragged himself along the ground, hidden from view by the wall until he'd reached a spot where he figured Roscoe wouldn't expect him to be – and one that brought him within shooting range of where he thought Roscoe was. He now took out his revolver and checked that there was a bullet already in the chamber.

He positioned himself behind the step in the wall and risked half of his head to take a look at where Roscoe might be. Two more shots rang out, both hitting the wall twenty yards away, where he'd first gone down and, more importantly, showing him exactly where Roscoe was. He took sight along the short barrel, rested it on his left forearm and trained the revolver on the dark, moving shape. Like Roscoe, he knew he must make this first shot count. The one thing Sep knew about this .357 Smith was the muzzle velocity. The bullet would leave the gun at a speed of 1,500 feet per second, which meant it would arrive at its target in around a tenth of a second with almost no loss of trajectory; all he had to do was set it off in the right direction. Roscoe got to his feet and looked over the walkway handrail to get a better view of where he thought Sep might be. Could be, Roscoe thought, that Sep was dead already. In that case he'd need to go down and check. Very dangerous in view of what a sly bastard that copper was. He was leaning on the handrail when Sep exhaled and, before inhaling, with his body completely motionless, he took the shot. The shot was good and the bullet would have hit Roscoe had it not pinged off the handrail. Eaten away by rust, the bracket that fastened it to a steel column sprang loose with the sudden vibration and the handrail gave way. Roscoe, shocked by this unexpected turn of events and unbalanced by the sudden pain in his wounded side, was teetering on the very edge of the walkway, now with no handrail for protection. He dropped his gun as he windmilled his arms to try to regain his balance, but he was beyond the point of no return.

He plunged to the ground, thirty feet below and landed with a sickening thud on the concrete road. Sep had watched the whole fall and had noted that Roscoe had landed head first, no doubt ending his life.

Sep now knew that even if he himself survived this, he'd be in serious trouble for killing a man with an unauthorized weapon. He put the gun back in his pocket and took out his mobile phone to summon help. Then he cursed himself yet again.

'Oohh, No! Shit, shit, shit bloody shit! You idiot! You are a dead man!'

In his hurry to get going, he hadn't checked the charge on his phone battery. His battery was stone-cold dead, as he would be if he didn't get help. The gate was a quarter of a mile away and even if he managed to drag himself there, he probably wouldn't find anyone out there to help him. Distant thunder rolled and the rain began to pour down as he lay in a miserable lump, alone with his thoughts. Just thoughts, no ideas. What he needed was help and there was none available. He hadn't told anyone where he was going or why and he'd brought with him no means of communication. *Jesus! What an idiot!* The pain in his leg was bad now and he was losing a lot of blood. The bullet had probably broken his femur, as that's where the pain was. He was also aware that a wounded thigh could lead to terminal blood loss, if it wasn't treated quickly; something to do with a femoral artery. The light was beginning to fade and, with it, Sep's hopes of surviving this bloody awful night.

He rolled over and lay on his stomach in the mud, mainly to keep the rain from hitting his face. In his confused mind he also thought the mud might act as some sort of poultice and stem the flow of blood from his leg. He turned his coat collar up as much as he could and resigned himself to whatever fate had in store for him. The rain had soaked through every layer of clothing he had on him and he began to shiver. Then he felt something else: a warm snuffling near his ankle. He rolled over and was immediately face to face with a Rottweiler. He cursed for the hundredth time. It had to be a bloody Rottweiler, not a friendly dog like Lassie which might go and seek help for this wounded man. He was saddled with an ugly bloody Rottweiler who could taste his blood in the air and wanted more. He pulled himself back before the dog could do more than growl and kicked at it with his good leg which was his left leg. He caught it at the side of its head and made it back off with bared teeth now; eyes staring angrily, snarling with menace. Jesus! He'd just aggravated a hungry Rottweiler that had come to eat him. He took the gun out of his pocket.

The dog came at him once again. Sep shot it in the head, causing it to drop dead on his wounded leg. The pain was agonizing. He managed to shuffle out from under it, which only worsened the pain. As he lay there he heard what sounded like an ice-cream van, and wondered what the hell was an ice-cream van doing in this godforsaken place and in this weather? Was he hallucinating? Had he gone mad? He knew that severe blood loss affected the brain, so was there really a dead dog at his feet and an ice cream van nearby? He looked down at the dog once again. The music had stopped but the dog was still there. Maybe he was only half mad.

He began to shiver again and wondered which would come first: death from hypothermia or death from exsanguination? Which would be preferable? Either would be a miserable way to go out. Maybe he should just lie there and go to sleep as his life blood drained out of him.

TWENTY-NINE

'Fiona, is Sep with you?'

'No, he's not . . . why?'

'Because . . . well, to be honest, I think he's gone after Roscoe Briggs and I don't think he's in any state to be doing that on his own. He said he was just going to find out where he is, but I doubt if Sep'll stop at that, once he finds him.'

'No, nor me. What makes you think he's gone after Briggs?'

'He went to Jimmy's to see Stanley Butterbowl and ask him if he knew where Roscoe Briggs was, but he's been gone a while. I've just rung Jimmy's and they say Sep left over an hour ago. He should have been back here ages ago.'

'I hope he hasn't been impulsive in going after Briggs, who may well be armed and Sep won't be.'

'Would he be in trouble if he was armed?'

'He would, yes,' said Fiona. 'He'd need to follow a proper procedure and apply to take an authorized weapon with him and to discharge it and I doubt if he's been authorized to do that. Not by Superintendent Hawkins anyway. Are you saying he's taken a gun with him?'

'I don't know. I'll ring you back.'

Two minutes later Winnie rang back. 'I think he might have taken a gun with him.'

'Has he now? Well, he's just rung me this second and he's in trouble. He's in a disused foundry in Hunslet. He never mentioned a gun but he sounded in a bad way. What sort of gun has he got?'

'It's a revolver that he, er, found at a crime scene.'

'Any idea what kind?'

'I think he said it was .357 Smith & Wesson.'

'Shit! That's a serious gun. Winnie, why would he even go after Briggs?'

'Peace of mind's what he told me. He thinks Briggs won't rest until he kills Sep, so the only way is to catch Briggs and get him locked up.'

'I suppose that makes some sort of weird sense.'

'Actually, it makes a lot of sense to me, Fiona. And you know where he is, do you?'

The rain was hammering against the windscreen as they pulled up behind Sep's hired Mondeo.

'This is definitely where he is,' said Winnie. 'I don't suppose you have an umbrella, have you?'

'Yeah, there's one in the boot.'

A minute later Winnie and Fiona were huddled under a spacious golf umbrella, looking at the broken lock, then through the bars of the gate at the grim frame of the South Leeds Foundry.

'It's huge,' said Fiona. 'How are we going to find him in here?'

'By shouting,' suggested Winnie, 'and hoping he shouts back.'

'Supposing Roscoe Briggs hears us first?'

'I suppose it's a gamble we'll have to take.'

'That's exactly what Sep would have said.'

'And that's exactly what he'd have done.'

'True.'

They pushed the creaking gate open and made their way along the concrete road. 'I reckon he was going by guesswork,' said Fiona, 'so I reckon this is the way he'll have walked.'

'Pity we couldn't get the car through the gate.'

'Yeah, too narrow. In any case, we might miss him in the car.'

'We could have hooted the horn a few times.'

Darkness was falling. Fiona took a powerful torch from her pocket and shone it into the falling rain, which reflected most of its light back to her. She didn't switch it off; the light it afforded was better than nothing.

'Sep!' shouted Winnie. Fiona joined in and they repeated the shout several times but got no reply.

'It's this damned rain,' said Fiona. 'He won't be able to hear us for the rain. We'll stick to this roadway and keep a lookout either side. It's pretty much all we can do.'

'You could call for support,' suggested Winnie.

'I know, but Sep's breaking all the bloody rules doing this on his own, especially if he's got a dodgy gun with him. I'd rather us find him. Let's give it fifteen minutes and if we don't find him I'll ring Hawkins and tell her what's happening.'

Winnie looked at her watch and noted the time. 'Fair enough,' she said.

They continued their trek along the cracked concrete road, passing the truck and its uncomplimentary Maggie Thatcher slogan, then coming to the low wall, behind which, Sep had taken cover from Roscoe. The rain eased off, allowing the torch beam to properly illuminate fifty yards ahead.

'Oh God, what's that?'

'It looks like a body,' said Fiona. They both stopped as the torchlight played on the prone figure lying on the concrete road, neither of them keen to go any nearer lest they identify it as Sep.

'It could be him, Fiona.'

'I know.'

Fiona took a deep breath and said, 'OK, let's take a proper look.'

As they approached, Winnie exclaimed, 'Fiona, I think there's two of them!'

'Oh God! I think you're right.'

A sudden rush of dread enveloped Winnie as she looked at the two prone bodies, knowing that one of them might be Sep; in fact knowing that one of them *would* be Sep. What she didn't know was if he was alive or dead. For him to be dead was something she wasn't ready for, nor would she ever be. The big lump was the light of her life, a man she was deeply in love with and a man whose dead body she didn't want to find. As Fiona walked forward, Winnie remained glued to the spot.

Fiona half turned, saying, 'Coming?'

'I – I can't, Fiona.'

Fiona also paused in her step; she also wasn't looking forward to finding Sep dead. She took a deep breath, knowing it was some-one's duty to take a look and she was the copper, not Winnie. Her torch shone first on Roscoe who was the nearest. She ascertained he was definitely dead, with a broken neck if nothing else. He'd no doubt fallen to his death. His body had exploded somewhat with the fall and his intestines were protruding from his stomach and being washed by the rain. Then she shone her torch forward onto the body whose head was hidden beneath a fisherman's hat. She removed the hat. It was Sep. The very fact that it was definitely him set her heart racing. She also had affection for him, albeit not of the romantic kind. She could see lots of blood on his trouser leg but nowhere else. However he'd arrived there, it wasn't from above, thank God! Still breathing deeply to steady her nerves and watched by Winnie from a distance, she knelt down beside her boss and put her head close to listen for breathing. She called out to Winnie.

'It's Sep – he's alive.'

Sep had dragged himself over to where Roscoe was lying and was now wearing the thug's fisherman's hat. He'd begun to need it badly, if only to make the time he had left on Earth a little more comfortable.

He was barely conscious when Fiona and Winnie found him. Winnie was in tears as Fiona rang for an ambulance, then she turned Sep over. He peered up at her through the rain and narrow eyes, but she was shining her torch on him, so he couldn't see her for the glare.

'Who – who the hell are you?'

He said it with as much belligerence as he could muster, which wasn't much. Maybe they were cronies of Roscoe. If so, their presence wasn't good news. Fiona pointed the torch away from him and at herself and Winnie.

'It's Winnie and Fiona.'

His dejection took a turn for the better. Here were the two people he most wanted to be with him at this time.

'Wha—? How did you, er, know I was here?'

'Sep, you rang me, that's how. We've rung for an ambulance. It should be here in ten minutes, as will the police. I'm sorry but I had to tell Hawkins. Couldn't cover something like this from her.' She nodded in the direction of the body. 'That's Roscoe, is it?'

'Is it? Oh, yeah, I think it is.'

'He looks dead. How did he die?'

'He shot me. I shot him . . . He er, he fell.'

Sep managed to raise an arm and point from where Roscoe had fallen.

'You shot him? What with?'

'Gun.'

'Of course a bloody gun. Where is it?'

Every word was an effort to him. 'Pocket . . . shot dog . . . there.'

He pointed again. Winnie went over and saw the dead dog. 'Yeah, there's a dead Rottweiler over there. Fiona, is Sep going to be all right?'

'Roscoe shot my leg . . .' said Sep. 'Bloody dog bit it.'

'He'll probably need a tetanus injection,' said Winnie, determined to make light of what she knew might be a terminal injury. 'We'd better tell them he's been bitten.' She was still standing at a distance, as if her proximity to him might affect Sep's chances of survival. Fiona had no such reservations.

'Bloody hell, Sep!' she said. '*You'll* get shot if Hawkins finds out you've been using an unauthorized weapon.'

Fiona took the gun from his pocket and examined it. Winnie recognized it but said nothing. Then Fiona went over to Roscoe and tried to find out where Sep had shot him. No obvious bullet wound to his head and none to his body.

'Winnie, I need your help to check this murdering bastard for bullet wounds.'

'Oh right. Didn't he take a couple of bullets back at the cottage?'

'Yeah, but they'll have healed up more or less.'

Winnie's eyes were on Sep as she and Fiona rolled Roscoe over and shone the torch on him, searching for a fresh bullet wound.

'Sep. Are you sure you shot him? We can't find a bullet wound.'

Sep's voice was now almost inaudible. 'He fell.'

'I can see he fell, but did he fall because you shot him?'

'Up there.'

The two women looked up to where Sep was pointing and saw the broken handrail hanging loose high above them.

'I bet he fell because the handrail broke,' guessed Winnie, in defence of Sep. Speaking on his behalf was all she could do to help him right then.

'Better that than Sep shooting him,' said Fiona.

'Well, he was shooting at Sep, surely Sep's allowed to shoot back.'

'I very much doubt that he's allowed an unauthorized gun to

shoot back with,' said Fiona. 'Anyway, I've got an idea, but we need to make absolutely sure Roscoe hasn't taken a bullet.'

The two women spent the next few minutes closely examining Roscoe's pulped body for a bullet wound but they found nothing. It was a grisly task. The body was twisted and he'd probably sustained many broken bones. His head was bashed open by the fall, but there was no indication that a bullet had entered it or passed through it before it landed on the concrete.

'Could the bullet still be in his head?' asked Winnie, 'or maybe in his innards?'

'I don't know,' said Fiona, turning the gun over in her hands. 'Not if he's been shot with this from down here. They're small but bloody powerful, these guns. If the bullet struck his head it'd go straight through – probably land a mile away. She sat back on her haunches and said, 'I think you're right about the handrail breaking and causing him to fall. So first we need to throw that dog in the canal. We don't want anyone asking who shot it and where's the gun?'

'What if someone asks where it is?'

'Who's going to ask? Not me, Winnie, it's just gone, that's all.'

Between them they dragged the heavy animal to the canal, threw it in and watched it sink beneath the water out of sight. Fiona wiped the gun free of prints and threw it over to the far side of the canal.

'Greasy fingerprints can survive in water,' she explained to Winnie.

'Why would Sep have greasy fingers?'

'Who knows what he might have put his hands in while he was grovelling about around here.'

'Good job you know your stuff.'

'It was just a precaution – probably unnecessary. The story is that, as far as we know, the only person with a gun was Roscoe Briggs. It'll be around somewhere. She looked upwards. 'Maybe still up there. Wherever it is we just leave it to my colleagues to find. Oh, Sep's got some bullets in his pocket we need to get rid of them as well.'

Winnie was throwing the bullets into the canal when they heard the sound of an ambulance siren. Fiona ran to meet it. Winnie went back to Sep and knelt beside him, stroking his head, having now regained some of her composure. This man needed her to be cheerful and optimistic not miserable.

'You're going to be all right, Sep. How long since all this happened?'

'Dunno . . . a while.'

'So, why did you leave it so late before you rang Fiona?'

'My phone was flat . . . Heard his phone ringing . . . Thought it was ice-cream man.'

'Ice-cream man?'

'Wasn't an ice-cream man. I thought it might be a phone ringing . . . Crawled over here.'

Winnie took a while to understand what he'd said, then she nodded.

'So it wasn't an ice-cream man, just a ringtone? What was it, "Greensleeves"? It's always bloody "Greensleeves" with ice-cream vans.'

'It was in his pocket . . . ringing,' Sep said.

'You did well to remember Fiona's number. Why didn't you ring me?'

'Couldn't remember your number.'

Winnie thought a little banter might not go amiss. 'Oh, you remember Fiona's number but not mine?'

Sep's voice was little more than a croak but he managed to protest. 'My leg hurts . . . I'm frozen silly . . . Don't need a . . . b-bollocking!' He paused for a breath and added, 'I thought – thought I'd had it, 'specially when he shot me.'

'Yeah, I can imagine how you'd think that. Anyway I think we got to you in time. The ambulance is here.'

'So I'm not going to die, then?'

'Not if you don't want to.'

Winnie tried to put as much conviction as she could into her answer, but she couldn't even convince herself that he was going to survive. He looked like death warmed up. What the hell did she know?

'No,' he said, 'I don't want to die today.'

'Sep,' said Fiona who had come to his side ahead of the ambulance crew. She spoke earnestly and into his ear so that he would hear every word. 'It's important that you remember this. Are you listening?'

'Yeah,' he wheezed.

'Right, we've got rid of the dead dog and your gun and the ammo in your pocket. We can't find any new bullet wound in

Roscoe. I repeat, *we can't find a fresh bullet wound in Roscoe*, so you didn't shoot him; he just fell. That's your story.'

'Didn't shoot him . . .' repeated Sep. 'He just fell.'

'That's it. Sep, your story is that he just fell. The handrail broke when he was shooting at you. You didn't bring a gun. I repeat, you *did not* bring a gun. Can you remember this? He was shooting at you and you saw him fall.'

Sep nodded his head, closed his eyes as he took all this in. Despite his pain and dizziness he saw the value in what she said.

'I didn't . . . bring gun . . . He shot me . . . fell.'

Fiona nodded. 'Yes, please keep that in mind. That's the story. It'll save a lot of trouble in the long run. I imagine you'll be in trouble enough with the story you're giving, but you did catch Roscoe, which has got to be in your favour.'

'Just do as you're told for once, Sep,' said Winnie who had been nodding in approval at this conversation. The ambulance crew arrived, fitted a neck brace to him, wrapped him in a blanket, loaded him onto a stretcher and carried him to the ambulance.

'Do you want to come with him?' asked a paramedic of Winnie.

She hesitated. She didn't know how she'd cope if she was there when he died. Fiona understood this, from both sides.

'Winnie, he'll want you with him. It'll help him.'

'Of course I'll go with him.'

'Are you with the police?' asked the paramedic.

'Sort of . . . yes.'

'The other man's dead, I'm afraid. There'll be another ambulance coming to take him.'

Winnie didn't take her eyes off the white face of her lover during the fifteen-minute ambulance ride with blues and twos flashing and blaring and creating a clear path for the driver to put her foot down.

The paramedic tending to Sep half turned to Winnie. 'We've got Mad Angela driving. She'll have us there in no time. She used to drive Formula One, but Ferrari kicked her out for speeding.'

Winnie gave his joke a bleak smile and asked, 'How's he doing?'

'He needs stabilizing as soon as possible.'

The ambulance skidded to a halt outside A&E at St James's hospital and within seconds Sep was being wheeled inside by the paramedic and Mad Angela, who pushed a trolley with the same urgency as she drove an ambulance. Winnie was running to keep up as the paramedic called out the baseline observations: 'This is Septimus Black, forty-eight; police officer; shot in the right femur; pulse – ninety-eight; blood pressure – one ten over seventy-five; GCS – eight.'

'He was bitten by a dog,' added Winnie.

'Yeah, dog bite as well,' confirmed the paramedic.

A doctor called out, 'We have a theatre ready and waiting for him. Follow the porter and take him straight through. Mr Griffin's already scrubbed up and waiting for him with a full team.'

Winnie stopped in her tracks as the trolley was pushed away from her. The urgency and efficiency with which the medics were treating this scared her. If experienced professionals who dealt with death night and day were worried, what chance did Sep have? She sat down on a lone chair in a corridor and tried to stem the flood of tears and control the awful sickness in her stomach.

She knew all she had to do was ask where they'd taken Sep and she'd be taken to wait outside the theatre, but that was not where she wanted to be. What she wanted was to be out of this bloody awful existence she had with him, never knowing if he was going to live another day. After sitting there for a while she got to her feet and went home where she had a bottle of illicit sleeping tablets she kept to take care of the extreme emergency which she had always suspected might arise, such was her life. In the end, she took just three and cried herself to sleep.

It was the ringing of her house phone that woke her up the following morning. She looked at the bedside clock and at her bottle of sleeping tablets. She'd taken enough to knock her out but not kill her. She wasn't ready for that, yet. Although she might be if she picked that bloody phone up. Before she left she'd given the hospital her landline phone number to keep her advised of Sep's situation and she knew they would only ring her if the worst happened. It was a number which very few people had; she almost always used her mobile. She glared at the phone with fear and hatred, swearing at it.

'Oh, shut the fuck up! I'm not answering. I know it's happened.'

The ringing stopped and a few minutes later her mobile rang. She knew this wasn't the hospital. They didn't have this number.

'Hello?'

'Hello, is that Winnie?'

She didn't recognize the voice. It sounded male and juvenile.

'It is, yes. Who's that?'

'It's me . . . Adam Piper. I'm ringing because of what happened to Mr Black.'

Oh God, she thought. *Adam will know the worst . . . or was it the best?*

'What about him?'

'It was on the television news that he'd been shot and I wondered how he was, because if he was dead me and Simeon have nothing to worry about.'

'*What*?' Winnie screamed the word down the phone. 'You stupid bastard! What do you want him dead for?'

'Because he's the one who knows about me and Simeon.'

'What does he know about you?'

'He knows about Snowball. Why was it on the news? Is he famous or something?'

'In his own way, yes. But he's famous for being a good man, not a dead one.'

'Oh, I'm very sorry for saying I want him to be dead. Anyway, he isn't dead; he's alive.'

He sounded as if he'd somehow regressed into a former existence which wasn't quite of this world.

'Alive? Are you absolutely sure?'

'Yes, I am very sure. You can ring the hospital if you don't believe me.'

'Did you say you were Adam?'

'I am, yes. Adam Piper.'

'Oh, you sounded like Simeon.'

'That's because we're brothers. I would like to come and see you.'

'What about?'

'Me and Simeon are scared and we'd like to get away from here and I don't know how.'

'How did you get here in the first place?'

'Mr Santiago helped us to come and work for him, but he's dead now.'

'Adam, did you say you were scared because Sep knew about Snowball?'

'Yes, I'm sorry for saying that.'

'Why would that scare you? Was Snowball your idea?'

'It was, yes. Can I come and see you?'

'Oh right. OK, why not? Do you know where I live?'

'I do, yes.'

She didn't bother asking him how he knew. His thought process was a mystery to her.

'Can you be here in two hours?'

'Yes, I can. Shall I bring Simeon?'

'No, just come on your own.'

'I'll be there in two hours from now.'

'I've no doubt you will,' she murmured, looking at the clock – three minutes past eight. After five minutes of pacing up and down her mobile rang again. The screen told her it was Adam ringing back.

'Yes, Adam?'

'I rang the hospital and asked how Mr Black was doing. I told them I was his brother, because they don't tell you if you're not his brother. Is that all right?'

'Er, I suppose so . . .' She hesitated for a while, before asking, 'How is he?'

Adam took a while to answer as he collected his thoughts. His hesitation told Winnie it was bad news.

'For God's sake, Adam! Spit it out!'

'He's been . . .' He paused as he tried to remember the word. '. . . Stabilized.'

'Stabilized? So he's alive.'

'Do you have to be alive to be stabilized?'

'You do, Adam. Sorry to disappoint you.'

'I'm not sorry. I'm very glad because it makes you glad.'

'It does, Adam. Very glad indeed.'

'I will see you at three minutes after ten o'clock.'

THIRTY

Sep's journey to the hospital had been a time of intermittent consciousness, mainly due to the pain-killing injection he'd been given. He was operated on with the alacrity befitting a senior policeman seriously injured on duty. When he awoke in a recovery ward he was told by a nurse that the operation had been a success and that his femur had been broken by the bullet on its way through his leg but it had been fixed with a metal pin that he'd be wearing for all his days, which was OK by Sep, who was just glad to be alive.

'It's not the only . . . piece of metal holding me together.' His voice was raspy but his mental faculties were returning.

'So we've noticed. You're apparently held together like a Meccano man. How are you feeling?'

'Woozy . . . like . . . like I'm drunk.'

'That's the anaesthetic wearing off, but you're hooked up to a morphine drip.'

She handed him a small plastic gadget with a red button on it. 'Whenever the pain gets too much just click the button and it'll give you a small booster dose.'

Sep took it and clicked it twice.

'I said when the pain gets too much. There's a timer on it limiting you to no more than one click every five minutes. We don't want you overdosing. Do you understand?'

'I was just trying it out.'

'Right, a porter will take you on to a ward. Are you up to having visitors? I believe one of your colleagues would like a word. First you need to get some rest. You should be OK in three or four hours or so. It's half past six now so I'll tell her half past ten, shall I?'

'It's a woman, is it? Did she give her name?'

'I believe she said her name was Hawkins. Do you want to see her?'

'Not really, but I might as well get it over with.'

'I gather you found out where Briggs was from Stanley Butterbowl. Why didn't you call this in?' said Hawkins.

Her manner was a little brusque but not too unfriendly. Sep thought he might be getting away with a reprimand and possible loss of seniority. This was perfectly OK by him, in fact, after his ordeal. Just being alive was OK by him; he'd only be back to where he was before Wood lost his marbles. During his three-hour recuperation he managed to remember Fiona's pep talk about him not saying he'd gone armed and that Roscoe had no fresh bullet wound, he'd just fallen. He also managed to get the rest of his story straight.

'If I'd called it in it would have delayed matters and I thought I needed to get to him straight away before he took off. I thought I could take him on my own. Didn't count on him being armed.'

'Well, he was armed as you now know. We're having ballistics check it out right now. What did you promise Butterbowl for the information on Roscoe?'

'A lot of time off his sentence for being cooperative.'

'Not every villain believes these lies of yours, Sep.'

'I know – shame, that.'

'Maybe you've lost your touch.'

'I'd like you to cut to the chase, ma'am, and tell me what's going to happen to me.'

'You're to be given a written warning as to your conduct and hope it keeps you on your toes if you want to stay with us.'

'No loss of rank?'

'That's not what I'm recommending, more fool me. Next time I'll recommend you to be bumped right down to sergeant. Assuming you do stay on, where do you want to work?'

'I'd like to work with you, no matter what rank I am.'

'You want to stay with the Cold Case Unit?'

'I do, yes.'

'I see.'

Hawkins walked away from Sep's bed, deep in thought, looked out of the window at the rooftops of Leeds, then returned to his side. 'Look,' she said, 'I'm of the opinion that Roscoe Briggs might well have been the one to have killed Charlie Santiago, on Redman's orders.'

'It's not a bad opinion, ma'am. He was certainly one of Redman's hitmen and he was all for killing me just for fun. I think the world's a better place without him in it.'

'And we apparently have a rusty handrail to thank for that . . . do we?'

There was a challenge in her last two words. Their eyes met; hers with the challenge in them, his with well-practised innocence.

'You tell me, ma'am. I've no doubt you've established the cause of his death. He must have been leaning on the rail looking to see where I'd got to. After he shot me I crawled behind a two-foot-high wall. I was in bad shape down there. That broken handrail saved my life, no doubt about that.'

'Yes, that's pretty much our forensic conclusion, although the rain washed a lot of stuff away. After that, you managed to get yourself over to Briggs's body and use his phone. How did you know he had a phone?'

'Well, mine was dead. I heard his ringing and I needed someone to know where I was.'

'*We'd* have known where you were, had you bloody well told us where you were going!'

'True, and that's a mistake I'll never make again. There's no bollocking you can give me that's worse than the one I gave myself back there.'

'And yet you asked DS Burnside to come on her own without alerting any of her colleagues.'

'Did I? Back there I certainly really wasn't thinking straight. If I told Burnside to come on her own, it was my responsibility, ma'am, as her senior officer.'

'There's a limit to how much I believe to be down to your disturbed mind, Sep. Personally, I believe you told her to come on her own so that she might help you cover up your stupidity.'

'Possibly, but she *didn't* cover it up, did she?'

'No, she notified me and I told her to get straight out to you, but I notice she picked up your fiancée on the way.'

'Yes, I remember asking her to do that as well. You see, I was fairly certain that I was going to die and I thought it only right to say goodbye to Winnie.'

'How very polite of you, but you don't die from a leg wound, Sep.'

'You do if the bullet clips the femoral artery. On top of which, I thought I might be dying of hypothermia and I did lose about half a gallon of blood. I'm told was on the verge of bleeding out and that I was suffering from something called hypovolemic shock, which is what happens with major blood loss. It affects a man's thinking, so I can't be held responsible for my actions at that time. The ambulance got me here for a transfusion in the nick of time. A few minutes later and I'd have been a goner.'

'Hypovolemic shock, eh? That's a real beauty, Sep. I must write that down so that I remember it the next time you try and use it on me. For now, it might well justify me recommending that you're not reduced in rank.'

'Who told you she's my fiancée?'

'She did.'

'Oh. I was hoping she might keep that quiet, with me being a copper.'

'I imagine there's a lot of people in your life keeping quiet about you, Sep.' She stared at him for a long moment and asked, 'So, you think searching for Santiago's killer might well be a waste of police resources, do you?'

It pleased Sep that she thought his opinion was of some worth to her. 'Well,' he said, 'I imagine we're still looking for Graham Feather's killer.'

'We are, but it was Santiago's murder that kicked this whole thing off and we're still no wiser. Us saying it was Roscoe Briggs is no more than convenient guesswork and we're better than that. I mean, throwing victims out of high windows, would that be Briggs's usual MO? That's an act of violence, not cold-hearted killing for money.'

'I've got no idea, ma'am – never heard of him until this thing kicked off, but it'll do no harm to keep Santiago's unresolved death in mind during the Feather enquiry, which, I strongly suspect, is connected with Santiago's case and if a definite lead drops into our lap, to follow it up.'

Hawkins nodded her approval of his thinking. 'You know, Sep, you might do better keeping yourself off the streets and spend more time in the office where we can make better use of your strategic mind. I've heard talk of us being disbanded and we really need a good result to head it off.'

'There's always a lot of bollocks banded around police stations, ma'am.'

'I'm aware of that, Sep, but I'm not sure this is bollocks.'

'I'm not much of an office boy, ma'am. If you're wanting to keep me in the office I'd rather go back into CID. I believe they're short of a DCI right now, with Wood gone.'

'You're a damned nuisance, DI Black! You know that, don't you? I'm sure your fiancée would prefer you to be kept in the office. Where is she, by the way? I expected her to be with you when I got here.'

'I'm wondering where she is myself. You don't think she's left me, do you? Why would she do that?'

'Because you're a hard man to love, Sep. A lot of the time she doesn't know if you're going to live or die. It's too hard for her to take.'

'You think that's it, do you?'

Hawkins nodded. 'Sorry and all that, but I think it might be, Sep.'

THIRTY-ONE

Four weeks went by and Sep hadn't had a visit from Winnie. Fiona had been to see him several times, as had his daughter, Phoebe; but no word from his fiancée. He had a mobile with him and he'd rung her every day but had only got a woman's voice telling him that the number he was ringing was unavailable. Roscoe was out of the way for good, so that was something, but with Winnie also gone for good it took the gloss off everything.

From a purely practical point of view, he would need her help when he was discharged, but he missed her, mainly because she was the only woman he had ever loved and he was desperately worried as to why she'd hadn't rung him.

'The odd thing is that the Piper brothers have disappeared as well,' he told Fiona. 'I wanted to have a word with Adam but the troops can't find either of them. Both them and Winnie are connected in some way to Carl Redman. I hope he's not exerting some sort of influence from beyond the grave. Is there some Mafia Mr Big behind all this that we don't know about?'

'I honestly don't know, Sep, except that the Mafia don't work much in Leeds. Oh, by the way, an estate agent from York's been trying to get hold of you. He's rung the station a couple of times. I told him I'd get you to ring him. I've got his number in my book.'

'If it's the one I'm thinking about, he's the one responsible for the attack on the cottage.'

'Oh, so you don't want to ring him, then?'

'Of course I do. If only to tell him what I think of him. Could you get him for me, please?'

Fiona stabbed in the numbers and handed the phone to Sep.

'Dunhill and Broome?'

'My name is Black I wish to speak to Mr Dunhill please.'

'What is it in connection with, Mr Black?'

'If you tell him it's Detective Inspector Black, he'll know what it's about.'

Dunhill came on the line within seconds. He spoke quickly without giving Sep a chance to berate him.

'I need to apologize to you, Inspector, for giving Wood the location of your cottage. I understand it caused you a heap of trouble.'

'It cost a dear friend of mine his life, Mr Dunhill and it destroyed my cottage.'

'Yes. I understand Mr Wood is in custody right now.'

'Wood will end his life in a secure loony bin, Mr Dunhill! What was it you wanted me for?'

'Oh yes. Well, I might have some good news for you. You see, the land on which your cottage used to be has just been re-designated as residential building land. It's to do with the government saying we need to build more houses.'

'And how is that good news for me? I'm not a builder.'

'No, but I know at least two building companies who would be interested in buying it. With it being next to a main road and all services, it's three hectares of quality building land, just waiting to be developed.'

'Really?' How much is it worth?'

'Well, it would take at least fifty quality homes, so my estimate is around one hundred and fifty thousand, although if I get these two firms bidding against each other it could well be more and if other firms become interested, who knows? Would you like me to handle the sale?'

'Er, yes, I suppose I do.'

'Good, I'll send you details of our terms, which are quite reasonable. Our fee will be 1.5 per cent of the sale price plus costs. Does that sound agreeable?'

'Er, yes, I think so. Yes, go ahead with it. I'll give you my address and bank and solicitor details.'

'That will be excellent, Mr Black. Oh, there is one other thing which I imagine you're well aware of.'

'What's that?'

'The cottage was insured for building and contents and your payments were up to date.'

'How would you know that?'

'Well, we're also insurance agents, Mr Black. We specialize in building insurance with it being connected to our main business.

I arranged the insurance myself as well as the standing order from your bank.'

'Did you? I didn't realize that.'

'No, you were a busy man back then, Mr Black. Anyway, all is in order and if you wish to make a claim, I'll send the forms and help you with the details if you like.'

'Yes, I'd appreciate that. How much is it insured for?'

'Well, back then it wasn't in very good condition so we kept the insured amount down to one hundred thousand buildings insurance and twenty thousand for the contents. I imagine you could put in a claim for those amounts and have it approved without any trouble.'

'Could I really?'

'Yes. If you give me your details I'll send the paperwork through to you and we'll get this started immediately.'

Sep handed the mobile back to Fiona with a frozen look on his face.

'What?' she asked.

'I think my luck's changed. I've just come into a bloody fortune!'

It was during the following week that Sep's mobile buzzed with an incoming call.

'Hello.'

'Sep it's me, Winnie.'

Sep almost screamed her name. 'Winnie! Jesus, Winnie! I'm really glad to hear from you. I was beginning to think the bad guys had got to you.'

'What bad guys?'

'Oh, I don't know. Both you and the Piper brothers disappear off the face of the Earth. What the hell was I to think?'

'I'm sorry if I've worried you Sep, but if I have, it's no worse than the worry you've caused me.'

'What are you saying, Winnie?'

There was a long pause, then, 'Sep, I'm saying I can't marry you and live like this, never knowing if someone's going to hurt you or even kill you. Your lifestyle's too much for me to cope with. I'm really sorry but I've left you for good, Sep.'

'Left me for good? Bloody hell, Winnie! I'm in hospital with a leg that won't be better for weeks and no end of other problems.'

'Yes, I know you need someone, Sep, but that someone can't be me. I love you too much and I couldn't bear to be around when bad news comes through about you, which it will one day. This last thing really shook me, seeing you half-dead out there in that awful place. And don't tell me you're giving it all up for me, Sep. I know you can't. It's in your blood. It's what makes you tick.'

'Where are you now?'

'I'm ringing from New Jersey.'

Sep only caught the last of that. 'The Channel Islands? Whereabouts in Jersey? St Helier?'

'No, *New* Jersey, It's next door to New York in America. I'm with the Piper boys.'

'What? You're in America? Bloody hell, Winnie! What're you doing over there? If the Mafia find out about this Snowball racket, you three are toast. How come you haven't gone to Auntie Maude's in New Zealand?'

'I came with the Piper brothers, Sep. I'm kind of looking after them and they need some looking after, I can tell you. Adam's got his old job back so he's OK, but Simeon doesn't know his arse from his elbow at times. When Adam got picked up for drunk driving, he thought he'd had it, especially with you interviewing him. Was it your doing that he was let go?'

'Not really, but I didn't object to him being released, if that's what you mean.'

'Well, thanks for that on his behalf.'

'What are you doing for money?' he asked her. 'Living off their ill-gotten gains?'

There was an angry silence that told Sep he'd maybe gone too far, accusing her of this.

'No I'm not, Sep,' she said, quietly. 'As a matter of fact I brought a lot of money with me. Got a loan against my house, which is up for sale and I've sold my business. I don't need to live on anyone's ill-gotten gains!'

'Well, you didn't do that overnight. You must have been planning this for a while!'

Then he realized that he was still on the offensive against this woman he loved. 'OK, sorry I'm having a go at you. You can do what you like with your stuff. None of my business. Although I'm curious as to who would buy your business. Are they aware of who your suppliers are?'

'He's actually my main supplier. He's been buying shops to cut out the middlemen.'

'It also makes him more high profile with the police and customs people,' Sep commented. 'Not having a middleman has certain disadvantages, I'd have thought.'

'I agree, Sep, but he's bought it and paid my asking price.'

'And the goods will still come from Naples, will they?'

'Sep, if you're asking this so you can nail him and I hear about it, you'll also put the final nail in our particular coffin.'

'Really? I thought that was already nailed shut.'

'I just said your way of life's too much for me to handle – right now.'

'So, there's hope for us yet, is there?'

'Oh, I don't know, Sep, but I love you too much to rule it out completely. Look, I've been planning on cashing in my assets for a while, but I wasn't planning on leaving you until that last awful business. It shook me up more than you'll ever know, Sep. It was a hell of a wake-up call.'

'And for me.'

'But that's just it, Sep – it probably wasn't a wake-up call for you. I wish it had been. It's just the way things have panned out. The boys aren't short of money either. Truth is, they've got this scam of theirs working over here.'

'Like I said, if the Mafia find out about that you'll all be toast.'

'The Mafia's practically out of business over here, Sep.' There was no reply, so she continued: 'Adam thinks you can't do anything without knowledge and proof, neither of which you've got and even then, if this became public you'd cause a major financial panic in the stock market.'

'He's too clever for his own good is that lad.'

'Nails in coffins, Sep! Leave well alone! Anyway, one of the reasons I'm ringing you is to tell you about Santiago and who killed him.'

'What?'

'I know you still don't know who killed Santiago.'

'We have a good idea.'

'Come on, Sep, you don't have a clue. All you have is guess-work, which means you haven't charged anyone. Tell you what, I'll do a deal. You leave the boys alone and I'll tell you how Santiago died.'

'I know how he died. He fell out of a high window.'

'I know but did he jump or was he pushed?'

'How would you know that?'

'Do we have a deal?'

'Oh, go on then.'

'No come back from you, for me or the boys?'

'You have my word.'

'Thanks, goodbye, Sep. I'll tell you the story when I'm good and ready.'

'When will that—?'

The phone buzzed to tell him she'd gone. He stared at it for a full minute, then he smiled, ruefully, as he realized that she had every right to leave him. He wasn't fit to be a husband to anyone, the way he disregarded his own safety. He thought back a few weeks to his ordeal in the old foundry compound and how he'd cursed himself for his stupidity, a stupidity that had ended with him lying there with a shattered leg and no hope of survival – until he heard the ice-cream van. Jane Hawkins's suggestion that he spend more time in the office might not be a bad idea. He brought up Winnie's number on the screen and made sure he had the right number on his list. One day, when he was ready, maybe he'd contact her and bring her home. That's if she hadn't taken up with someone else – someone who made her happy. That very thought sickened him. Was he able to make *any* woman happy?

A nurse came to take his temperature and blood pressure.

'My blood pressure might be a bit on the high side,' he told her. 'My fiancée has just left me and gone off to America. Why do women do such things to me?'

'I don't know, Mr Black, but I do know it's good news about your leg. The surgeon is of the opinion that you'll make a full recovery within six weeks and that you can be discharged from here in a couple of weeks or so.'

Mrs Boswell arrived at Sep's bedside as he was settling under the covers.

'Oh hello.'

'Hello, Sep. I just heard about you being shot and wondered how you were going on.'

'Heard about me? Who from?'

'It was on the television news the night it happened. I haven't heard anything since.'

'The Home Secretary put a D-notice on the story.'

'Because of the money market connection?'

'What else? It certainly wasn't for my benefit.'

'Well, my James had many contacts, including quite a few police people. They keep me up to date with events.'

'Ah, say no more. I've more or less recovered from my operation and I'm now convalescing, but I've just been assured of a full recovery if I do as I'm told.'

She grinned. 'So, no absolute certainty of a full recovery then?'

Sep grinned back at this woman who hardly knew him, but enough to take the piss. He was a man with a serious job. Why didn't people take him more seriously?

'I heard you'd got engaged to Winnie as well,' she said.

'Good God! Who have you been talking to?'

'I cannot reveal my sources.'

'And has your source told you my engagement is off as of ten minutes ago?'

'Oh, sorry to hear that. Look, I've come because I know you like Jaguar sports cars.'

'I really liked the one that got blown up. Mind you, I'm happy I wasn't in it at the time.'

'I saw it when you came to see me. It was a beauty and I know where there's one for sale just like it. Same colour, one year old.'

'How much?'

'They're asking fifty-six and a half thousand. It's only done fifteen thousand miles and it's still under warranty. I know the man at the dealers and I've already agreed fifty grand cash with them. All I have to do is buy it in your name.'

'And it's red, is it? Convertible?'

'Yes, same red as yours.'

The very thought of it perked up Sep's spirit. 'You couldn't take a photo of it. Could you?'

'I've got one on my tablet, plus all its details, horse power and all that stuff. It looks brand new to me, not a mark on it, new tyres, beautiful upholstery, satnav, everything.'

She took a tablet out of her bag and showed him various photographs of the car as well as a sales sheet from the dealer giving all the car's details. It was identical to the car he'd had, only this was a newer model and with far fewer miles on the clock. His despair at the loss of Winnie lessened slightly as he studied the pictures.

'And you can get this for the fifty, can you?'

'I can. All you have to do is say the word. I can keep it in my garage under a cover until you're fit to drive it.'

'Best give you the cheque back then. My wallet's in the drawer.'

As Sep gave her the cheque, he commented, 'In the space of ten minutes I've lost fifty grand and a fiancée, but I've gained a car.'

'Would you rather have Winnie back and not have the car?'

'In a heartbeat, but this helps.'

'Right, I'll be on my way back to the dealers then and do the deal. I'll bring you all the papers in the morning.'

'By the way, I'm not quite as skint as I thought I was.'

'Really?'

'Yes. The cottage that was blown up has some value, or rather the land it was on has. It's up for sale and, to be honest, taking your money was always a dangerous move on my part. It might well have ended my career.'

'I wouldn't have wanted that, Sep, although I don't think Winnie would have minded. No one would ever have found out from me. I'd prefer it if you kept the fifty grand. If not, I could give it to Winnie.'

Sep gave her words some thought and said, 'You know, as part of all this trouble, a good friend of mine was killed. He was an old reprobate but a good man at heart. Winnie really took to him. His name was Eli McMurphy. Winnie and I went to his funeral and a bloke turned up who claimed to be Eli's son.'

'*Claimed* to be? You sound as if you doubted him. Why would he pretend to be the son of a reprobate, unless he thought Eli had left some money behind?'

'No, Eli left nothing. To be honest he had a look of Eli so I believed him. In fact he brought his own son with him who would have been Eli's grandson, although he'd never met his grandfather. The lad's at university right now, no doubt struggling for money.'

'You want me to give the fifty grand to the grandson?'

'Not to him, to his dad. He'll make sure it does the lad a power of good. Winnie's not exactly short of money so she won't object.'

Mrs Boswell held out a hand. 'OK, Mr Black, you have a deal.

When you give me the fifty grand back I'll pass it straight on to Elijah McMurphy's son.'

'That would please Elijah no end. It'll please Winnie as well. By the way, are you still a journalist?'

'Sort of. I haven't officially given it up.'

'I seem to remember you saying you'd like to finish the story that James was working on.'

'I would, yes.'

'Well, I'm very near getting the whole story if you want it. When I'm ready I'll fill you in with all the details.'

'That would be great.'

As he watched her leave, Sep realized that what he really needed was Winnie O'Toole, but that Jag, now that was definitely acceptable. All legally paid for by him.

THIRTY-TWO

The following week Hawkins paid him a second visit. 'How are you doing, Sep?'

'Well, I think I'm wheelchair capable, ma'am, if only I could get someone to bring me a wheelchair.'

'And where would you go in this chair?'

'Is Stanley Butterbowl still in this hospital?'

'Yes, he is, but he's due to be moved over on to the Armley Prison hospital wing any day now.'

'In that case, it's him I'd like to visit and I'd like you to come with me.'

'Why?'

'Because in this case there's only one unresolved murder and that's the murder of Graham Feather and I think I know who killed him and why.'

'In my book, Sep, there are two unresolved murders: Santiago's and Feather's. Is there something about the Santiago case that you're not telling me?'

Sep looked up at her and said, 'There's nothing I'm not telling you. It just strikes me that the people with all the answers might all be dead.'

'Well, it's a strong possibility. We're talking about Santiago himself, James Boswell, Carl Redman, Graham Feather . . .'

'And Roscoe Briggs,' added Sep. 'And two more of Redman's heavies – Bazza and Animal; and my pal Elijah and the old woman from the Grimshawe hotel. How many's that?'

'Nine,' said Hawkins. 'Nine people dead, all connected and we still don't know who's behind it all. We can't just leave it at that and hope the main culprit's dead or all these cases will remain on file, which will do our unit no good at all. I don't want us to be disbanded. I like the work we're doing and I think we're good at it. Success in these cases will prove that beyond all doubt.'

'I'm with you on all that,' said Sep. 'And I want to know how I came to end up in this state. Car blown up, Winnie's left me and I don't know if I'll be able to walk properly again.'

He paused for thought and then asked her, 'How much do you know about Snowball, ma'am?'

'I know it was a stocks and shares scam that never got off the ground.'

'I tend to think it has an American connection, ma'am. The connection being Adam Piper who's a computer genius and who once worked at the New York Stock Exchange, servicing their computers, and then he came over here to work for Santiago.'

'That's a fairly weak connection.'

'It's the only connection I've got,' said Sep.

'And am I right in thinking that the Piper brothers are back in America?'

'They are, along with Winnie.'

'Well, if we notify the NYPD of our suspicions, it might well get Winnie into serious trouble, which could possibly result in her arrest as an undesirable alien. They're very fussy about such things, are the Yanks.'

'I wouldn't want that, ma'am.'

'I assume you still have hopes of a reconciliation.'

'Er . . . yes.'

She stared down at him with narrowed eyes. 'Quite. If this is now an American scam and it's dead in the water over here, perhaps we could let America deal with it with no interference from us. Nonetheless, while you've been in here, the Home Office have ordered us to tread carefully. I understand it might cause a panic in the stock market if it all becomes public knowledge that such a thing is even possible. Not that I know what this "thing" is. Right now I'm interested in the Feather killing.'

'Ah, well, that might be more doable. In fact, if you could get me a wheelchair and take me to see Stanley Butterbowl, we might be able to solve that case.'

Within minutes Hawkins was pushing Sep along a corridor and into a lift that would take them to Butterbowl's ward. When he got there Butterbowl was dozing.

'Wakey, wakey, Stanley!' called out Sep. 'I've brought my boss to see you.'

Butterbowl opened his eyes and sat up, looking at Sep. 'Oh, shit! Are you still alive? Yer've just ruined me fuckin' day!'

'Your mate Roscoe tried to shoot me, Stanley, but he got himself killed doing it. You see, he probably thought I was lying when I said I could get him a reduced sentence. I reckon you thought I was lying as well which is why you told him I was going after him.'

'I did no such thing.'

'Stanley, we found your mobile phone and checked the calls which included one to Roscoe just after I left you.'

'Well, I know you were fuckin' lying about me sentence.'

'Just watch your language in front of the lady, Stanley. We're here to do you a favour but we want one in return. And it's not a favour that'll do anyone any harm. No one who's alive that is.'

'What's this favour and what do I get?'

'Well, this lady is Detective Superintendent Hawkins, Stanley. A very senior officer in the West Yorkshire Police Force and she's not allowed to lie to scumbags like yourself.'

Jane Hawkins held out her warrant card to verify what Sep had just said.

'OK, she's a top copper, so what?'

'So I just want you to verify what I know already. That's all.'

'What is it you know?'

'We know that a man called Graham Feather used to work for Santiago and he got banged up for something he didn't do and this was all down to Santiago setting him up for it. Do you know about that?'

'Yeah, I knew all about that.'

'So it was true.'

'Course it was.'

'And you knew that Feather had a grudge against Santiago?'

'Yer mean about him bein' banged up? I do, yeah.'

'Have you heard of a scam called Snowball?'

'Yer mean that stocks and shares thing? Yeah, I heard of it. No idea how it works, though.'

'And did you know that Feather had found out about it from the Piper brothers, most probably so he could use it to do damage to Santiago. This was before Santiago was killed.'

'Yeah and I heard that Redman were very pissed off that Feather knew about it.'

'Why would he be pissed off?' Sep asked.

'Because them Piper lads knew how ter work it and Redman didn't and after Santiago died, if they hitched up with Feather, who knew the stocks an' shares side of stuff, they could run the whole scam between the three of them and leave Redman out of it. Redman told me that himself. He reckoned it were Feather what killed Santiago.'

'So what did Redman do?'

'He were very pissed off. I think you know what he did.'

'I do know, but I want you to tell me. I don't want to put any words into your mouth. I want the superintendent to hear the truth.'

'He put out a hit on Feather for three grand.'

'Who took the job?'

Butterbowl looked up at Hawkins. 'Not me. Yer not layin' that one on me.'

'We know it wasn't you, Stanley,' said Sep. 'We want you to tell us who earned the three grand.'

'It were Roscoe, who d'yer think it was?'

'Are you saying Roscoe Briggs murdered Graham Feather?'

'Jesus Christ, Yeah! Roscoe Briggs killed Graham Feather. Do I have ter spell it out for yer?'

'No, we think it was Roscoe Briggs as well,' said Sep.

'If you could make that statement in an affidavit to the CPS and perhaps in court,' said Hawkins, 'I will see to it that your cooperation is taken into consideration at your sentencing.'

'If it helps me. Why wouldn't I?'

'No reason at all. Roscoe's dead,' said Sep. 'You can't harm a dead man by telling the truth about him. On top of which the strangulation marks on Feather's neck match Roscoe's hands and the murder scene's got Roscoe's DNA all over it.'

'Bloody hell! It took yer long enough ter figure that out.'

'That's because I wasn't working on it back then,' retorted Sep.

'You know he'll get life, no matter what I say on his behalf,' Hawkins said to Sep as she wheeled him back.

'I do, but it might get him a shorter tariff. They might let him out after forty years.'

'I will speak on his behalf as I promised, but I don't intend being all that persuasive. That's a loathsome man who should never be let loose on the streets again.'

'Agreed.'

Hawkins now wheeled Sep back to his bed in silence as she mulled over what she'd just heard and added it to the complexity of crimes that had revolved around Charlie Santiago's death. She summed up the cases so far: 'So, we have the death of Charles Santiago and the death of James Boswell, both unsolved. Whoever killed Boswell killed the old woman, Agnes . . . whatever-her-other-name-is, we'll have it on file. Graham Feather was killed by Roscoe Briggs on the order of Carl Redman. That's four murders, one resolved and two offenders still at large.

'I suggest we leave Santiago's death in abeyance for the time being and concentrate on catching James Boswell's killer,' said Sep, before adding, 'There is one other murder we haven't mentioned, ma'am.'

'Oh?'

'Elijah McMurphy who was killed at my cottage.'

'Well, that will be put down to Redman and his thugs. That's five murders and just one solved.'

'On the other hand,' suggested Sep, 'you could stick with your previous theory that Roscoe killed Santiago on Redman's orders. That's two murders solved. Good for the unit, that.'

'On what evidence?'

'Just the balance of probabilities. Roscoe Briggs is dead and he's the hot favourite and you can't take a life from a man who hasn't got one to give.'

'For once I agree with you. We could stick to Roscoe Briggs being Santiago's killer on balance of probability. By the way, have you given any further thought to your taking a desk job from now on? I suspect that would please your friend Winnie.'

'I'm not too sure, ma'am. The only thing that would win her

back for sure is for me not to be a copper anymore and to get myself a safer job – maybe as an English teacher somewhere.'

'And you value your job above all things?'

'A copper is exactly who I am, ma'am. If having her back meant me not being an active copper any more, it would put a strain on our relationship. I'd probably resent the price I'd be paying. Up until now she's always accepted what I am and who I am, as I've accepted who and what she is.'

'If she doesn't come back to you, will it be a problem you can't cope with?'

'I wouldn't know how to deal with it, ma'am. I've never been in this situation before.'

'What, never been in love?'

'Not until now.'

'Not even with your ex-wife?'

'Knowing how I feel about Winnie, I know for certain I never loved my ex-wife, nor any other woman for that matter.'

'Well, if Winnie's your one and only, of course you'll miss her. It's a horrible feeling. I had a dose of that once.'

'Yes, it is. It's bloody horrible. I could really do without it. How did you deal with it? Did you get over it?'

'No.'

'Oh.'

Sep felt oddly proud that she'd taken him into her confidence over such a delicate matter. 'Are you saying I should go after Winnie no matter what the cost to me?'

'Sep, if the cost to you is staying in the office I'd say it's a small price to pay for getting yourself the right person to spend your life with – especially at your age.' Hawkins got to her feet, looking pensive. Sep looked up at her, expecting some further comment, perhaps some advice. It was this:

'You're a resourceful and impressive man in many ways, Sep. I know I moan about you and I probably always will, but you're a one-man army and I'm lucky to have you on my team.'

'Hang on!' Sep exclaimed. 'You've missed my ward – just gone past it.'

'No, I haven't. You've been moved to a private room for the rest of your stay in here, which won't be long, I'm pleased to say.'

'Who's paying for this?'

'The West Yorkshire Police, on my recommendation.'

'Why are you spoiling me all of a sudden?'

'I'm not spoiling you.'

She opened the door to a spacious room with one bed and pushed him through. 'We need the privacy of this room for a meeting we're arranging.'

'A meeting? In here? To do with work is it?'

'Of course. Do you have some objection?'

'Not really. Who's coming?'

'Well, the two of us and, given our conversation, Stanley Butterbowl.'

'Will Gibbs be coming?'

'No, I need to be the senior officer at this meeting and responsible to no one present. This is why there won't be a solicitor present. Apart from the witnesses there'll be just three coppers: me, you and Sergeant Burnside, who seems to know quite a bit about it.'

'It would really help,' said Sep, 'if we could get Winnie and the Pipers over from America.'

'I agree,' said Hawkins. 'I'm trying to keep the meeting down to a minimum, but there'll also be Butterbowl and Julie Rogerson making statements. I make that eight altogether. Where is Mrs Rogerson, by the way?'

'She'll be at home. She isn't being held on remand on our recommendation.'

'And you want this Mrs Rogerson to come to the meeting, as well as Winnie O'Toole and the Pipers?'

'That sounds about right,' said Sep. 'With that lot all in one place I think we could clear the whole lot up.'

'I wish I could say "I see", but I don't see. How do you propose we get Winnie and the Pipers back?'

'You get them immunity and leave the rest to me.'

Hawkins looked at him and shook her head, amazed at his self-confidence. Sep heaved himself out of the wheelchair and on to the bed where he settled himself down on top of the covers and looked around the room.

'Oh yes! I like it in here.'

'They'll be bringing your clothes and stuff through from the ward.'

'I get a telly as well, do I?'

'I believe you have to pay through the nose for it.'

'I suggest,' said Sep, 'that we make this meeting for one week's time, to give Winnie and the Pipers time to get back and to give you time to get their immunities approved.'

'OK, Sep, I'm going along with you on all this, but if things go wrong with Winnie and the Pipers I'll be down on you like a ton of bloody bricks!'

'You can trust me, boss.'

This had her smiling as she left him staring at his pot leg which was pristine white and hadn't been decorated with a single signature. Long ago, there had been a time when it wouldn't have a square inch free of names and rude comments. Could a person's worth be measured by the number and quality of comments they collect on their broken and plastered limbs? If so, he wasn't worth much. With his visitor gone, a nurse came to take his readings, which were to her satisfaction.

'And how are you today, Mr Black? Any problems?'

'Just one that's causing me grief.'

'Just the one problem, eh? I'm guessing it's to do with a woman.'

'Yeah. It's a win or lose situation . . . not easy.'

'Yes, it is. If she's worth keeping, you let her win. That's what my husband always does and I make damned sure he doesn't lose in the long run.'

Once again he was left alone staring at his pristine white leg, hoping that he'd be able to persuade Winnie to come back. He had a plan but it wasn't foolproof. He looked around the room and pictured it in a week's time with everybody there. He wondered where Winnie would be sitting, or would she be standing, looking down at him, thinking what a pathetic bastard he was? There was a lot hanging on this meeting.

THIRTY-THREE

It was almost ten o'clock and Sep was ready with a sheaf of notes, most of which he'd memorized. He was sitting in a bedside chair with his right leg resting on a stool. Not wishing to feel at a disadvantage by wearing a hospital gown as such a gathering, he was washed and shaved, hair neatly cut and in his best suit, wearing a regimental tie.

What he wasn't sure of was who exactly was coming. He'd have been more than happy if only one person had turned up, provided that person was Winnie O'Toole. He'd spoken to her on the phone to persuade her to come but she hadn't been exactly definite as to whether she'd turn up or not, nor whether she'd bring the Pipers. Since then he'd heard nothing.

Needless to say, Jane Hawkins was the first to arrive, closely followed by Julie and Fiona. The three of them struck up a meaningless conversation about the excellent hospital facilities as Sep looked at his notes. After a while Stanley Butterbowl arrived, with a uniformed constable pushing his wheelchair. He was unshaven and had an obnoxious look on his face as if he'd been brought into court to do something against his will.

Sep's ears were attuned to approaching footsteps. At exactly the appointed time, he heard them. The door opened and in came Adam and Simeon Piper, who closed the door behind him.

'Is Winnie with you?' asked Sep.

Simeon gave a blank look and said, 'We don't know, do we, Adam?'

Sep looked at Hawkins. 'I hope this isn't because you couldn't get her immunity.'

'The Home Office approved the immunity for the Pipers,' said Hawkins. 'Winnie didn't get it because she doesn't need it. She's not involved in the NYSE scam.'

'She's definitely coming,' said Adam.

The door opened again and in walked Winnie. Without sparing a glance at anyone else in the room she went over to Sep's bed and kissed him on the lips. It was a prolonged kiss that made the others feel slightly uncomfortable. Then she found a chair and sat down, without speaking a word to anyone.

'Hiya, Winnie,' said Sep. 'Really glad you came.'

'Glad I came, Sep.'

'Yes, I think we can all see that,' said Hawkins.

'I assume everyone's here now?' said Sep, casting his eyes around the room.

'You assume correctly,' said Hawkins.

'Right,' said Sep. 'We're here to resolve the sudden deaths of Charlie Santiago, James Boswell, Agnes McGinty and finally

Graham Feather. All suspicious deaths; all presumed to have been murdered; all connected in some way, but the mystery is: who would benefit from killing all four of them?'

There were no answers, so Sep continued. 'The answer is – no one. That is, no one person. I think we can get one matter on the agenda out of the way fairly quickly and that is the murder of Graham Feather. I believe Detective Superintendent Hawkins can bring us up to date on what we have so far.'

Hawkins opened a folder and read from a sheet: 'Forensic tests on marks around Graham Feather's neck proved beyond doubt that he was manually strangled before his body was arranged to make it look like suicide. The marks on his neck are an exact match to the unusually large hands of the late Roscoe Briggs, who died while attempting to murder Detective Inspector Black. Our medical experts assure us that there is no doubt that Feather was strangled by Briggs. On top of which, there is much DNA evidence proving that Briggs was at the murder scene.'

Butterbowl spoke with some derision. 'Why has it taken yer so long figure it all out? I'll tell yer why. It's cos yer a bunch of useless bastards, that's why.'

Sep was glad it was all down to Wood and not him. Hawkins put the sheet back in the folder and sat back in her chair to indicate that she had no more to say.

'The useless bastard investigating it was one of your own useless bastards, Stanley,' said Sep. 'Now residing in one of Her Majesty's Secure Nuthouses.' He went on to add: 'Mr Stanley Butterbowl, I believe you have information that will strengthen that evidence.'

'Er, what?'

'Tell us about the contract on Feather. Oh and what you say is being recorded on video.'

'Is it? Oh right. Redman put a three-grand contract out on Feather because he reckoned Feather were goin' ter muscle in on a scam he had goin'.'

'This was a contract to murder Graham Feather, was it?' asked Sep.

'Course it was. That's what a fuckin' contract is.'

'Just moderate your language, Stanley!' snapped Sep. 'And who took this contract?'

'Roscoe took it.'

'Roscoe Briggs?'

'Yeah.'

'How do you know?'

'I know cos it were offered ter me at first, only I wouldn't do it with it bein' too complicated.'

'Complicated?'

'Yeah. Redman wanted me ter make it look like suicide. He wanted me ter make it look like he'd strung himself up. I mean, toppin' someone's a hard enough job as it is, without havin' ter piss about like that afterwards. That's just askin' ter be captured.'

'So, you know for certain that Roscoe Briggs murdered Graham Feather?'

'I do. He told me how he made it look like suicide. I knew he'd make a bollocks of it an' leave bits of himself all over the place.'

Sep looked at Hawkins. 'That's as much evidence as we can gather to resolve the murder of Graham Feather, ma'am.'

Hawkins glanced at the constable accompanying Butterbowl. 'Constable, could you take Mr Butterbowl back to his ward and return to your normal duties?'

'Ma'am.'

They all watched in contemplative silence as Butterbowl was being wheeled from the room, then Hawkins said, 'I'd say that's more than enough to satisfy the CPS regarding the Graham Feather murder. Which leaves us with three suspicious deaths. Have we got any further regarding the death of James Boswell?'

'Yes, we have, ma'am,' said Sep, 'but it hangs on our witness, being given immunity from prosecution for perverting the course of justice.'

'This immunity has been granted,' said Hawkins, passing a letter over to Sep, who read it carefully. He then passed it over to Winnie, who read it and commented drily, 'So this is what an immunity letter looks like . . . I did wonder.'

Sep then turned his attention to Julie Rogerson.

'You are Julie Rogerson?'

'I am.'

'Then you have been granted immunity. If you could pass her the letter, Winnie.' Winnie gave the immunity letter to Julie. Sep waited until she had read it before continuing: 'Are you happy to speak your piece safe in the knowledge that nothing you say here will be given in evidence against you in a court of law?'

'I am. What I have to say is short and to the point. My husband,

Martyn Rogerson, killed James Boswell. I was there in the room in the Grimshawe Hotel when it happened.'

'Would you like to explain why you chose the Grimshawe, which is about as downmarket as you can get?' asked Sep.

'Well, Martyn saw a text message on my phone about me arranging a meeting with James and he was sure I was having an affair. I wasn't. I told Martyn that it was purely to do with my work, but he didn't believe me, so I told him to come with me if he didn't believe me. I rearranged the meeting for it to be in the grottiest place I knew about, to make Martyn believe it couldn't possibly be a meeting place where I'd ever go to meet a lover. I told him that I'd simply arranged to meet James in the Grimshawe to pass on information about Carl Redman, who James suspected had killed Mr Santiago – and that was the truth.'

'Why did James suspect him?' Sep asked her.

'Because of the Snowball scam that Santiago was running with the Pipers, who were friendly with James. He'd found out from them that Redman wanted in on it and I was trying to warn James to keep away from him.'

'How did Redman find out about it?'

'I'm very sorry, but that was me,' put in Adam. 'Redman threatened to kill Simeon if I didn't tell him all about Snowball.'

'Could someone tell *me* about Snowball?' said Hawkins.

'I think it might be as well if we allow Mrs Rogerson to finish her story first,' said Sep. 'Snowball's quite a complicated story.'

'Really?' said Hawkins. 'Then you must proceed, Mrs Rogerson.'

'There's not much more to tell. Martyn and I turned up at the Grimshawe, James turned up a few minutes later. Martyn came up behind him and hit him with an iron bar. Killed him, poor James.'

'And are you prepared to swear to this in court?'

'Yes I am. I know he's my husband and I still love him, but he also killed the poor old lady in the Grimshawe Hotel. I've given it all a lot of thought and I can't live my life keeping quiet about him doing all that. He really needs to get what's coming to him.'

'Excellent,' said Hawkins. 'That's three murders solved. I'd now like to hear all about Snowball, if I may.'

All eyes were now on Adam, who flinched beneath their collective stare. 'It's all right, Adam,' said Sep. 'You've got nothing to fear from telling the truth. You've got immunity as well. Start at the beginning.'

'Well,' began Adam, 'me and Simeon have a social anxiety disorder. My condition is quite mild compared to Simeon but I tend to concentrate my mind along a very narrow path which means that my brain works better than most along this path.'

'Yes, I understand that to be the case in some highly intelligent people,' said Hawkins, sympathetically. 'Carry on, Adam.'

Adam paused to give himself time to think. Speaking before so many people hanging on to his every word made him feel uncomfortable.

'Would anyone mind if I took up his background story,' said Winnie, 'and left the technical stuff to him?'

'Oh, please do,' said Hawkins.

'Well,' explained Winnie, who had spent a lot of time with the brothers over in New York, 'Adam's a genius with computers. You see, his mind isn't clouded with distractions, such as art and music and sport and relationships . . .'

'And sex,' put in Adam. 'I'm not interested in sex with women or men or anything.'

'And sex,' added Winnie, 'and all the stuff the rest of us think is important. He has the ability to channel his mind down a narrow path that focuses on him being interested in computers. In fact, I think it's only computers he's interested in. He and his brother grew up in children's homes. The people at Adam's home spotted his ability with computers and encouraged him and then got him a job working in the computer industry for a firm that serviced computers that had gone wrong. They also had the job of looking after the computers at the New York Stock Exchange and this gave him the bright idea of, erm . . . I think you'd better take it up from there, Adam.'

'I only want to talk to Winnie,' he said politely, 'if that's all right by everybody.'

'That's fine,' said Hawkins. 'Please continue.'

Adam turned his chair so that he was facing Winnie. He then cupped his chin in his hands and rested his elbows on the table as he thought of where to start.

'Go on, Adam,' encouraged Winnie, taking up the same pose and smiling at him. 'Pretend there's only silly old me listening.'

'You're not silly.'

'OK, Winnie the genius.'

'Well, it started when I worked at the New York Stock Exchange.

The firm I worked for was given the job of upgrading their network system. There were problems which I was asked to locate and put right. The NYSE as it's called is the world's biggest and most important stock exchange.'

'That sounds like a very responsible job,' prompted Winnie. 'Why you? Are you highly qualified or something?'

'I've got no paper qualifications, but I am gifted in that field and it's a field where genuinely gifted people are quite often more valued than qualified people. The computer company that I worked for gave me all the tricky jobs that no one else could handle. You may have noticed that my brother has a mental disorder which has never been properly diagnosed. It's a condition with a very broad spectrum, in fact I'm not entirely free of such a condition insofar as my brain tends to focus much more of my brain power on that which really interests me, to the exclusion of many other things.'

Sep remembered Winnie O'Toole's very similar assessment of him. Smart girl that Winnie, smarter than him in many ways. *Do no harm at all to marry her.* He dragged his thoughts away from her as Adam continued with his self-assessment.

'I'm quite brilliant at mathematics and anything to do with numbers and computers in particular – it's as if my brain was designed to work on computers. When I was three, I had a reading age of twelve. My IQ has been assessed at around one hundred and eighty, much the same as Einstein. My passion is computers; as far as computers are concerned, you could say I'm the man.'

'Go on, Adam,' said Sep, 'Tell us about this firm you worked for in America.'

'I'm only talking to Winnie,' said Adam without looking at Sep. It was a remark that amused everyone except Sep, who put his palms up and said, 'Sorry.'

'Well, the first place I worked at was just a computer company and I was pretty much a gofer until they realized that I had a real aptitude for the workings of computers and they gave me much more interesting work to do. Eventually I ended up as their senior expert. I know this sounds silly, but I got to a point where I thought I could beat a computer at its own game.'

'Beat it?' said Winnie. 'How do you beat a computer?'

'Computers are man-made,' he said, 'which means they can be man-*ipulated*, which is what I did.'

Adam paused and glanced sideways at Sep, as if reluctant to explain any further.

'I'm sorry, Adam, but you've no option but to tell us,' said Sep. 'You sit there with your mouth shut and your situation will get worse. You know, when you talk about computers it's like listening to a different Adam.'

'You mean I don't sound stupid?'

'That's not what I mean at all. No one thinks you're stupid. I mean you *do* sound highly intelligent – even more intelligent than Winnie the genius.'

Winnie grinned at this, then leaned forward and whispered a few words to Adam, who nodded and said 'OK. I'll tell you what I know about Snowball.'

'That'll do for starters,' said Sep. 'A bit of your background wouldn't go amiss either.'

'My background? Well, first of all, Simeon and I have dual citizenship both here and in the United States, as we were born over there and have English parents – that's if you can call them parents. They split up when we were children. Not sure if they were even married. Our mom looked after us for a while, then we became too much for her, with Simeon being like he is and apparently I was an awkward child, so she abandoned us. The courts put us into different children's homes. Simeon went to a home for children with special needs and I went to a normal place. It was harder for Simeon than for me because I was the only person who had ever shown him any affection. I was six and he was four. We didn't see each other for ten years. Simeon never learned to read or write, so without actually seeing him there was no way I could communicate with him. My life changed when the home I was in got a computer. None of the carers could work it properly but it came with an instruction manual which I read and it all seemed so simple and straightforward that I took to it straight away. It wasn't a very powerful computer, none of them were back then, but I learned how to upgrade it and convinced the people at the home to buy the necessary hardware to do this with. It got to the point where no one else in the home could use it but me. When I was sixteen this job came up in a computer firm and I was recommended for it by my carers. I got it and suddenly found myself surrounded by massively powerful computers. I was in heaven. After I'd been there a year or so they began giving me very interesting work and paid me quite a lot of money, presumably to keep me there, so I got myself a two-bedroom apartment in Brooklyn and went to Simeon's home and told them I would like to look after him. I was eighteen by then and he was sixteen. There was a lot of stupid red tape to sort out but I managed it and he came home with me to live in my apartment.'

'That was very good for me,' said Simeon who had been following his brother's story with intermittent nods of his head.

'Adam, you're doing really well,' said Winnie. 'Could you tell us who looked after Simeon while you were at work?'

'He looked after himself. He can't read or write, but he can make himself a sandwich and a bowl of cereal. I always cooked him a meal when I got home. I worked at the same firm for years and then I was headhunted by a much bigger company who gave me a massive salary.

'We moved into a proper house with a big yard and I got a woman in to cook and clean for a couple of hours every day – Mrs Hegerty; she was Irish. Looked after us very well, didn't she, Simeon?'

Simeon smiled and said, 'Sunday dinner, Adam.'

'Yeah, she always made us a lovely Sunday dinner. Me and Simeon, we were really happy. I thought he was coming along great. OK, his problem was always there and always will be, but he was enjoying his life with me. Then I was assigned to maintain the New York Stock Exchange computers in their headquarters in New York City. It's a massive place. There's a lot of men in suits there who call themselves number crunchers. I was very valuable to them. It was the most important contract our firm had and I was the main person doing it. I spent a whole day of every week there, just checking that everything was working correctly. Eventually I knew their computers inside out.'

'Is that the computer you thought you could beat?' said Winnie.

Adam smiled. 'It's the computer I *did* beat. You see, I got friendly with someone there who knew all about the workings of the money markets and stocks and securities and stuff. It all seemed so straightforward to me and I rather fancied doing a bit of dealing myself. I was earning five times as much money as I needed so I had a lot of money in the bank. That's when the idea came to me.'

'Thank God for that,' said Sep, who was becoming bored with

this life story, although it was essential to know as much as he could about the Piper brothers.

'At your request,' said Adam, stiffly, 'I've compressed my background story into as few words as possible and I'm trying to make the computer part of the story as simplistic as possible.'

'Your condescending remark has not gone unnoticed,' said Sep under his breath.

'Try and make it short but interesting, Adam,' said Winnie, 'and not too technical. None of us are as clever as you.'

'I know,' said Adam matter-of-factly, making Winnie smile. 'Well, as you know, stocks and other securities are traded all over the world by stock exchanges. As the value of shares rise and fall their latest values are sent to stock brokers. In the early days this was done in coffee houses, and then by tickertape and then by other means until nowadays by electronic mail, which is instant and efficient.'

'And secure,' added Sep.

'Not to someone like me,' said Adam. 'You see, brokers get to know the very split-second the share values move. In other words, split-seconds can be made to count when the investor is looking out for upward and downward trends. It occurred to me that if an investor knew five seconds before the broker did about the movement of a share it would put him in a great position to buy or sell within that five seconds. So I needed to create a piece of software that delayed the transmission of shares to the broker's computers by five seconds and at the same time, send the new share prices to my computer the very instant they moved, that is five seconds before they appeared on the brokers' electronic quotation boards. I believed five seconds was the optimum time I could afford to delay this transmission without arousing suspicion.'

'On what did you base that?'

Sep asked the question because he wanted to be part of the interview and not just sit there dumbly listening to a subject he didn't fully understand. Adam shrugged, now having accepted that Sep could ask him questions.

'Educated guesswork. It could have been ten seconds or a lot more, but there will have been a definite cut-off point where the delay would have been noticed. I didn't want to go anywhere near that cut-off point.'

'And did you created such a piece of, erm . . .?' Sep was stuck for the word.

'Software,' put in Winnie.

'Yes, I did,' said Adam. 'Not only did I create it, but I installed it very cleverly in the NYSE's main server, where it is to this day.'

'What? You mean you took the back off the computer and installed it?'

Adam looked at Sep as if he was an imbecile. 'I created the programme and put it on to a memory stick which I stuck it into a USB port in a certain computer, after which I removed the memory stick, leaving no evidence of what I'd done. It took about thirty seconds to transfer.'

'Easy as that, eh?'

'Hardly easy. The hard bit is me getting myself into a position to be able to do it. Very few people are allowed access to those computers. I just happened to know exactly which computer the memory stick needed to be plugged into.'

'So it's not physically noticeable. It's just hidden somewhere in a computer chip along with millions of other things,' said Sep.

'Something like that.'

'Almost impossible to find.'

'*Very* impossible, if you don't know what you're looking for.'

'Five seconds doesn't give you much time to do the trading.'

'True, so what I needed to do then was create an algorithm to pick up the trends, assess them and buy and sell shares for me before the five seconds were up.'

'And you created such an algorithm?'

'I did. It was horribly time-consuming but I needed to get it right. In fact, I'm still tweaking it now and again, as it's by no means as good as it could be. Assessing the trends is the really tricky bit.'

'And is this working for you right now, as we speak?'

'It works quite well,' said Adam. 'In fact, it's taking on average just 2.6 seconds for my algorithm to evaluate the share movements and trade them.'

'Sound like a very clever algorithm,' said Winnie who now took over the questioning.

'It's better than clever,' said Adam. 'It's a work of genius and it's getting better all the time.'

'But you left New York and came over here?'

'Yes we did and getting passports was a problem. In fact, finding our birth certificates was a problem. When you're abandoned to the state by your parents you almost become a non-person, you know. So I had to become Simeon's parent.'

'Seems to me that you did really well. Simeon was lucky to have you around,' said Winnie. 'Go on.'

'I was worried that if I was found out I could be locked up although I've no idea if what I've done was illegal. I can't afford to be locked up, if only for Simeon's sake. I wanted to put some distance between me and the NYSE computers. Also I needed someone who knew about running a business to help me make my system work efficiently. That's another of my problems – I'm not very efficient, which is why I came to work for Mr Santiago. I knew his name from my NYSE days and he knew about me and my computer expertise, although he didn't know about my new system until I got here.'

'I imagine he was impressed.'

'Oh yes, but he was also worried about the legality of it so he created the Snowball company, whereby clients would buy and sell shares, using our system and we would take fifty per cent of their profits. It was a way of generating large sums of money which we didn't have, to trade with and no one could trace the dealing down to us, because we weren't doing the actual dealing.

'We did a trial run with our first fifty shareholders, who each put a thousand pounds in and we doubled the value of their shares in two days. They each paid us five hundred pounds and they were delighted that they'd made five hundred for themselves. So were we, but we'd made twenty-five thousand using their money. Each of these shareholders was chosen for their ability to invest a million pounds. So, working on our very brief track record we could make fifty million pounds in a very short space of time, of which twenty-five million would be ours. At that point we could and would, have closed down Snowball as we'd have been satisfied with the money we'd made. I was worried that at some point our scam would be discovered so why wait for that point to be reached? We wouldn't know what to do with billions of dollars.'

'Could you close down remotely the file you installed in the NYSE computer without physically going into the computer?' asked Winnie.

'Hardly. If I could close it down remotely I'd have been able to install it remotely – and so could anyone. No, it stays where it is. You see, greed is where most criminals and a lot of business people come unstuck, which I believe is what happened to Mr Santiago. He saw himself as a multibillionaire, whereas I wouldn't know what to do with such wealth. My way would have made us twelve and a half million pounds richer. With that sort of money I could have given Simeon a much better quality of life.'

'And did Santiago split this initial twenty-five grand with you?'

'No he didn't and that was his first mistake. His second mistake was to believe I couldn't close down the system that Snowball operated on. Mr Santiago was a greedy man. He offered me ten per cent – £2,500. You see, in his mind the software in the NYSE computer was safe and beyond our reach: our computer was up and running in his office, the money was being paid into a bank account he'd opened in Snowball's company name and I had no shares in Snowball. His wife was the other director, so he didn't need me anymore, or so he thought. But he was wrong because I'd learned enough from Mr Feather for us to run the business on our own and I had all the data I needed to close the algorithm programme in Santiago's computer remotely, any time I wanted and start trading with my own computer.'

'And this is what led to Graham Feather's death,' said Winnie.

'I think it was, yes. He was a very nice man was Mr Feather, wasn't he, Simeon?'

Vigorous nods from Simeon.

'Very nice indeed.'

Winnie pressed on before they both got maudlin about Graham Feather. 'I assume the Snowball computer was in Santiago's offices before he was killed?'

'It was and that computer is still working properly, but only as a computer. I just wiped any trace of the software from the Snowball system and installed it in my own computer at home, which means Santiago's Snowball is effectively inoperable.'

'You did that *after* he was killed?'

'Yes. Right now I just use my own money to trade. With the investors, it was their intention to trade in millions and make quick killings before we shut the whole thing down. On my own I just trade in thousands, which is not a quick killing but nor is it all that noticeable. I work very much under the stock market radar.'

'And how many thousands is that?'

'It's basically everything I've accumulated up to now, after I bought my house and car.'

'How much?' Winnie asked.

'With your money,' Adam said, 'we currently trade with around two hundred thousand pounds, which might seem a lot, but in the world of stocks and shares it's peanuts. The big guys trade in billions.'

'What do you mean, with *Winnie's* money?' asked Sep.

Adam was nonplussed, Winnie helped him out. 'I gave him some of my own money to invest.'

'How much?'

'A hundred thousand, which I got from the sale of my house.'

'Oh, bloody hell, Winnie! That makes you part of the scam. You've just dropped yourself right in it,' said Sep, 'and you haven't got immunity.'

'Let's see how this pans out,' said Hawkins. 'I'm not sure that Winnie has anything to worry about as yet.'

'I estimate,' said Adam, 'that if it was still working, since I've been talking to you we'd have made about a thousand pounds, which we hadn't stolen from anyone. It would have been automatically paid into our trading account and used by my algorithm to make us even more money and it would all snowball from here. I was just taking advantage of a vulnerable system.'

'It's got to be against some law or other,' said Sep.

'I don't know about that,' said Adam. 'Mr Santiago went into this and couldn't find any specific law which we'd broken. We weren't insider trading or anything, we were simply taking advantage of the system.

'You've tampered with a very important computer programme to further your own ends,' said Sep.

'Look, this is all very interesting,' said Hawkins, impatiently 'but this is not America, this man has immunity and I want to know how Charles Santiago died.'

Adam looked to have come to the end of his verbal tether. Winnie looked him and said, 'Would you like *me* to tell them, Adam?'

'I think so, yes, please.'

'Is that all right with everyone?' asked Winnie. 'I know the story as well as Adam does.'

'Then I wish *someone* would damn well tell us!' snapped Hawkins.

'Right,' said Winnie, 'Well, when Santiago reneged on his agreement to split the profits down the middle and only gave the boys ten per cent, Adam plucked up the courage to tell him that he could shut the whole thing down any time he wanted and run the thing on his own.'

'In my opinion, Adam and Simeon aren't entirely blameless in all this,' said Sep warningly. Winnie looked daggers at him.

'Sep, is it possible for you to shut up for a few minutes?'

Sep shrugged. 'Am I right or am I wrong?'

'Well, I'll tell you, Mr Know-it-all!' she snapped. 'Santiago got really ratty about it and it all got very violent. He was apparently a real nasty bugger when he didn't get his own way. He grabbed hold of Adam and pushed him to the window which was stuck wide open and five floors up, threatening to throw him out. Adam said he was scared to death that he was going to die, but Simeon went to help and he's much the stronger of the two lads.'

She turned to look at both Sep and Hawkins, saying, 'There's something we didn't know about Simeon. Some years ago Adam booked him in for judo lessons to stop him being bullied by idiots. Simeon really took to it and ended up with a brown belt which, I imagine, would be plenty to deal with the likes of Santiago. Anyway, Simeon pulled Santiago off Adam and threatened to push *him* out of the window.'

'This annoyed the hell out of Santiago and he really lost it. He went ballistic and of course Simeon was very upset because Santiago had tried to kill his brother. They had a real ding-dong battle, with Simeon giving better than he got.'

She paused and looked around the room, from face to face before she said what she had to say next.

'Now Simeon said he didn't push Santiago out of the window and knowing Simeon as I do, I absolutely, one hundred per cent believe him.'

'Just tell us,' said Sep impatiently.

'Did you hear what I just said because it's very important.'

'Yes.'

'OK. What happened was that Simeon ducked out of the way when Santiago went at him like a steam train. Santiago stumbled over Simeon's feet and went clean out of the window like an escaping bird. The window was stuck wide open, as you know.'

'That's what happened,' confirmed Adam.

'Yes, it is,' said Simeon. 'It wasn't my fault, was it, Adam?'

'No, it wasn't.'

'And that's it, is it?' stormed Sep. 'That's what kicked all this stuff off? A bloody window that was stuck open? A window sticks and nine people die! And we're supposed to believe this crap?'

He looked around the room. There was a long silence broken eventually by Sep, whose mind was now more on keeping Winnie safe than solving the Santiago case.

'Do you know what I think?' he said.

'Oh, do tell us,' said Hawkins.

'I think this story is a load of rubbish. I know Winnie believes it because she believes in the boys, but I don't because I happen to know that Roscoe Briggs killed Santiago.'

'Really? How do you know?' asked Hawkins.

'Because he bloody well told me back there at the foundry. His last words were: "I might not have got you, but at least I got three grand for killing Santiago." Last words of a dying man. Death-bed confession to a senior police officer. A lot of dying villains like to go out boasting that they've got one over on us coppers before they go.'

'So,' said Hawkins, 'you're saying the fall didn't immediately kill him?'

'He was all but dead, alive enough only to talk to me for a few seconds.'

'You should have made a statement to this effect at the time and it could have been verified by our forensic people. It's too late now with Briggs having been cremated.'

'Sorry about that, but my mind was all over the place.'

'He didn't look to have much life in him to me,' said Fiona.

'He didn't have any life in him when you arrived!' retorted Sep, annoyed that she wasn't helping him to help Winnie. Surely she must see what he was trying to do.

Hawkins studied him, nodding slightly, as if to indicate that she knew what he was doing and that she approved. Then she asked him, 'Why would the Piper boys concoct such a story?'

'I don't know, ma'am. Their mental limitations might well come to their rescue in court. A half-decent defence brief will destroy their testimony and they have the money to hire the best. This will leave us police with egg on our faces.'

'So, DI Black, if you stick to your story how are we supposed to handle this?'

'Well,' said Sep, 'if Adam's outlandish statement about Snowball reaches the hands of the NYPD, which it would, it condemns all three of them, including Winnie, as having committed a very major crime in the US. Is that what we want? All three of them extradited to the States where the boys' UK immunity doesn't count? Long prison terms for them all, I shouldn't wonder. And we must bear in mind that all three of them came here of their own free will, at our request, to straighten this mess out.'

'And . . .?' asked Hawkins.

'And,' said Sep, 'We're here to find out who murdered who and why. We definitely know who killed Feather and James Boswell and Agnes from the Grimshawe. I say we now add Santiago to the other three solved murders. The two murderers being Martyn Rogerson and Roscoe Briggs.'

There was a silence in the room, broken only by Hawkins drumming her fingers on the desk, her thoughtful and narrowed eyes on Julie.

'Mrs Rogerson, Miss O'Toole and the Piper brothers, I wonder if you could leave us at this point. This is a matter to be resolved by police alone.'

'She means not to be discussed in front of a reporter,' said Julie to Winnie as they left the room.

'Think yourselves lucky you're all walking away from this without being charged with anything!' snapped Hawkins.

She waited a few seconds after they'd left before saying, 'So, what we possibly have in reality are three murders which we have solved, which is good, and one accidental death which is not good. The latter will make the police seem rather unprofessional, having spent so much time and money investigating what amounts to a no offence. After our success in solving the other murders it would seem foolish to blemish our success with what is, at worst, death by misadventure.

'On balance,' she went on, 'It would save us enormous trouble to simply take your version as the most likely cause of Charles Santiago's death, Detective Inspector Black.'

'Everything to gain, nothing to lose, ma'am,' said Sep. 'Roscoe Briggs is dead. We already know he was a hitman. Let him make our job easier.'

Hawkins continued: 'With regard to the programme in the NYSE computer we've already been in contact with the New York police to tell them, in absolute confidence, about a scam some of our criminals were running to defraud their stock exchange. I did tell them that the two main perpetrators were dead and the rest locked up and that the scam is dead and buried and no longer running. I heard yesterday that a top expert has been all over the NYSE computers and had found a programme that seemed surplus to requirements which he's deleted. They're happy to leave it at that because any story about the stock exchange being defrauded would cause unnecessary panic in the world money markets.'

'So, what's the outcome, ma'am?' asked Sep.

'Well, I anticipated something like this, which is why I made myself the senior officer present. First of all we must thank Winnie O'Toole and the Piper brothers for coming over here to clear things up for us. Our reward to them is that they will have no charges to answer to. I suggest we use Roscoe Briggs's deathbed confession to our advantage. DI Black will of course need to make a sworn statement to this effect.'

'Not a problem, ma'am.'

'Excellent. Then Roscoe Briggs's death and his confession wraps up this whole bloody pantomime very neatly. So, all the crimes are solved and no one present at this meeting is to be prosecuted for any of them.'

'What about Martyn?' asked Julie.

'Martyn will need to be caught and brought before the courts,' said Hawkins to her, 'so if you have any clue at all as to his whereabouts, you need to tell us.'

'I've no idea where he is,' said Julie.

Sep looked, keenly, at her to see if she was telling the truth. Julie looked back and gave him a challenging smile. Hawkins looked around the room and added, slowly and clearly: 'For obvious reasons I expect that every word spoken at this meeting to be forever cloaked in absolute secrecy by all who are present.'

Heads nodded all around the room. Everyone understood the gravity of her words.

'Then this meeting is concluded.'

Sep winked at Winnie, who mouthed *Now will you marry me* to him.

EPILOGUE

Sep had been discharged into Winnie's care. She was driving him home in his recently acquired Jaguar.

'Last words of a dying man, my arse. Jesus! Septimus Black, you really are a world-class liar!'

'How do you know he didn't confess to me?'

'Because I saw his brains scattered all over the concrete. That man was stone dead when he hit the deck.'

'Was he? I must have been hearing things – things very much to your advantage I might add.'

'I know and thank you, but Hawkins will know all that. She's not an idiot. Shouldn't a copper of her rank have gone by the book?'

'She *is* going by the book. There's firm proof that Roscoe killed Feather and it clearly follows that he killed Santiago as well. Sometimes we have to go on circumstantial evidence. This way, no one's going to be unjustly punished. Anyway, why are you upset? She's got you off the hook.'

'She's let you get me off the hook, you mean. You coppers twist things to suit yourselves.'

'Suit ourselves? To suit you, you mean. You and Mrs Rogerson and the Pipers. You were the winners here, not the coppers; and for your information *we are* going by the book. Roscoe's confession won't form any part of the evidence against him. We have him nailed on the Graham Feather murder without his confession and enough circumstantial to pin the Santiago murder on him as well. Legally, we've got all we need.'

'I know but . . . bloody hell, Sep! You've got to sign a sworn statement.'

'I'll be doing no such thing and Hawkins won't press me on it. Winnie, did you not think justice was done back there?'

'I don't know. I wasn't allowed in the room when it was done.'

'If Julie had been allowed in she'd have made a story out of it and sold it to a national paper and you and the boys would be on your way to the States very shortly to face major charges. Winnie, the law isn't always black and white. If we can, we like to be fair whenever possible. I just saw a way of making it possible. Hawkins picked up on what I was doing and made it work. Neither of us wanted to see you banged up, especially after all the trouble you lot took to help us sort this mess out.'

'The two of you have it all nicely sewn up, haven't you?'

'Rank has its privileges and it's been our privilege to see justice done.'

Winnie pressed the button that had the hood come up. She waited until it had clicked into place before saying, 'Talking of justice, you told me that if I came back, you'd give me this car and your word to me is your bond. You've often told me that.'

'So, you're back for good, are you?'

'I am, if I get to keep this car.'

'What? You'd take this off me, after I've saved you a ten stretch in an American prison and you call that justice?'

'Why not? Your word is your bond, Sep. Oh, by the way, Hawkins had a word with me on the way out.'

'Yes, I saw you two talking.'

'She's offered me a job. In fact, she's offered both me and Adam jobs. The West Yorkshire Police are opening a Yorkshire Cyber Crime Unit based in Leeds and they need someone with Adam's expertise to run it. I did tell her that Adam couldn't run a bloody whelk stall, which is why she offered me the job as his mouthpiece, so to speak. With me understanding what he's talking about I'd be able to pass it on to our minions with some authority. That's what Adam lacks, you see, my authority. We'd make a good team, don't you think? I stay a civilian but I get sergeant's wages.'

'Winnie, are you really going to keep my car?'

She grinned and said, 'Hey, do you know who the top expert is who did the impossible and found the file in the NYSE computer? The only person in the world who could find such a thing.'

Sep chewed this question over in his mind for a while, until realization hit him.

'Oh, please, no!'

'Oh, please, yes!'

'So, it's still in there?'

'Who knows?'

'Jesus, Winnie!'

'Sep, if we get married, this'll be our family car.'